The VALLEY of the BLUE MISTS

THE SKY ELDERS

The VALLEY of the BLUE MISTS

R.J. YOUNG

4 Horsemen
Publications, Inc.

DEDICATION

To my good friend Liz. Thank for being so supportive, when I was doubting myself.

TABLE OF CONTENTS

HISTORICAL MAP REFERENCES

Shipapa-Lina—Mesa Verde in Colorado

The Land of Everlasting Summer—The Four Corners

Kolhu—Chaco Canyon, NM

Ulah-Nane—North America

Kuwahi the Mystic Mountains—Clingman's Dome, TN

The Valley of the Blue Mists—Monument Valley, Utah

The Endless River Agazzi—The
Mississippi River

The Pisas Vaya River—The Colorado River

The Swimming Bear River and Night Way
River—Mancos River and San Juan River

Norumbega (The High Seat)—The Great
Lakes Region

Gitche Gumee—Lake Superior

The Shouting Mountains—The Coso
Mountains Range

The Blue World—The Pacific Ocean

CHAPTER ONE

AD 1252—The Long Debi-Kway
Season of the Great Turtle's Trek

A god cried in the ravaged, devastated fields. Mournful wails echoed across the barren landscape like the roar of a dying beast.

Pahana was riding atop the mighty bison, Mountain Fury, who had once belonged to his father Tawa. Young Pahana was surveying the damage done by the fire locusts, who had devoured the forest, where the Itiwana tribe foraged and hunted, near Shipapa-Lina. *I never imagined I would see a wasteland where the majestic forest once stood.*

At the age of 20 summers, Pahana was charged with ruling the village of Shipapa-Lina while his father was away. Pahana's mother, Pinga, had once been a northern Sky Elder, but her quondam divinity had been stripped from her. However, her hallowed blood still possessed deific quality. Pahana had inherited his albino skin from her.

Pahana heard a wailing, weeping sound reverberating from beyond a hill. The sad sound was haunting. "Do you hear that, Mountain Fury? Or am I ill in the mind? Forward, Large One. I need to know what that sound is."

The old bison galloped forward, ascending the hill. Pahana saw that the source of the strange noise was a crying figure. It seemed, from the distance, to be a tall, muscular man with dark brown skin, and multi-colored speckled dots all across his body. When the strange being turned, it had the head of a ferret.

Pahana paused, taken aback by the unexpected sight. *By Awona'Wilona's grace! What am I seeing?*

Tears rolled from the bizarre creature's eyes as he spoke in a high-pitched, shrill voice. "Woe, the Land of Everlasting Summer is sorely wounded. Muyingwa the Germinator cries for it."

Muyingwa the Germinator? Pahana thought. *I know of him. Manabazo has taught me the names of the Sky Elders. Muyingwa is the deity of vegetation, crops, and germination.*

Manabazo had told Pahana that the wandering Muyingwa germinated the corn crops across Ulah-Nane. The many colorful spots that covered his form represented the different types of corn that the indigenous tribes of Ulah-Nane grew. Pahana slid off Mountain Fury and warily approached the weeping Elder.

"Muyingwa weeps," the Elder said sadly. "Dagwona, the whirlwind witch and Agwara, the snow fox spirit, have regrettably succeeded. Alas, the living forest of the Land of Everlasting Summer bleeds."

"I destroyed the witch," Pahana said, respectfully.

The Germinator's shoulders sagged as his nose twitched. "Pahana, the son of Tawa, has failed. Dagwona, the witch of the whirlwind, lives and the sacred forest lay devastated."

Pahana was taken aback. "She lives? But I skewered her with a lance of pure ice. How could she..."

"Pahana, the son of Tawa, should have finished what Pahana began," the Germinator said. "The sacred mission trusted to the family of Morning Star is in jeopardy. Pahana, the son of Tawa, disappoints Muyingwa the Germinator."

"But I protected the Tree of Life," Pahana protested. "Yaxche still stands."

"Yaxche, the majestic Tree of Life, stands for the moment, but it is not safe," Muyingwa replied. "Agwara, the snow fox spirit, and Dagwona, the witch of the whirlwind, now know the area where Yaxche, the Tree of Life, stands. Never has Yaxche the Tree of Life been in greater danger."

"What danger?" Pahana asked, dreading the answer.

"The Spear-Finger!" Muyingwa said, with a worried sob. "He comes! Beware the Spear-Finger!"

Tawa was unconscious and defenseless, dying from his wounds, blood loss, and a virulent infection. The courageous leader of the Itiwana, who had fought stone monsters and defeated the Vykans with his skill, intelligence, and strength of will, was now hovering helplessly at the edge of death.

He had received a mortal wound while battling the powerful poshayanki bear spirit, Nanook. Tawa had done the impossible by slaying the beast, utilizing the advantage of his magic spear, Dragonfly, and his formidable bison mount, Brave Fire. His success had come at a terrible cost.

After days of travel, he collapsed, but was fortunate enough to have been found by Naya-Nazgani, the legendary monster hunter. A mastop-kachina, like Tawa, he had been sent by the Wind People to hunt skinwalkers and had succeeded in his mission, luckily finding the dying Tawa in the process.

The Itiwana chieftain was hunched, unmoving, atop his bison mount, Brave Fire. The big bison came to trust Naya-Nazgani and allowed itself to be led. The monster hunter didn't know that there was an ancient, sacred arrow stashed in the mount's harness. Nor did he realize that the simple-looking spear tied to the bison's woven netting was a magic weapon.

I can't stop his bleeding, Naya-Nazgani thought. *He won't last much longer. I hope help lies in this direction. I saw smoke coming from this vicinity earlier. It may be a village. It's a slim hope, but there's nothing else in the area.*

Naya-Nazgani heard a repetitious pounding in the distance. The strange sound became more perplexing when he felt the impact tremor. Brave Fire reacted with agitation each time the ground shuddered. Tawa's eyes fluttered open as he was brought back to consciousness by the ever-increasing pounding.

The resounding footsteps alarmed the travelers. Determining the direction that the heavy footsteps were coming from, Naya-Nazgani's muscles tensed. He anticipated imminent danger. An experienced monster fighter, his instinct was always to presume peril. He held up the battle ax he had been given centuries ago by his mentor Red Horn. *Whatever this heavy-footed beast is, it will find a formidable adversary in me.*

A gigantic figure pushed its way through the trees. Its face peeked out through the leaves of the tallest branches. Even Brave Fire backed away, alarmed. The towering man's head appeared from behind the treetops.

Gah-Oh the Wind Giant looked down at the monster hunter and the unconscious Itiwana chieftain. Gah-Oh was one of the Cheenook giants and happened to be one of the largest. He stood

26 feet tall and had brown skin. He was of portly build, with broad shoulders, a large nose, and a full, gray beard. He had a bald head and a pair of bull-like horns. His attire was made from tree bark and vines. The giant had stripped the inner bark from trees and beat it until it was thin, then he dyed it with plants found in the area. After it dried, he made it into clothing, adorned with vines. In his huge hand, he carried a log that had been carved into a club.

Gah-oh looked over the scene and spoke in a booming voice that resonated and reverberated like the echo of thunder. "Yon intruders upon our land, be thou warned. Towering Gah-Oh feels a burning fury at the sight of those who would bring their violence here. Immense Gah-Oh strongly demands that all who thrive on combat and blood must depart this peaceful domain. Thou will keep thy deadly war from this peaceful abode of life. Run swiftly, strangers. Fear my mighty wrath."

As the giant lifted his massive club over his head, preparing to strike, Naya-Nazgani backed away cautiously. *In three centuries, I have never fought a foe so large. I must be wise and cautious.*

As one who had hunted monsters for so many years, it did not occur to Naya-Nazgani that there was any other way to resolve this situation other than combat. As he debated his strategy, a weak voice broke the tense silence.

"You have ... no enemies here, my large friend," Tawa said softly. "Be at peace. I seek help. I am ... dying."

Only now did Gah-Oh notice the blood on Tawa's limp body. The giant kneeled to inspect the wounded Tawa. He saw how pale the man on the bison looked. Clearly, this man was close to death.

"Yon lethal wound is very deep indeed," Gah-Oh commented, rather calmly. "Seeping red blood. Very bad. Giant Gah-Oh is greatly dismayed. Yon ailing human is frighteningly weak. A sad death is rapidly coming."

Naya-Nazgani had long heard the rumors that giant blood had miraculous healing powers. Perhaps this encounter was fortuitous. Even if this giant was hostile, Naya-Nazgani was plotting a way to spill the blood of the massive opponent.

"Essential aid must indeed be quickly supplied," Gah-Oh said, his shadow falling over Tawa.

"Will you ... help me?" Tawa managed to say, barely able to speak.

"Gah-Oh will assist thee," the giant said. "Indeed, I doth know of one who can heal thy wounds."

"Can you ... take me there, please?" Tawa asked.

"Agreed, it is," the giant said. "If yon armed warrior with the bloodied ax vows he shall refrain from all violence in this beneficent realm."

Naya-Nazgani was initially reluctant since his long-established instinct was to kill monsters, including Cheenooks. Still, this one was surprisingly calm and willing to talk.

True, it could be a trick, but Tawa needs help, and this being may be the only hope for the Itiwana. Aside from that, Naya-Nazgani did not know how to slay something so large. He felt it was better to feign cooperation and look for a weakness in this giant. If the Cheenook did reveal itself to be an enemy, Naya-Nazgani would need to know its vulnerabilities.

"Very well, giant," Naya-Nazgani said. "I vow not to strike the first blow while in your home but be warned that I will defend myself and my ailing companion if need be."

"Gah-Oh accepts your promise," the giant said. "Come. A long walk must begin immediately if we are to save thy companion."

Gah-Oh gently lifted the limp form of Tawa off the bison and cradled the Itiwana leader in his arms. He began to walk swiftly, taking giant strides. Brave Fire hesitated, but finally chose loyalty to its master over fear of the giant and trotted along behind.

Gah-Oh glanced down at Brave Fire. "Ah, yon shaggy, horned beast dutifully follows towering Gah-oh. Yon dying mortal inspires much devout loyalty, eh? Come swiftly then, devoted animal. We four have many long miles to traverse this day."

Naya-Nazgani began jogging to keep up with the ponderous pair who walked with protracted paces he could not match. *I am beginning to wish I had never come across this Itiwana. But I am now forsworn to this course of action. Whatever happens, I must be ready. I only hope I can keep pace with this giant. Curse him, he's fast.*

CHAPTER TWO

oraging and hunting had become a challenge for the Itiwana. With so much of the forest eaten away by the Fire Locusts, the children and elderly were no longer able to spend a leisurely day wandering the local woods in search of nuts and berries, while hunting parties were deprived of large game since the animals had fled. If they wanted to find any food growing in the area, they had to trek southeast, beyond where the locusts had reached.

Fortunately, a supply of nuts arranged by Pahana's grandmother, Atira, helped alleviate the shortage. The longhouse that had once been the meeting place of the Shakowin was now a food storehouse. They also had a healthy corn crop and bison meat. Still, the loss of the forest beyond the mesa was a worrisome situation for the Itiwana.

The tribe used wood and plants beyond just sustenance.

As Atira was rationing the nuts, she recalled the last time the Itiwana faced a food shortage. Twenty-two summers prior, before the White Buffalo Woman had supplied them with their herd of bison, the tribe struggled to find large game because the terrifying poshayanki, Achiyala, had chased the animals away. Atira's long-departed husband, Yana-Luha, who was the leader of the tribe at the time, had suggested evacuating the village and relocating. They had avoided that option back then, and Atira hoped they could do so again.

As she sorted through the stored nuts, the lithe form of Pinga glided into the longhouse. Her albino skin immediately caught Atira's attention. Atira was often envious of the fact that Pinga did not seem to age. She looked as young and beautiful as she had 20 summers ago.

Pinga looked over the stored foods. "This One sees that you are hard at work. She does not mean to disturb you."

"I'm never disturbed to see my son's wife," Atira said. "Is something on your mind?"

"This One has been thinking about the dire situation with the forests," Pinga said. "She thinks we must find my Tawa and bring him home."

"Tawa?" Atira asked. "My son is quite formidable, but what can he do about this?"

"He has Dragonfly," Pinga said. "It has a special bond with the grass and dirt and the energy of nature. It is bonded with Ulah-Nane."

Atira let the nuts fall from her grip. "Do you mean to say it can restore the forest?"

"Perhaps," she said. "If his will is strong enough. This One thinks it is. We must locate him."

"Then we shall, somehow," Atira replied. "And when he comes home, it will be a relief to know he is here. I worry about this Spear-Finger Pahana told us of."

"As does This One," Pinga said. "The legend of Spear-Finger fills her with dread."

"Things are indeed dire," Atira said. "My dearest Yana-Luha would be weeping to see this. Now we have this Spear-Finger threat hovering over our heads, like a vulture. What could this creature be?"

The mood was somber in the Great Lodge Cliff Palace. Pahana sat on the floor, cross-legged, next to the chieftain's raised stool, where his father would have been sitting, if he were there. Pahana, in the shadowy chamber, lit by the flickering light of the burning embers in the fire pit, wondered what his father, Tawa, would do if he were present.

In Tawa's absence, Pahana consulted with Tawa's most experienced, aged advisor, Manabazo, the shape-shifting avatar of the Sky Elders. He was in his snake form. His scaly body was coiled, except for his serpentine head, which raised to Pahana's eye level. He spoke in his strange way of carrying his words through his hissing.

"The Spear-Finger is fierce and has great power," Manabazo said. "His coming makes my mind worried and dour. You must react with great alarm. He will cause much destruction and harm."

"But what is this monster?" Pahana asked. "Why is he coming here?"

If a snake could look worried, Manabazo showed his concern. "The Spear-Finger is a living tree. She has long hated the sacred Yaxchee. She wants the elemental power of the ancient world tree. The Yaxchee will be a casualty. The Spear-Finger won't be dissuaded by any plea."

Pahana barely managed to hide his nervousness. He and his family had long been responsible for protecting the Tree of Life. In order to keep winter from covering the world once again, the Itiwana tribe would be asked to risk their lives to defend the tree.

"How can I stop it?" Pahana asked worriedly.

Manabazo lowered his head to his coils. "I do not know if that can be done. If we fail, the Enemy Way will have won."

An arrow pierced the rabbit. Hayoka collected the dead animal for its meat. Both large and small prey were abundant in the area since they, like Hayoka, had fled from the swarm of locusts that had razed most of the forests in the Land of Everlasting Summer to an area beyond Shipapa-Lina where the trees and bushes still stood.

Hayoka had been in this evergreen area for more than a week. He had a strong, personal reason to tarry here, instead of returning to Shipapa-Lina. He knew Pahana would be wondering where he was. He also knew that others in Shipapa-Lina were most likely glad he was gone and wished that he would never return.

However, he had something more important on his mind at the moment. He returned to the campsite with the dead rabbit in his hand. He saw the glow and the smoke of the campfire beyond the shrubbery. Pushing through the bushes, he saw the small hut, along with its owner.

A man in a hooded robe sat on a log, poking the campfire. He turned toward the returning Hayoka to reveal his hideously burned face. The unnamed man rarely spoke or showed any emotion. Hayoka referred to him as Burned-Faced Man.

While in one of his rare talkative moods, the disfigured man had explained that he was of some odd religious order known as monks. These strangers had come here over the Great Water for the purpose of spreading the word of their beliefs. Hayoka didn't understand this behavior. *Very odd ritual. Why come so far merely to pontificate about your religion to strangers?*

The monks had the misfortune of running into the Vykans, who preferred their own belief system to that of the monks. They preferred Odin to this

Jesus person. As a result, they killed the monks and burned their bodies. One monk was allowed to survive, to return to his home and spread the word of Odin to his far-off people. But as punishment for his sacrilege, they had engulfed his face with fire. The monk had run off into the night, screaming in pain.

He had miraculously recovered but was too embarrassed by his horrific deformity to return home. As a monk, he was used to solitude and private prayer. He chose to remain in his strange, green realm. He had wandered for years until he settled in the warm, green realm of the Land of Everlasting Summer. He had lived as a hermit for quite some time.

Hayoka stumbled randomly upon the Burned-Faced Man after finding the dying form of Dagwona, the Witch of the Whirlwind. She had been stabbed by Pahana while she attempted to destroy the Tree of Life. Hayoka had carried her off, looking for some assistance, before it was too late.

The Burned-Faced Man seemed to have some expertise as a healer and helped tend to the wounded witch. Despite her heritage as a kachina, he was able to help her. In fact, he credited her spiritual physiology with her survival. He would not have been able to save her had she been human.

The Burned-Faced Man held out his hand. "I'll cook that for you."

Hayoka handed the rabbit to the monk. "How is she?"

"She's awake," he replied, preparing to cook the hare.

Hayoka entered the small hut, which was lit by a candle. Hayoka had never seen a candle before. *Clever creation*, he thought.

The Witch of the Whirlwind lay silently in a bed made of grass, hay, and leaves in the flickering light. She seemed frail. Hayoka had developed intense feelings for the mystic mistress of the elemental winds. Dagwona had saved his life by warning him of danger, and he was physically drawn to her. He was risking the wrath of the Itiwana if they should ever find out he was caring for her.

Dagwona stared at the roof of the cabin, watching a spider devour a fly in a web. Her face was a mix of sadness and anger. Clearly, her defeat at the hands of Pahana still tormented her.

Hayoka sat on the floor beside her. "How do you feel?"

Dagwona didn't look at him. "Prodigious pain. Terribly tired. Woefully weak."

"The monk says you're recovering nicely," Hayoka said. "The pain and weakness will be gone soon."

"Dagwona's distraught," the witch said. "Malicious memories. Nagging nightmares."

"Because of Pahana?" he asked.

"Indeed. Infernal Itiwana," she muttered. "Witch was wounded. Pierced painfully. Requiring revenge."

Hayoka was torn on the subject of killing Pahana. It was true that Pahana had impaled Dagwona with an icy spear, and was the son of Tawa, the man Hayoka's mother hated more than anyone. His mother had raised him to despise the Itiwana. And Hayoka's introduction to the Itiwana had been rather cold and unpleasant. They disliked and distrusted him because his father, Hobomok, was seen as a traitor to the tribe. The Itiwana would never accept him. All this seemed like sufficient reason to hate Pahana and the Itiwana.

However, Hayoka liked Pahana. Of all the Itiwana, Pahana was the only one who had completely accepted Hayoka. Despite his father, Hobomok, being vilified by the tribe, Pahana accepted Hayoka as a friend. Pahana continually defended Hayoka against his own family and had taken it upon himself to train Hayoka as a Two Horn Rider. *He's my only true friend.*

"Retaliate ruthlessly!" Dagwona insisted. "Punish Pahana. Slay savagely!"

Hayoka paused, considering his next words carefully. "We need to be cautious. Pahana is no fool. The Itiwana are a resourceful lot. We must be wise. We should plan."

"I'm impatient," she replied. "Bloody brutality beckons."

"I know, but you've underestimated them before," he said. "It will be worth waiting for. Let's think this through so we don't make any mistakes. Do you trust me?"

"Dagwona does," the witch said softly. "Please plan perfectly. Witch will wait."

Hayoka felt uncomfortable misleading her. He hadn't decided what he was going to do. "I brought you some food. The monk is cooking it now. After I bring it to you, I'll take my leave. I should go back to Shipapa-Lina to see what Pahana and his people are doing. I'm curious about their condition since the locusts came. If they're vulnerable, we should gather information and I need to be there."

"Hasten, Hayoka," she responded. "Make me mirthful. Deliver death!"

Black Crow flew with an unerring, unshakeable sense of where he needed to go. The black-plumed bird had been bonded to Tawa for 22 years and served his master with devotion. Pinga had sent him to find Tawa.

Whatever the old bird needed to find, it always flew directly to, merely by instinct. Black Crow had been specially bred with that ability. Just as the avian had found the cave of the Na-Ash-Jai spider women years ago, its keen senses now directed it unerringly to Tawa.

After hours of flight, the avian agent of the Itiwana flew over a field and spotted a giant carrying the limp figure of Tawa in his arms. The bird saw Brave Fire and an unknown man following behind them. The giant was heading directly for the Mystic Moon Mountains.

Satisfied that it had carried out the first part of its assignment, Black Crow changed course and flew north to find Tawa's family.

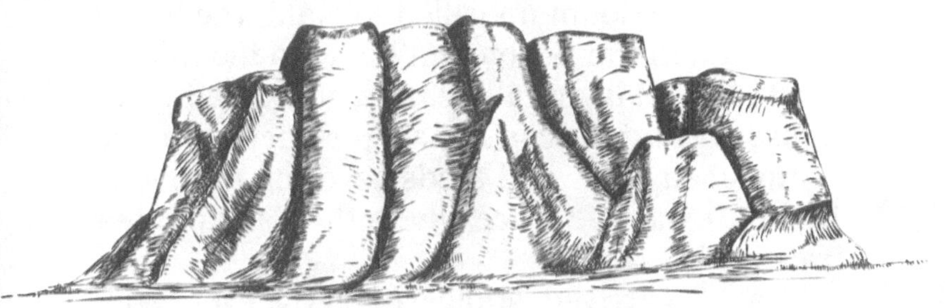

CHAPTER THREE

Gah-Oh had reached the Mystic Moon Mountains in a single day because giants walk extremely fast. He walked up a path to the top of an escarpment on the western fringe of the grand plateau. The mountainous region was familiar to Gah-Oh because it was the home of the sacred Earthmother.

Naya-Nazgani had been fortunate enough to induce Brave Fire to allow him to ride atop the bison. He had been having great difficulty keeping up with his two massive companions and attempted to mount Brave Fire. At first, the bison bucked and refused to allow the monster hunter to ride him. In time, however, as they traveled together, and the monster hunter kept speaking gently to the animal, Brave Fire relented and accepted Naya-Nazgani as his rider.

The divine grass house of the Earthmother sat far from curious eyes peacefully enhancing the top of a mountain called Kuwahi, the tallest mountain in the region and home to the mighty White Bear, king of all bears. The exalted grass house was a tall, cone-shaped structure made of thatched grass and reeds covering a wooden frame. It was the place where the Earthmother preferred to reside.

Gah-Oh arrived, still carrying the ever-weakening Tawa. Brave Fire managed the long climb with Naya-Nazgani. After the arduous climb was completed, the bison needed to rest. Naya-Nazgani hopped off the animal, patting it gratefully.

Naya-Nazgani watched as Gah-Oh gently placed Tawa down on the stone path leading to the divine grass house of the sacred Earthmother. His large shadow fell over the entrance.

"It is I," Gah-Oh shouted with his thunderous voice. "Earnestly, I call to the resplendent Earthmother. Immense Gah-Oh humbly implores the luminous one's aid for yon dying, fragile mortal man."

A curious Naya-Nazgani waited and watched, wondering who or what would emerge from that hogan. *I've never heard of the Earthmother in 300 years of wandering.*

From out of the grass house stepped a tall woman with brown skin and light brown hair. She wore an unusual type of garment made from tree bark. She was also adorned with a cloak made of jewels and seashells, connected by seaweed and vines. Her head was crowned by a headdress made of iridescent tail feathers from the quetzal bird. She walked with regal elegance. Her name was Eithinoa, the Earthmother.

"In familial devotion I come," Eithinoa said.

He gave a slight bow. "Towering Gah-Oh gratefully thanks majestic Eithinoa for generously coming to help."

"In curiosity, I ask what you need of me," she said.

Gah-Oh pointed to Tawa. "Yon ailing, frail mortal is in great need of beneficent healing help from wondrous Eithinoa."

Eithinoa stepped closer to Tawa and looked at his wound. "In concern, I ask what has happened to this poor man."

Gah-Oh shook his head. "Immense Gah-Oh has learned that this unfortunate wanderer ran afoul of vile skinwalkers. Only sacred Eithinoa has the amazing power to successfully aid yon dying mortal."

She studied the wounded man with sympathy and curiosity. "In perception, I say this is more than a mere mortal. In accuracy, I say he is a mastop-kachina."

"Does this unforeseen information mean the blessed Earthmother can save yon unlucky stranger?" Gah-Oh asked.

Eithinoa put her hand on Tawa's chest. "In alarm, I say that he is too near death. In sadness, I say that I cannot save this man."

"Is there nothing imminently helpful that sacred Eithinoa can do to assist yon dying wanderer?"

"In doubt, I say that I see little hope," Eithinoa replied. "In optimism, I say I will try."

Niya Nazgani stepped into view, catching the eye of the Earthmother. They sized each other up for a moment.

"In clarity, I say you are a mastop-kachina, as well," Eithinoa said. "In apprehension, I say that I sense within you a history of blood and violence."

The monster hunter responded with a slight nod. "I'll not deny my past, and I've fought with pride. But I did not come here to kill. Only to help. I came across this man by chance. If it would ease your mind, I will depart, leaving him in your tender care."

Gah-Oh stomped a large foot in between them and raised his club. "Shall faithful Gah-Oh remove yon dangerous stranger from your divine presence?"

Eithinoa hesitated, looking at Niya-Nazgani's intense eyes. "In perspicacity, I say he may stay. In positivity, I say such an act of kindness indicates a good soul. In expediency, I say to bring the injured one into my home."

Naya-Nazgani lifted the bloodied Tawa and carried him into the grass house. The Earthmother gestured to her bed, made of something that looked like interlocking lily pads floating in a ditch of sparkling jade water. Niya-Nazgani expected to see Tawa sink into the water and therefore prepared to hold his head above the surface. Surprisingly, the Itiwana chieftain did not sink. Somehow, those little lily pads supported him. *Even after centuries, there are things that surprise me.*

Eithinoa laid hands on Tawa, trying her best to heal the wounded Itiwana, even though she did not seem confident. He assumed that Tawa was beyond her help, assuming she was sincere in her efforts. Though he had not dismissed the possibility of a trap.

After a long trek, a hot and tired Hayoka reached Shipapa-Lina. He was still unused to the heat of the Land of Everlasting Summer, having come from the cooler north. While he was glad the trip was over and he could get some water, he was also worried about his reception. *I don't anticipate the most genial of welcomes.*

The stamping thud of bison hooves grew louder, and he spotted one of the Itiwana sentries cantering toward him. He hoped the rider would not simply trample him. When the sentry got close enough, he recognized Yoki of the Moon Clan. Yoki, who was the age of 40 summers, glared down from his bison, Running Fist.

"So, the son of Hobomok returns," Yoki said. "I suppose it was too much to hope you had scurried off forever."

Hayoka offered an infuriatingly polite smile. "You'd have preferred, perhaps, that I was as dead as a beaver pelt? Life is so disappointing. Have you no kind words for my return?"

Yoki scowled. "Do you find yourself charming? Well, we do not."

"Undoubtably," Hayoka agreed. "Still, I would see Pahana before I leave. Perhaps he will greet me a bit more kindly."

"I should have my loyal Running Fist stomp you under his hooves," Yoki replied. "But I imagine Pahana would like to have words with you in person. Come along."

Yoki nudged Running Fist and the bison trotted toward the cliffs of Shipapa-Lina. Hayoka rushed to keep pace with the animal. For the first minute, they traveled in a tense silence.

"We are kin," Yoki said, sounding like he was spitting something distasteful out of his mouth.

"What?" Hayoka asked.

"I am of the Moon Clan," Yoki said. "Your father, Hobomok, was the leader of my clan when I was a boy. We shared the same blood. I respected him as a child. He taught me to hunt. He was a great hunter."

"I've heard he was."

"And he betrayed our trust!" Yoki said. "His action was the darkest blight upon our clan that has ever occurred. We've had to bear the shame of his actions ever since. To this very day, there are still those who remind our clan of this dishonor. And I curse Hobomok because of it."

"You seem to have a lot of company in that respect," Hayoka said. "But it's good to meet kin."

"You won't think so if you betray us," Yoki said. "The Moon Clan does not forgive."

"I am grateful for the warning," Hayoka said. "Be assured that I take it seriously."

The pair reached the buffalo pens. Many of the Itiwana glared at the returning Hayoka. He did not look directly at any of them. All that mattered was how the acting chief would receive him. Hayoka was still unsure what he would say or how he'd be greeted by Pahana. Yoki did not speak another word to him during the tense walk. Hayoka kept thinking about Dagwona.

Pahana and Ashiwi, the master of mounts, were looking over a group of large, sturdy bison. Pahana was examining them all carefully. Yoki simply rode away, giving Hayoka a warning glance.

"A good selection," Pahana said. "Sadly, none of them matches my wonderful steed, World Giant. I miss that loyal beast."

"A sad loss," Ashiwi said. "I've rarely seen a beast so formidable. Aside from Mountain Fury, he was the mightiest of the bison."

"Agreed wholeheartedly," Pahana said. "And my father's old steed has been a valuable replacement, but I can't turn back his years. Mountain Fury deserves a rest."

Ashiwi gestured toward the assembled bison. "As soon as you make your choice, I will begin preparing him for battle."

"I think..." Pahana started to say when he caught sight of Hayoka nearby. He stared coldly at the returning Hayoka, who approached with trepidation.

"Hello, Pahana," Hayoka said.

Both men continued to stare silently. Hayoka was seeing the Itiwana for the first time since learning that Pahana had stabbed Dagwona. Mixed feelings flooded his troubled brain.

"Come with me," Pahana ordered and turned his back. He marched toward the cliffs and Hayoka reluctantly followed. The son of Tawa trod ominously through the sandstone and mortar walls of the Cliff Palace. Hayoka had been here once before. On his last visit, Pahana had also led him into the consecrated structure, although on that occasion, it was to meet the chieftain, Tawa.

Then, when they had entered the chamber of the Shakowin ruling counsel, Tawa had been sitting on the seat of honor reserved for the chieftain. Pahana, as the acting leader in his father's absence, seemed comfortable taking Tawa's spot. Hayoka was reminded of his first visit and the intimidating view of the regal-looking Tawa greeting them in that same seat. Somehow, Pahana did not look quite as impressive. He looked more like a boy trying to fill his father's shoes.

"I hate being wrong," Pahana said, glowering at Hayoka. "When every man and woman among the Itiwana told me not to trust you because you were the son of the greatest traitor in our history, I rebuked them. I said you weren't to blame for what Hobomok did. I gave you my friendship, thinking you a man of good character. I hate being wrong."

"I'm sad to hear you say so," Hayoka replied. "You were good to me on my last visit."

"Then why did you run out on us when we were attacked?" Pahana asked. "I took the time to personally train you as one of my Two Horn Riders, despite the protests of my people. When I needed you, you fled. To say I am disappointed in you is immensely inadequate."

Hayoka felt some shame at disappointing Pahana but was also glad he left Shipapa-Lina when he did. He would not have been in the proper place to save Dagwona had he not. He was torn between his guilt and his feelings for the witch.

"I never claimed to be of heroic character," Hayoka said. "Perhaps you think too much of me. I appreciate your view of me as being worthy of joining your warriors, but you may have misjudged me. Not everyone is suited to be a warrior, even if he was trained by the noble Pahana. And don't forget, the people of your tribe view me as the undesirable son of a traitor. If they had their way, I would be sent away forever. Should I truly be expected to risk my skin to defend a village that would happily see me skinned alive?"

He felt as if Pahana's eyes were boring into his soul with that cold stare. *Will he accept this explanation or stab me the way he did Dagwona?*

"I suppose the fault is mine," Pahana said. "I wanted you to be something you weren't. You are not strong. Why have you returned here?"

"It is just as I told your father," Hayoka said. "I want to know about my father and the events leading up to his departure from the Itiwana. And more importantly, I need to know what happened the day your father killed my father."

"So you said," Pahana responded. "Mentioning your father won't win you many friends here in Shipapa-Lina. But I do owe you for your part in my rescue from the Puk-Wudjies. Also, my father decreed he would speak to you about Hobomok. Therefore, with very little enthusiasm, I permit you to walk among the people of Shipapa-Lina."

"Thank you, my friend," Hayoka said. "I—"

"Don't presume a comradeship still exists between us," Pahana said. "Respect stronger men."

"Greatest of apologies," Hayoka responded. "You're a good and just man."

Pahana replied in a low, stern voice. "If I'm wrong about you, you will not like Itiwana justice."

"Clearly understood."

"Perhaps it's best you take your leave while I talk to the Shakowin," Pahana said. "They may take some convincing to welcome the son of Hobomok for a second time. You should return on a later day."

"Very wise counsel," Hayoka replied. "I would regret being murdered solely for someone else's sins. I leave in haste."

"Go."

Hayoka backed slowly out of the room and sped up once he was out of Pahana's sight. As he made his way out, getting lost before stumbling upon the door, he was surprised at how emotional the dispute with Pahana had left him. Despite everything, part of him still felt a strong affection for Pahana. This made him feel wretched for running out on Pahana during a crisis. Yet he simultaneously felt equally wretched about liking the man who stabbed Dagwona. *I'm glad to be getting away from this place. I need to think.*

Stepping outside, he only proceeded a few paces before stopping. He had come face-to-face with the person he least wanted to see. Calian, son of Pogum, had arrived.

"First locusts and now a new type of vermin," Calian said. "Neither one is welcome here."

"Hello, Calian," Hayoka said. "I don't imagine you have any words of touching welcome for me."

Calian's eyes burned into him. "When Yoki told me you were back, I prayed to Awona'Wilona it was a cruel jest by him. Now I see it was a cruel jest by the Sky Elders."

Hayoka offered a polite smile. "The whims of the gods can be a curse, as well as a blessing, wouldn't you say?"

Calian moved nose-to-nose with Hayoka. "This is Shipapa-Lina. This is where Tawa and the Shakowin rule. It's been farmed and defended by the Itiwana for generations. It's where we raise our children. We live here and we try to live as well as we can. And take care of each other. It is our home—our world! It will never be yours!"

"I believe you're asking me to leave," Hayoka said. "But Pahana has permitted me to continue to enjoy the hospitality of the Itiwana. Ask him yourself."

Calian's face was expressionless. "Your trickery and manipulations may work on him, but I am not susceptible. If he commands that you remain, I will concede to his wishes. But nothing you do will escape my eye and the moment I have demonstrable evidence of your treachery; you and I will fight, and your blood will stain Ulah-Nane."

Hayoka remained stubbornly cocky in his response. "I sense a tone of displeasure directed toward me. Is it my imagination, or are you threatening me? My good friend Pahana would not like that. Surely, I misunderstood you."

"Was I not clear?" Calian said. "Must you hear the words? Then hear them now. I am the enemy you should fear, and if you do so much as sneeze aggressively upon one of my people, I will kill you in a bloody fashion. I state it plainly and unmistakably. Now you know my mind."

"I do admire honesty," Hayoka quipped.

"You know nothing of honesty," Calian said. "And you know even less about me if you do not take heed of my promise. Not a warning. A promise."

"Your feelings are as clear as ice crystals," Hayoka said. "And just as cold. To spare you the need of thinking up further threats, I will take my leave of this place."

"That is the only thing you will ever take from Shipapa-Lina," Calian said in a low growl.

Hayoka circled cautiously around Calian, half-expecting a physical blow to match his verbal assaults. "Have a pleasant afternoon, Calian. I look forward to our next battle of words."

"That is the only battle against me you could ever survive," Calian sneered.

The nearest members of the Itiwana tribe overheard this final verbal strike and showed their support. Some of them chanted Calian's name in approval of his actions toward Hayoka, while the rest just stared distrustfully at the visitor. As for Hayoka, he ignored the hostile glances of the tribe as he gratefully departed Shipapa-Lina.

I don't know whether my fate is to be friend or foe of the Itiwana, he thought. *But whatever I decide, Calian is going to be my biggest obstacle.*

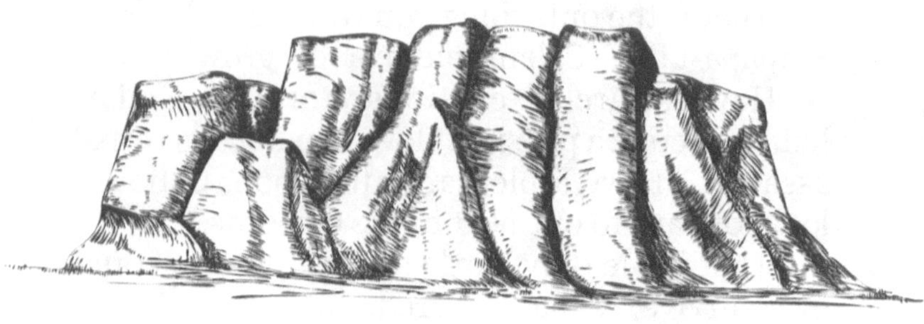

CHAPTER FOUR

The feeling of panic increased for the people of Kolhu. The eerie purple light now completely surrounded the Sun Dagger House. The holy dwelling was the center of religion and government for Kolhu. The four-level, nine-hundred-room semicircular structure with its great kivas was always a reassuring sign of hope and optimism for the Itiwana of Kolhu. It was here that Molowia ruled the city and protected it, with her shamanic powers and her mystic bond with the mighty guardian Wishpoosh. Seeing the Sun Dagger House seemingly under attack caused rampant fear among the population.

Molowia was as confused as everyone else. She rushed back to the Sun Dagger House as quickly as her aging, portly body could. She spent most of her time in the great house, and this was the first time she had left in days. She had spent the past few hours visiting the corn crop, to use her magic as protection against a locust attack similar to the one Shipapa-Lina had suffered. She knew it was more than a coincidence that this bizarre incident happened while she was away from the great house. *Someone knew I was not there to protect my house.*

A crowd had surrounded the great house by the time Molowia reached it. She calmed the frightened tribespeople with confident words although she was not as assured as she seemed. "I will see to this. Have no fear. Our fear only serves the enemy."

She hesitated before walking into the bizarre glow. For all her vast experience, she had no frame of reference to understand what was happening here. *What could this be?*

Firming up her courage, she stepped into the glow and entered the Sun Dagger House. Being inside that purple glow felt like moving through warm water. The sensation confirmed what she had suspected. This was not a freak natural phenomenon. It was magic. And she feared she knew who had cast this mysterious spell. *Where is Kia?*

She made her way to the chamber deep within the Sun Dagger House. If Kia was responsible, she had to be stopped and if she was not the cause of this, she could be in danger. Either way, finding Kia was her priority.

Molowia heard strange noises, and inhuman, incomprehensible voices coming from Kia's chamber. Her heart beat faster as she crept closer to the room that reeked of dark magic. *What's happening in there?*

To her surprise, when she was 10 steps away from the chamber, the eldritch light instantly vanished. The voices stopped. That feeling of unfathomable, otherworldly power was gone. In the blink of an eye, every hint of the strange event had disappeared.

The perplexed Molowia stepped into Kia's chamber, unsure of what to expect. She peered through the dim light, made more oblique by the smoke from the small fire emanating from a small pit. All she saw inside was young Kia sitting cross-legged atop a wooden bench, cushioned with animal pelts. The petite girl, who was only twelve summers old, had her eyes closed. One arm was reaching out in front of her, palm down, while the other was stretched out to the side, palm up.

Before Molowia could speak, Kia opened her eyes and looked at the older woman. "Hello, Cacique. May I do something for you?"

Molowia was uncharacteristically speechless. She did not understand what was happening here, and she didn't like the feeling of being so bewildered. She was the one people turned to for answers. It was a foreign feeling for her to be the one struggling for those answers.

"What happened here, Kia?" she asked. "Are you unharmed?"

"I am completely well and content," Kia replied. "Why do you ask?"

Molowia felt a mixture of surprise and anger at the response. "Why do I ask? Are you claiming you're oblivious to the uncanny events of the past minutes?"

"I was meditating," Kia said with infuriating calmness.

Molowia marched forward and stood before Kia. "Why are you lying to me, Little Woman?"

Kia tilted her head, looking innocent and adorable. "What do you mean? Why would I lie?"

Molowia struggled to control her anger. She was normally a very controlled person, but she had become increasingly concerned about Kia, as she was acting increasingly strange and clearly hiding things. Molowia cared dearly for Kia, who was the daughter of her nephew, Tawa, but that did not mean the girl was allowed to be deceitful and endanger Kolhu.

"I am giving you a chance to tell me the truth, Kia," Molowia snapped. "I ask you once again, what happened here while I was absent?"

Kia shrugged innocently. "I noticed nothing. I was meditating."

Molowia narrowed her eyes. "I don't think you're being honest with me, child."

"Don't you trust me, Cacique?"

Molowia barely controlled her rage and decided to try a different tactic. She used her shamanic skills to open her third eye and expand her mind. She reached into Kia's mind, intending to read her thoughts. She did not like doing this because it was a violation of the mind and the soul, but occasionally she found it necessary. *I must know what she's hiding.*

Molowia tried forcing her way into Kia's mind, but to her alarm, she could not. It felt to the aging shaman like her thoughts had hit a solid rock wall. That had never happened before. Redoubling her efforts, she still found herself unable to break through the girl's impenetrable defenses. The shocked Molowia hadn't realized until this moment how powerful her student had become. *This is insane! What in the name of the gods is happening?*

Molowia stood befuddled. For the first time in her life, she didn't know what to do next. If Kia was not being honest with her and she was unable to read the girl's thoughts, she had to do something to ensure that Kia was not endangering Kolhu. Should she order Kia to leave Kolhu? She hated to do that, but it may be necessary. However, was it wise to allow the girl to wander off on her own while her power was growing faster than a weed? If she was unmonitored, Kia could become a danger to both Kolhu and Shipapa-Lina.

Molowia kneeled in front of Kia, changing her strategy once again. "Kia, my sweet. Listen to me. We are kin. I have cared for you and taught you since the day you came to live with me. Your parents entrusted you to my care. They expect you to listen and learn and be loyal to the Itiwana. We are in a time of great peril, and we need to be able to trust each other. I have always been honest with you. I ask you now to be honest with me. Tell me what happened here."

Kia hesitated, and there was a moment of sadness in her cold eyes. But she quickly resumed her dispassionate demeanor. "I wish I could speak words that would soothe you, but I have already told it all."

Molowia stood up and shook her head. "I can do nothing more here, except to pray that my suspicions are wrong. If I am, I will humbly ask your forgiveness, but if I'm correct, we will have an unloving confrontation. Remain here and please refrain from mischief."

"Of course, Cacique," Kia replied softly.

The distraught Molowia left the chamber, utterly at a loss about what to do with the girl. She could only think of one possible course of action. *I must speak to her parents. If she won't obey me, perhaps her respect for Tawa will compel her to comply.*

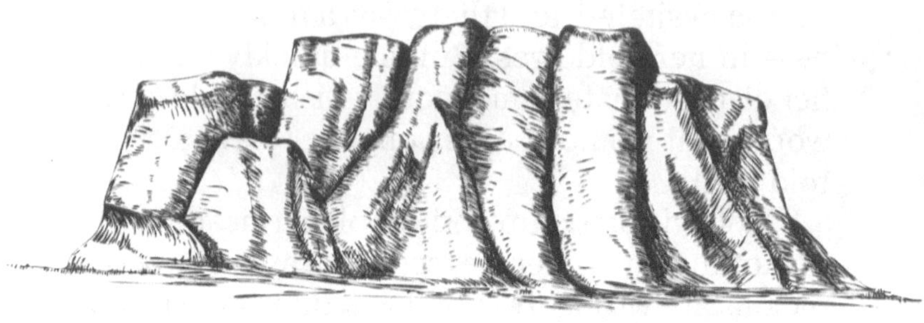

CHAPTER FIVE

I'm not alone, Hayoka thought nervously, as he strode across the ravaged plains.

While making his way back to the Burned-Faced Man's cabin, he caught sight of something out of the periphery of his eye. He could not see anyone or anything, which should have been reassuring since there were no bushes or trees remaining for an enemy to hide behind. If some threat were nearby, surely he would be able to see it.

Yet he kept detecting something in the corner of his eye, skittering rapidly but vanishing when Hayoka looked in its direction. Hayoka had seen too many strange things to accept that this was just his imagination. *I think I have a serious problem.*

He stopped, hoping to track the evasive entity with his hearing. Surely a running beast or man would make a sound. Yet he heard nothing. *Concentrate. Focus on the sounds.*

"Panicky, you are," said a voice from behind him.

The alarmed Hayoka spun around and saw a large, white snow fox glaring at him with a toothy grin. After a moment of fear, Hayoka calmed down, recognizing the strange being.

"Agwara," Hayoka said. "Must you continually find sport in alarming me with intimidating arrivals?"

"My impishness, you must forgive," Agwara said mirthfully. "Mischievous fun I need for relief. Tense these days are."

"That much is certain," Hayoka replied. "To what do I owe this humorous visitation?"

"Information, I have," Agwara said. "Things you need to know, there are."

"My ear is yours," Hayoka responded.

The snow fox spirit circled Hayoka unnervingly as he spoke. "A place there is, which you should know about. Important to our plans, they are."

Our plans! Hayoka thought. *Agwara is taking for granted that I'm going to help him and Dagwona destroy the Itiwana. I've not yet made up my mind about that.*

"The Valley of the Blue Mists, it is called," Agwara said. "Go there, you must."

"Why?"

"Strange powers, they have," Agwara said. "Power to be great allies, or great enemies.

Enemies to the Itiwana, they could be. Contact them, you must."

As Agwara talked, Hayoka considered his options. While he remained undecided about the Itiwana, it might be advantageous for him to make powerful allies. Whatever he ultimately decided to do, having formidable confederates would make him feel more secure against which-ever side got mad at him. *I'll make some allies for myself, not for the Winter Gods or their servants.*

"Very well, my friend," Hayoka said. "Tell me where to go."

Feeble moans filled the sacred grass house. Eithinoa held her hands inches above Tawa's wound, concentrating her nature powers on the Itiwana leader. She drew energy from the ground, which channeled up through her body and into the dying man. His mournful groans distressed her, as her efforts to heal him came to nothing.

She sensed the inherent nobility and integrity in Tawa. He had a rare strength of spirit, which had probably kept him alive. That, and his phys-ical nature as a mastop-kachina, had prolonged a life that should have ended days ago.

Naya-Nazgani paced silently, having ambig-uous feelings about this situation. He hardly knew Tawa, and he did not trust the giant out-side. He had never heard of an Earthmother in all his centuries of traveling and had no idea of how her powers worked. Was she genuinely trying to save Tawa, or was she deliberately failing due to a hidden agenda? He kept a close eye on her, trying to spot any deceit. *I hope she is what she seems. I don't want to have to kill her.*

"In dejection, I say he is not long for this realm," Eithinoa sighed. "In guilt, I say I can do nothing better than to give him a few more sunsets."

"What about the giants?" Naya-Nazgani asked. "Is it not widely known that giant blood can heal?"

"In fairness, I say that your information is false," Eithinoa said. "In admission, I say many untrue stories have spread about my friends. In truth, I say giant blood will not save him."

Naya-Nazgani did not know what the truth was. "So, you say there is no hope?"

"In disgrace, I must concede this," she replied.

They were both surprised when Tawa opened his eyes. He looked up at Eithinoa's face. Something similar to a smile formed on his dry lips. He whispered weakly. "Thank you. For your help ... and your honesty."

Eithinoa brushed his sweat-moistened hair from his face. "In surprise, I say your words are unexpected. In shame, I say I deserve no thanks."

Naya-Nazgani came closer. "Can I do anything for you, my friend?"

Tawa managed a slight nod. "Y-Yes. My family. I need to speak to my wife. My son. Must contact them ... before the flickering fire of life fades."

"I will do whatever I can to see it done," Naya-Nazgani replied.

"I earnestness, I say I will also," Eithinoa said. "In compassion, I say I will see you reunited with your family somehow."

Hayoka marched a very long way. He had been directed on this journey by Agwara. He was still undecided about Agwara's plan, but he also did not disagree there was potential in paying a friendly visit to people with power although he did not know whether these people would end up being friends or foes. If they become involved in this matter, who would they help at the end of the day? Would they help either side? Or maybe they will just kill him. He would find out very soon.

Hayoka continued his march, following the path Agwara had indicated. It was a hot day, as it often was in the Land of Everlasting Summer. He walked at a slow, steady pace, not wanting to exert himself too much because he may need all the energy he could muster when he arrived at his destination. He might have to fight or run. *I hate the not knowing.*

Part of the trip took him over the devastated wasteland that had been ravaged by the locusts. Another part was over green plains and plants and trees, in areas outside the scope of where the locusts had ravaged the land. And yet another part was on fertile, wide grassy green fields, comfortable under his feet as he walked. Thinking about many things, he daydreamed about Dagwona, wondering what she knew about the plan Agwara had concocted. *Had he told her what he planned to do? If he had, she would no doubt have been in favor of it.* Hayoka himself was not so enthusiastic. He wondered what Dagwona would think if she knew about his misgivings. In her mind, he was completely devoted to the cause of getting revenge for her. While he had strong feelings for her, possibly even love, he was not yet committed to killing the Itiwana, particularly not Pahana, who he still saw as a friend, despite everything that had happened recently.

Hayoka had been brought up by his mother to distrust the Itiwana because they killed his father, Hobomok, just as the Itiwana distrusted him because of what Hobomok had done to them. Yet something inside him vehemently wished that he could spend his days riding alongside Pahana, as one of his Two Horn Riders, having exciting adventures and good comradeship. Sadly, he did not think that was how his life would end up being.

He had yet to decide what he was going to do when he finally reached the mysterious place known as the Valley of the Blue Mist Agwara had told him about.

The legendary mist swirled like a living thing. If there were people living in the valley, the mists cloaked them completely. There was something eerie about the strange blue mist. It seemed he could almost hear it. He definitely felt it caressing his skin, making him feel as if he were walking through a pile of feathers. It was simultaneously relaxing and menacing.

He had been warned that he might not find these people overly welcoming. He feared falling into some hole or running into some unfriendly creature as he made his way through the mist, unable to see beyond the reach of his arms.

This second thought seemed prophetic when he heard strange noises echoing around him. He could not identify the sounds. They were like distant voices but seemed to be whispering in his ear. Were they warnings or words of welcome or were they not directed to him at all? He couldn't guess. His heart pumped and his instincts told him this had been a bad idea and he should depart quickly. However, he had to keep going. The enigmatic voice that had long whispered to him spoke. *Far too late to be cowardly now. I'm in this quagmire too deeply.*

Something moved inside the mist. Something with a heavy tread. He heard heavy breathing. *That's not Agwara.*

He had asked the snow fox spirit to accompany him, but Agwara intimated that he was either unwilling or unable to enter the Valley of the Blue Mist. Was the cunning animal spirit afraid of these people or did his machinations depend upon the people of the valley not knowing Agwara and the servants of the Winter Sky Elders were involved? *I hope I can trust that damnable fox.*

Whatever was hiding in the mist came nearer. Hayoka could feel the vibration from the heavy footsteps. Was it a deadly threat, or possibly just their way of investigating a new arrival to determine if defensive measures were needed? The sound seemed to be behind him now. Hayoka turned and spotted a towering silhouette for a moment, but it moved to his right, vanishing into the mist. The footstep sounds told Hayoka that the creature was still close by. The breathing increased as if it were preparing to make its move.

Hayoka decided to address whatever unknown beast was stalking him. He had always been a good talker. "Whatever you're planning to do, there's no need to hurt me. I'm obviously no threat to you. I am very small. I vow I am not your enemy. I'm merely here to talk. I'm just a harmless visitor, and I want to speak to someone. I would kindly ask you not to kill me."

After an ominous silence, a voice answered them from the mists. It was a throaty female voice. "A visitor? Visitors should be invited. You were not. This is a threatening gesture. We do not look kindly upon threatening gestures."

"I do not mean to threaten anyone," he replied. "Believe me, I am harmless. I run from fights. I'm a rabbit, not a wolf. I see no glory in violence. I have come only for conversation. Nothing more."

"You have been warned once," the female voice said sternly. "How many warnings do you require before you depart? Our patience is very limited."

"Please," he said. "How can I persuade you I have no evil intentions? You have no reason to be afraid of me. Surely my docile nature is evident.

If you'll simply let me speak to you, we could be great allies. I implore you to listen to me. I don't ask for your trust. Just for your ears. You can kill me afterward if I prove deceitful."

A different female voice spoke in a more honeyed, soothing tone. "It shall be permitted."

The first voice interrupted, "But that is not our way."

"I wish to give this man a chance to speak," the second voice said. "My instincts say we should listen."

"We must solve this disagreement," the first said.

As Hayoka listened, hoping the new voice would win the debate, something in the darkness grabbed him. Clutching him in an unshakable grip, it pulled him off his feet, as if he were a baby chick.

"Wait, There is no reason to hurt me!" Hayoka cried.

The large, unseen creature held him so tightly around the waist and chest that he could hardly draw a breath. His attacker was a solid mass of muscle and had a strong, strange odor. Hayoka assumed it was perhaps an ogre or sasquatch, but he wasn't sure. He only knew it was huge and strong. Then a hairy hand clamped over his mouth. A third arm. As he vainly struggled, a fourth arm struck him on the head, and he knew nothing else.

CHAPTER SIX

Get out of my head, Hayoka thought. He felt violated in his own brain as unfamiliar thoughts intruded forcefully. He moaned and jerked fitfully in his unconscious state, repulsed by the foreign minds rooting through his deepest dreams. *Get out!*

He woke later. The feeling of being defiled was still churning in his brain. Opening his blurry eyes, Hayoka saw that he was no longer outside in the blue mists. He was now inside some type of structure. *Where am I?*

Hayoka found himself in an adobe dwelling, lit by candles. His head was aching from the blow that knocked him out. He tried to focus his mind to take stock of his situation. Thinking and planning were what he excelled at.

The strange place had an abundance of various types of plants in clay pots. On the walls were petroglyphs and pictographs that Hayoka could not identify. He rose from the feather and leaf bed where he had been placed. Looking around suspiciously, he expected the four-armed beast to pop out of the shadows and batter him to death.

Why have I been brought here? he wondered. *To dig through my mind for information? So far, I have been treated very well, but will that last? What are their future intentions? Am I being held for torture or execution?*

He debated leaving the small chamber he was in. *Should I risk wandering through this unknown place? Should I look for the people who brought me here or just wait? They might be peeved if I wander into a place they don't want me to see. Maybe it would be wise to sit here and wait for my headache to pass.*

He rubbed the back of his head and sat back down on the bed. He breathed deeply to calm himself, planning what he would say when his captors arrived. He hoped his glib tongue would serve him as well here as it had with Pahana. More often than not, he could talk his way out of trouble. True, there were people like Calian who would not give him any grace, but he hoped these people were not like that. *Just stay calm, Hayoka. Fear won't help you here. Maybe I can make friends with these strangers.*

He wasn't sure how long he waited there since he couldn't see the sun or moon. However, the candles melted down quite a bit. He had never seen wax candles before but deduced that their shrinking size indicated the passing of time. He began nodding off when he heard the shuffling of feet. His eyes opened wide, and he leaped to his feet and saw two silhouetted female figures standing in the flickering candlelight.

The older one was shorter, with a round, time-worn face and short-cropped hair. Clutched tightly in her fist was a tube made from a hollow bone. The other woman was leaner and angular, with a mop of curly hair. Both wore clothing made from various colorful pieces of cotton and silk. Their wraparound skirts were tied at the waist by a thin snakeskin belt. Their staring eyes were so intense that Hayoka felt an icy chill. Their faces were so hard to read; he had no idea what they were thinking. He debated staying quiet and waiting for them to address him but chose to risk taking control of the situation.

"I greet you," he said, as amiably as possible despite his feeling of dread. "My name is Hayoka. I represent the people of Ulah-Nane. I've specifically come to speak for those in the Land of Everlasting Summer although they do not know I've come here today. I seek an alliance."

"You are Anasazi," the older one said with a hoarse voice.

"I'm what?" Hayoka asked.

"Anasazi," the younger one said. "It is our word for the ancient enemies who once threatened us. All intruders are now deemed Anasazi."

"I pray I can change that perception," Hayoka said.

"You have a difficult challenge ahead of you in your hope to accomplish such a thing," the younger one said.

"You were warned to leave," the hoarse, antagonistic one said. "Visitors are not permitted here. Our message was clear and concise. Why did you not depart?"

Hayoka did his best to remain calm and confident. "I believe you have already looked into my mind. Very rude of you, by the way. You've seen that what I say is true. I came here merely to speak to you."

"There is a part of your mind we cannot pierce," she said. "There is a shadow concealing the hours before you came to see us. This concerns us."

So, they do not know about Agwara sending me, Hayoka thought. *That crafty fox did something to conceal himself in my memories. Plots within plots. Who can I trust? I'll attend to Agwara later. For now, I must make friends with these women.*

"No need for concern," he said with a smile. "I have nothing to hide. I can't explain the reason for this shadow in my mind you speak of. I can only assure you I come in peace. Just consider me a friendly visitor."

"The Valley of the Blue Mist is not a place for visitors," the elder said. "We do not wish to be involved in the affairs of the outside world. Do not bring your evil here."

"Do not be so harsh," the other said. "The man is nervous. I sense no intention to attack or to harm anyone here. This man's nature is not one of a predator."

Good, that one is championing my request to stay, Hayoka thought.

"We must be united on this," the elder said. "Do not divide us."

"Let me speak to this visitor, sister. Go attend to more important matters. Please."

"Very well," the hoarse elder said. "I will permit it. Be wise and be cautious. I shall return in time."

As the suspicious woman left, the younger one smiled at Hayoka. "Forgive my sister's suspicious nature. Caution has kept us alive. We are responsible for protecting those who live here in the valley. We must be wary of strangers."

"I understand," Hayoka said, relieved. "No offense was taken. Your caution is wise."

"Thank you for understanding," she said. "She carries heavy burdens. My sister is known as the Breathing Shaman, bearer of the bone tube. Her powers are formidable."

"And you are?"

"I am known as the Keeper," she said. "I oversee the care of our sacred objects."

"An honor to be in your presence, Keeper," Hayoka said, bowing his head slightly. "What is this place?"

"This is the House of Many Hands," the Keeper said. "It sits under the Full Moon Arch. Few outsiders have the honor of coming here."

"I imagine I have you to thank for my safe arrival," he replied. "I don't think your sister is overjoyed by my presence here. You have my gratitude."

"Unnecessary," she said. "I am of the mind that your arrival is fortuitous."

"How so?"

"I'll explain. Walk with me, Hayoka."

They left the square chamber and stepped into an adobe passageway with more pictographs on the walls. Several wooden stools, each one with a cairn of five crystals—four black onyx atop one obsidian—lined the walls. The onyx crystals glowed, emitting a strange black light.

Hayoka and his enigmatic guide passed another square room, where several more women sat on the ground in a circle around another cairn, humming melodiously. Hayoka felt something otherworldly about this House of Many Hands.

"This place was created long ago by the Great Shaman," the Keeper said. "He was the teacher of myself and my sister. He trained many powerfully magic women, including the Priestess of the Evening Star and Molowia, the Cacique of Kolhu. It is a place of learning, where we mastered ancient powers, aided by the charmed power of these crystals, which empower themselves by drawing the negative energy away from us. They were unearthed from within the circle of the sacred totem."

"I'm unfamiliar with this totem," Hayoka said. "But please continue."

The Keeper resumed her tale. "For many years, we have remained here, shunning the outside world. This is our sanctuary from danger. We're more interested in the spirit than the material world. Here in the valley, we want only peace and self-improvement. We wish to grow spiritually. That is our goal. Nothing else matters to our order."

"Laudable self-control," he said.

"Perhaps," she said. "I have long been of the opinion that we of the valley have been secluded from the affairs of the others for far too long. We know that a war of gods has begun, and my sister has foreseen that it will become much worse. She sees this as a reason to remain in hiding. I, however, have challenged this. We must reach out to the world. We must know them and let them know us."

Hayoka was very glad to hear this. His task might be easier than he thought. "I am in complete accord with your opinion. This is why I'm here. The world is tumbling toward chaos, and we need allies such as yourself. You have a power that can save many lives and perhaps end this war sooner."

"We want nothing further of the gods, nor do we expect any mercy from them," the Keeper said. "But I feel for those who suffer from their callous conflict."

"Indeed," Hayoka said. "I have no stake in this war. I was born to the people up north who were done wrong by this conflict. I came south to the Land of Everlasting Summer to visit a tribe because of questions about a father I never knew. However, I found them unwelcoming."

"Yes, we saw some of this in your mind," the Keeper said.

"I have wondered why they are so suspicious and hostile," he told her, rubbing his sore head. "They are very eager to go to war. Why is it so many people are eager for that? I find there are warriors everywhere, but not many intellectuals. I blame the gods for that. They've instigated this war."

"I agree," the Keeper said sadly. "Someone should stand against them."

"That is why I'm here, to help you, and hopefully persuade you to help me."

"But how would you help us?" she asked.

"You don't know much about the people outside the valley," Hayoka said. "But I know. I've spoken to many people since I left the north lands. I have spoken to people in the north and south. I've spoken to warriors and snow spirits and witches. I have traveled across Ulah-Nane, and I have seen war. I can be a source of information for you when you make contact with those who are unknown to you. I can help you to understand these people before the war comes. Because the war will come, inevitably. You will not be able to stop it or avoid it once it arrives. Therefore, you'll need all the information you can gather."

The Keeper closed her eyes for a few moments, contemplating all this information. "The Breathing Shaman feels the war will not come here if we do not antagonize the gods. She fears you may have brought it to us."

"Others have believed they could avoid the conflict," Hayoka said. "Molowia, the high shaman of Kolhu, thought she could remain neutral, but she was disappointed."

"We know Molowia well," the Keeper said. "The Breathing Shaman thinks we can do what Molowia could not."

"And what do you think?" he asked.

She paused for an uncomfortably long time before answering. "I think our involvement is inescapable and that you are the great hope for peace in Ulah-Nane. We will need knowledge, and we will need allies. You can help us with both."

"I would be happy and honored to help you," Hayoka replied. "We must parlay with the Itiwana and reason with them to quell their zeal for war. You must be the peacekeepers before the war reaches you. Don't make the mistake Kolhu made, sitting in the shadows, hoping the war passed them by only to be dragged into it."

The Keeper stared at a pictograph. "The Breathing Shaman would argue that Kolhu's involvement came due to its connection to Shipapa-Lina. While we, on the other hand, are far removed from—"

"You are not as far removed from the war as you'd like to think," he interrupted. "The tribes of the north who were ravaged by the Vykans had no antagonism with anyone. They imagined their non-involvement led to safety. They no longer exist."

The Keeper's lips tightened, and her posture stiffened. "You speak of unhappy days."

"I've seen many such days," he answered. "I hope to prevent you from seeing the same. In the near future, the Sky Elders will force you to choose. They'll insist that you must be on their side or pay the price. I do not wish to see your beautiful valley harmed in any way. You are the only ones who can stop this war. By creating an alliance with the Itiwana and controlling the area where the Tree of Life stands, you will be a force unlike anything ever seen before in Ulah-Nane. The human servants of the Winter Elders will fear you and be forced to negotiate. You can induce them to stop fighting. Without human servants, the war will no longer vex the land of Ulah-Nane. But only you can do this."

The Keeper folded her hands in a prayer-like way, pressing her palms together. Hayoka could tell that she was struggling with her decision.

"I can talk to the Itiwana," Hayoka said. "Pahana, the son of their chieftain, is my friend. I can persuade him to come here and parlay with you. They need allies, just as you do. Allow me to bring a delegation of the Itiwana here to speak to you, as friends. Just a small number. I ask you to trust me. Surely there's a way you can verify that I am not here to destroy you."

The Keeper gestured for him to follow her. "There is, indeed. Come."

Hayoka followed the Keeper to another chamber, where he saw a black pool in the ground.

"Look into this pool," she said. "Your reflection will change if you lie. I wish you to look into the Water of Veracity and speak the words you just told me, and we will find out what your genuine intentions are."

"Very well," he said, not hesitating. Looking at his reflection in the pool of liquid, he said, "I have not come here to destroy you. I want you to survive. I want the Valley of the Blue Mists to be strong. I need you to be the strongest power in Ulah-Nane. And when I bring the Itiwana here, they will be small in number. And if anyone is to be destroyed, I would pray it be them, not you, because their warlike obedience to the gods is the cause of all our problems. I wish you to have the advantage over them. I will do anything to see that you survive and triumph over any hostile warriors from Shipapa-Lina. You have my blessing to destroy any of them if they are hostile. I would encourage it. If the Itiwana prove treacherous, kill them with my blessing."

The Keeper saw that the reflection did not change at all. She relaxed, seeing that he was not a threat to them. "Excellent."

"And you see I've told you the truth," he said with a chipper voice.

"I believe you," the Keeper said. "And I am willing to work as your ally. But I must convince the Breathing Shaman. It is she who makes the final decision. She will be difficult to persuade, but I will somehow change her rigid mind."

"Shall I go with you?"

"No, certainly not," the Keeper said. "Your presence will not be advantageous. I deduce that it is better if you leave the valley. Although it goes against our normal rules, and my sister will be angry, I allow you to leave here unharmed. Soon, I will contact you. Do not ask how. You will know my message when it comes to you. At that time, I will instruct you to bring a small party of Itiwana to this place. When they arrive, the Breathing Shaman and I will look into their hearts and learn their true nature. They will then become either allies or enemies. Until then, you must leave us."

"I will do as you say," he said, rubbing his sore head once more. "Your promise makes the pain worth it."

"I apologize for the guardian's aggressiveness," she said. "Let me make amends."

The Keeper produced a wooden stick, seemingly from nowhere. She waved it over his head, muttering some unintelligible words. After a few moments, the pain began to subside, and the throbbing faded away.

"The pain will be gone very soon," she said.

He touched his head and could barely feel the lump any longer. "Miraculous. I am in your debt."

"Not at all, dear Hayoka," she said.

"You are certainly miracle workers," Hayoka replied charmingly.

"A simple spell for a simple injury," she said. "You showed great courage coming here, and you may be the savior of our valley. But you must leave now. You may rest for a few minutes but leave as soon as possible. There are many here who do not relish your presence."

"I leave at once," he said. "I feel rejuvenated. Thank you. Thank you for your ministrations. With your permission, I go now. It was an honor to meet you."

"And you," she said. "I hope to convince the Breathing Shaman and see you again soon."

She led him to the nearest egress point and smiled a warm smile. "Travel safe, Hayoka. Your visit was a blessing."

"Thank you for everything," he said. "Be well until next we meet."

Hayoka stepped back out into that blue mist. He glanced back and even the exit he had come out of seemed to vanish.

The oddest of places, he thought as he walked through that blue mist. He heard that large creature moving in the mist. It growled with primal menace, and Hayoka hoped it was not going to attack him again.

"I'm leaving," he shouted. "I'm leaving. No need to be angry."

He walked briskly until he came to the edge of the valley. He climbed a hill and left the blue behind. Once outside the valley, he took a minute to look back, seeing only the swirling mist.

Strange and intimidating people, he thought. *I wonder what sort of powers they truly have. They seem confident about their capability to defend themselves. They certainly have healing abilities and control whatever creature lurks in that mist. Their spell to hide their home under the blue mist is a formidable trick. In truth, this may be the most powerful community of people I've ever encountered.*

As he walked away, he thought about what he had said to the shaman. *I did not lie to them. Everything I said was true. I want them to be able to defeat the Itiwana. If I ultimately declare the Itiwana to be my enemy, I want them to know I have formidable allies who would destroy the Itiwana for me. Perhaps the Breathing Shaman will declare them unfriendly and save me the decision by destroying them herself. Or perhaps they'll make an alliance with the Itiwana. If I choose to make them my friends, the united power of both can help me defend myself against the anger of Agwara and Dagwona, who will not be happy with my betrayal.*

Hayoka didn't like the word "betrayal" because so many people thought he was already destined to be a traitor due to what his father had done. The shadow of Hobomok still loomed over him.

While the hopeful Hayoka walked unhurriedly back to the Land of Everlasting Summer, he thought about the sad fact that he had never found a place where he truly fit in. Even among his own people up north, he was unpopular due to his intellectual aloofness and the fact that his father Hobomok had been an ally of the Vykans. *The acts of my father will forever haunt me.*

He heard the voice in his head again. The strange voice, which had been his one constant companion, was badgering him, insisting that he follow Agwara's plan. It was in his loneliest moments that Hayoka most attentively listened to that inexplicable voice. All he knew of this ghostly whisperer was that it was called "Coyote."

Feelings of kinship and desire for a friendship with Pahana were the biggest reasons for doubts in Hayoka. He felt some guilt about his plan to manipulate the only person who had ever shown him outright friendship, regardless of what Hobomok did.

He continued to walk back toward the Burned-Faced Man's cabin to check on Dagwona. *I will tell her Agwara's plans, if she does not know them already, and I hope she does not detect my doubts because she would surely be furious. After that, I will go to the Itiwana. I'm not sure yet what I will say to Pahana, but he needs allies, so I will find a way to persuade him. I do have a way of speaking, don't I? I want to be his friend. I would like to be friends with the Keeper. When this is over, one or the other may feel indebted to me and need my council. Perhaps both. Yes, I feel more positive about Agwara's plan. This could end up very favorably for me.*

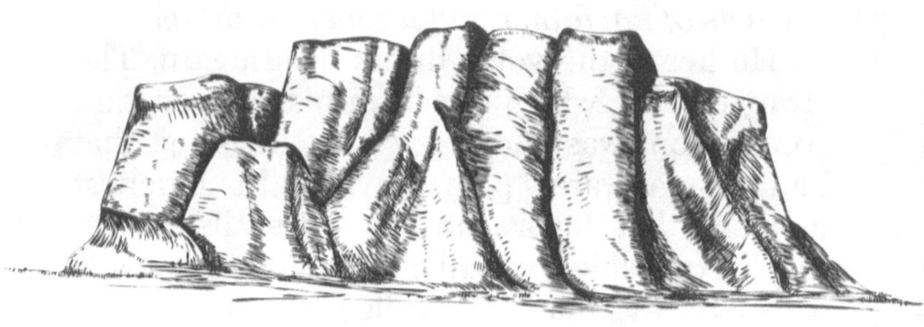

CHAPTER SEVEN

"This One begs you to listen." Pinga was standing on the edge of the precipice above the cliff housing. She looked up to the clouds, beyond which were the beings to whom she addressed her plea. "She asks your indulgence. Although This One is no longer one of you, she once shared the skies with you. You must remember that she was the emissary of the Winter Elders. They stripped This One of her divine powers because she wanted peace between those who live in the skies. She suffered due to her compassion for the Summer Sky Elders, and so she asks your mercy now."

She spread her arms wide and spoke with passionate desperation. "Your war has inflicted much harm upon the Itiwana, who have served you diligently and faithfully. This One does not know if her husband still lives. Though you are not human, she implores you to be humane. Help us. We need to find Tawa. We need the Dragonfly to save the forest. This One implores you to assist us. Please help those who so dutifully serve you."

An answer came in a form that Pinga did not expect. Black Crow abruptly landed on her outstretched arm. The ebony bird startled the albino beauty, who then laughed at her own jumpiness.

"Hello, Winged One," she said. "This One must have frayed nerves if she is startled by Tawa's loyal pet. Where have you been?"

The crow chirped loudly and flapped its wings energetically. Pinga tilted her head, instinctively feeling that the crow was attempting to communicate some message to her. "What's wrong, Little One? What are you trying to tell This One?"

The crow continued to caw and flutter, making Pinga wonder what new bit of bad news could be coming their way. A worrisome thought struck her. "Is it Tawa? Has something happened to him?"

Black Crow reacted to the sound of his master's name. The bird outstretched its wings and squawked piercingly. "You have seen him. Something's wrong! Tawa is in danger!"

Descending the mesa, after having inspected the nut reserve for distribution, Pahana was heading to the field where Aholi, the war chief of the Two Horn Riders, was drilling the warriors. Aholi was an elder member of Pahana's Sun Clan, but since Pahana was the acting chieftain, Aholi served him loyally. The redoubtable Aholi had been War Chief for 20 summers and faithfully obeyed Tawa.

Pahana thought about his father, wondering if Tawa would approve of his stewardship of the tribe. Pahana was brash and confident, but still strove for Tawa's praise. He wondered what Tawa would do about the looming threat of Spear-Finger. *My father has left the Itiwana in my care, and I must devise a defense as clever and effective as he himself would formulate.*

He spotted his mother rushing in his direction, with Black Crow on her shoulder. Even from a distance, he could tell she was upset. *What's happened now? Will there never be a moment of tranquility?*

Pinga relayed her concerns about Tawa, while Pahana listened patiently. Pahana thought his mother was overreacting to the crow's return, interpreting every sound as a projection of her own fears. "Stop your fretting, Mother. You, beyond everyone, know how capable and clever Father is. Surely, whatever hardship he is facing, he will overcome and return with his prize."

"Tawa has been gone too long," she said. "He would have somehow sent word of his well-being were he able to do so. And we need him here to help heal the forests. This One insists we take action to find Tawa and hurry his return."

Pahana took some of this personally, thinking that his mother had no faith in his stewardship of the tribe, but he could agree that only the holder of the Dragonfly could replenish the forests. "Very well, Mother. We'll gather the Shakowin to discuss ways of finding Tawa. Where are Grandmother and T'Soona?"

Atira and T'Soona were feeling more peaceful than they had felt in many weeks. They had chosen this particular afternoon to have an afternoon outing beyond the mesa, in the green area that was undamaged by the locusts. T'Soona had managed to collect some fruit, despite the local damage. He also cooked some meat and carried the woven basket to his perfectly chosen spot. He knew that Atira had been very tense since her son, Tawa, was absent. Before Tawa left, he had burdened her with supervising the temporary chieftain, Pahana, and possibly stripping him of power should he fail in his duty. It was a difficult thing for a grandmother to consider, but she promised that she would do so for the good of the tribe if it became necessary.

"So peaceful," Atira said as she sat on the grass eating an apple. "After all we've been through, I'd forgotten what peaceful moments felt like."

"You take too much to heart," T'Soona replied, in his mirthful way. "Your family has burdens heavier than boulders. Don't let them crush your joy. The Sky Elders will not be enraged if Atira has a merry day. Savor every wondrous moment until your final one."

Atira beamed affectionately at the medicine man, admiring his ability to remain jovial. He'd possessed that capacity ever since they were young. She had always enjoyed his humor and puckish nature. Atira kissed him on the cheek. "The world feels solid underneath me once more. Thank you for your joyous spirit, dear T'Soona."

"Your happiness is my reward," he said.

She stroked his back and hair. "No woman ever had a better friend than T'Soona."

T'Soona's normally happy eyes suddenly darkened. "Friend, eh? Yes, of course. I had forgotten my place."

Atira hated to see T'Soona hurt, but they had had this conversation before, and it always ended up with him being hurt. "More than a friend, my sweet. When Yana-Luha was taken from me, my heart crumbled like a dry leaf. I thought I would have no further use for it. And then there was T'Soona. You made me laugh, and you let me lean on you. You've been my lover and my closest advisor. Your place in my heart is rooted like the grandest tree. Even though I will never be the wife of anyone other than Yana-Luha, I cherish you more than anyone, other than my son and grandchildren."

Before T'Soona could respond to her heartfelt words, he spotted someone in the distance, heading in their direction. "Wait. We're not alone."

Atira saw the unusually tall, unfamiliar woman with silvery hair walking toward them. Her weathered face indicated great age, and yet she walked with a brisk, youthful step that belied her appearance. She wore a strange outfit made of animal skins and tree bark. The stranger walked directly toward the two Itiwana.

Atira and T'Soona stood up, warily watching the stranger approach. Atira squinted in the sun to get a better look at her. "Do you recognize her?"

"Not at all," T'Soona answered. "But I am having unsettling assumptions."

Atira felt the same. Given the number of enemies who would love to see the Itiwana destroyed, the presence of a silent stranger created a sense of dread. "Who are you? Speak your name, old woman."

The mystery woman merely grinned and continued walking toward the nervous pair. She gave no outer sign of her intentions, and that somehow made her even more frightening. T'Soona stood defensively in front of Atira and grabbed a handy stone because it was the only weapon he could find. "Stay back, interloper. The Itiwana are no one's prey."

The sound of pounding bison hooves interrupted the nerve-wracking moment. The twin sons of War Chief Aholi arrived. Masewa and O'Yewa rode in on their mounts, Lightning Charger and Thunder Rumbler. Both T'Soona and Pinga were relieved by the timely assistance.

The old woman stopped, observing the two young warriors with that same enigmatic smile on her lipless mouth. She did not seem intimidated.

"You two are hard to find," O'Yewa said. "Pahana sent us to fetch you, and I was beginning to think we'd need Molowia's magic to find you."

"Who is this woman?" dour Masewa asked.

"We don't know," Atira said. "She will not identify herself."

"She is strange and off-putting," T'Soona added.

"Name yourself, old woman?" Masewa ordered sternly.

The strange woman gave no answer. Not in words. However, something happened that revealed her intentions. She began to grow, almost doubling her original height, and her skin began to change.

The four astonished onlookers watched as the woman's wrinkled flesh turned brownish-gray and hardened. It took on the consistency of a petrified tree. She lifted her now stone-like hands and her fingers stretched out into sharp spears.

"Spear-Finger!" Atira shouted, frightened. "She's come!"

"Stand behind us!" O'Yewa shouted to Atira and T'Soona.

Grim Masewa guided his bison into a protective position between Spear-Finger and the others. "Stay back, monster! The Itiwana have slain monsters before!"

The tree-like creature stomped forward, ignoring the threat. The monster did not say a word or make a sound as it advanced. O'Yewa and his mount joined Masewa in a defensive stance.

When Spear-Finger did not halt, Masewa urged his mount, Thunder Rumbler, toward the enemy. Spear-Finger was unexpectedly quick and slashed the bison with its long, sharp fingers. Thunder Rumbler instinctively backed away, hurt by the attack.

O'Yewa ordered his mount, Lightening Charger, to ram Spear-Finger since the Itiwana bison were bred to fight monsters. The impact rocked the tree-like creature, momentarily causing it to teeter. However, Spear-Finger recovered quickly and slashed at Lightning Charger. The bison squealed and backed away. With their mounts hurt, the twins tried firing their arrows at the strange creature, but Spear-Finger did not react to the impact at all. The brothers hesitated, unsure of how to proceed.

"We need to get help!" Atira yelled. "We have to get back to the village and warn everyone."

"Excellent idea," T'Soona said. "Strength in unity."

"Very well," O'Yewa said. "If you insist."

While the others headed back to the mesa, Masewa paused, glaring hatefully at the rock beast. He never accepted defeat well.

"Come along, Brother," O'Yewa cried.

"You go ahead," Masewa replied. "I'll keep a watchful eye on this abomination."

"Don't do anything foolish while I'm gone," O'Yewa said. "I'll return with reinforcements shortly."

Atira and T'Soona climbed upon Lightning Charger, and they rushed urgently back to Shipapa-Lina. Spear-Finger lumbered toward Masewa and his mount. Masewa backed away slowly, never taking his eyes off the monster.

"Prepare to fall, monster," Masewa said. "The Itiwana will not be gentle with you!"

Spear-Finger was not intimidated and continued its inexorable march toward Shipapa-Lina.

The long walk back from the Valley of the Blue Mists was almost over. Hot and tired, Hayoka was relieved to see some familiar scenery, indicating that the Burned-Faced Man's cabin was not very far away. He'd been lost in thought during his trek, musing about how he could leverage the shamans of the Valley of the Blue Mists to his advantage.

He was so focused on his plans that he was not as aware of his surroundings as he should have been. Passing a large stone surrounded by a patch of bushes, Hayoka was unaware that he was not alone.

It wasn't until the four large figures lunged at him that he realized how careless he had been. He heard the savage yelp and caught sight of his attackers in the periphery of his vision.

The Vykans had returned to the Land of Everlasting Summer. The wild Northmen, who had come to Ulah-Nane decades ago, had previously tried to conquer Shipapa-Lina at the behest of Hobomok, father of Hayoka. The Vykans failed, and Tawa killed Hayoka. After that, the Itiwana managed to slay Giwakna, the Wendigo, whom the Vykans worshipped. The Vykans had wanted to destroy the Itiwana to avenge their god, but Pinga had convinced their leader, Hunwulf, to call a truce. The Itiwana had not encountered the Vykans since that day.

Gunnar, the son of Hunwulf, was leading this small Vykan incursion. He was accompanied by Red Rolf, Grimhilt, and the mighty Drengar. They were all tall and burly, with either red or blond hair. Two of them had beards, while Gunnar had a thick, bushy crimson mustache. All four wore metal skull caps, although Gunnar's had horns to indicate his stature as the son of the leader. Drengar carried an ax, while the others had swords. Each of them had a shield.

Hayoka squealed in alarm as the four big men grabbed him roughly. Grimhilt struck him in the face, and Hayoka fell senseless to the ground. His dazed senses were brought back to reality by the pain of a boot to the gut from Red Rolf. The air was knocked from his lungs, and he gasped loudly.

"Pick him up," Gunnar ordered.

Red Rolf and Drengar yanked Hayoka back to his feet. Hayoka took stock of his situation, realizing that there was no way to fight or escape this group. He recognized the Vykans immediately, having grown up among the Thrown-Aways, who had been both victims and opponents of the Vykans before Hunwulf, and the Thrown-Aways's leader, Angakku, made peace.

Hayoka feared the Vykans. Although he was only a child the last time the Vykans attacked his tribe, the memories of their attacks had caused him nightmares for years. The Thrown-Aways hate the Vykans to this very day. The Vykans were known to be ruthless to their enemies and prisoners.

"Speak, little skraeling," Gunnar commanded. "What tribe do you belong to?"

Hayoka's mind was racing, debating the best things to say in order to prevent these savages from killing or torturing him. "I am a wanderer. My name is Hayoka, son of Hobomok, friend of Hunwulf and ally of the Vykans."

Gunnar knew the name well although he had not been born yet when Hobomok allied himself with Gunnar's father, Hunwulf. He had heard the tale of Tawa killing Hobomok, which denied the Vykans of a weapon for their god, Giwakna. Hunwulf had liked Hobomok.

"The son of Hobomok?" Gunnar said, surprised. "Here? Odin is a whimsical god."

"How do we know this skraeling is truly the son of Hobomok?" Grimhilt asked loudly.

Gunnar could only chuckle at the question. "Who would claim to be that if he were not?"

Hayoka knew he had to take control of this conversation. "I have been seeking you out. I have long wanted to meet the allies who fought beside my father when he died."

"Your father died long ago," Gunnar said. "Where have you been all this time?"

Hayoka came up with a lie quickly. "I've been held captive."

"By who?"

"By the Itiwana," Hayoka said. "Those who killed my father and your lord, Giwakna."

Drengar abruptly howled with rage, startling Hayoka. "The Itiwana! They must die! They killed Nanook and Giwakna! They must burn!"

Gunnar held up his hand for Drengar to be silent. "Tell me, Hayoka. How do you come to be here if you were a prisoner?"

"I escaped," Hayoka replied, as convincingly as possible.

Red Rolf grabbed Hayoka by the hair and yanked him. "I don't trust this little rodent! Is it mere coincidence that we come here to destroy the Itiwana and happen upon someone who claims to have just escaped from them and is looking for us?"

I have to gain their trust, Hayoka thought. "I can help you!"

"How?" Gunnar asked.

"I know them," Hayoka said. "I've been among them. I've observed them. I have information you can use. There are only four of you. The Itiwana are formidable. You must know that from the past. I'll provide you with knowledge of their weaknesses."

"I agree with Rolf," Grimhilt said. "I don't trust him. Let's kill him."

"Yes! Kill!" shouted Drengar eagerly.

Gunner folded his arms, considering the fate of Hayoka. "Hmmm. What shall I do with you?"

Hayoka came up with another idea. "If you want to destroy the Itiwana, you'll need more power. I know where you can find great power."

"What kind of power?" Gunnar asked.

"Shamanic magic."

The Vykans were very attentive to this news. "Continue."

Hayoka proceeded to describe the magic he'd witnessed in the Valley of the Blue Mist. Gunnar and Grimhilt listened intently, while Red Rolf seemed a bit dubious. Drengar paced, only wanting to kill something.

Hayoka prayed that the Vykans would be intrigued by his story. They stood silently when he was done. Grimhilt and Red Rolf looked at Gunnar for his decision.

"Where would we find this valley?" Gunnar finally asked.

Relieved that the intimidating Vykans were interested, Hayoka did his best to provide accurate directions, even drawing images in the dirt with a stick to mark the specific route more clearly.

"We shall verify the truthfulness of your odd tale," Gunnar said. "We shall travel to this supposed valley and determine if these strange shamans exist. If so, we will take these crystals and use their power for our own purposes. If there are no such mystics in this valley, we will return and carve you into pieces and feed those pieces to any animal we can find."

"Clearly described," Hayoka said. "Very vivid."

Gunnar put his hand on Red Rolf's shoulder. "You will remain here and guard this skraeling, Rolf. See that he does not escape."

Red Rolf looked disappointed. "I would rather go on this excursion with you than remain here with this pathetic excuse for a man. Guarding such a tiny man will be dull and lacking in any challenge."

"One of us must keep vigil over this weakling," Gunnar said. "I have chosen you. Do as I command. We will return as soon as possible."

"As you wish," Red Rolf said without enthusiasm.

"You'll find everything is as I said," Hayoka added.

"For your sake, this had best be true," Gunnar said. "If you waste my time, your death will be very slow and very, very painful."

"I understood that from your previous description of my death," Hayoka said. "But thank you for elaborating further."

Gunnar waved to Grimhilt and Drengar to follow him. "Come along."

As they left, Red Rolf grabbed Hayoka by the hair and shoved him to the ground. He waved his sword threatening in front of Hayoka's face. "Sit there and be silent."

Red Rolf tied some sort of stringy, rope-like material to Hayoka's ankle and then fastened the other end to his own as Hayoka watched disdainfully.

Those powerful shamans of the valley will no doubt eliminate those three buffoons, Hayoka thought. They won't even get past the guardian in the mist. It's they who'll die painfully, I predict. Now I need only figure out a way to dispose of this red-haired simpleton, and then I can be on my way back to Dagwona.

CHAPTER EIGHT

"**F**orm a protective line!" Pahana shouted to his warriors.

The Two Horn Riders rapidly arranged their mounts in a defensive formation, cutting Shipapa-Lina off from the area where Spear-Finger had been seen. The bison were to be the main defense against supernatural creatures although Spear-Finger was not a poshayanki. This strange being was something entirely unique. Faw-Faw stood with the Itiwana warriors.

Aholi the War Chief rode Stone Horn to the forefront of the defensive perimeter, supervising the warriors under his command. O'Yewa joined the line but kept looking in the distance for some sign of his brother. He prayed Masewa would not do anything reckless or foolish. *Don't you dare get yourself killed without me at your side!*

Pahana, who still did not have a properly trained mount of his own since his previous bison was killed, chose to once again ride into combat astride Mountain Fury, his father's aging but still powerful bison. After 22 years of battle, the old animal was still feisty and brave. *It's no wonder my father loved this loyal beast.*

The people of Shipapa-Lina pulled up the ladders to the cliff housing to prevent Spear-Finger from climbing up to reach the children and elderly of the Itiwana. The women of the Bow Sisterhood took up their positions on the cliff, armed with their ample supply of arrows. They had a clear vantage point to fire at any intruder. Atira was in command of the sisterhood, which included Evaki, the dour bride of Aholi, and Hani, the teacher.

Manabazo assumed his eagle form and took flight over Shipapa-Lina, getting an aerial view of the approaching enemy. It was the will of the all-powerful Awona'Wilona that divine beings who lived in Ulah-Nane would not indulge in direct conflict and risk escalating a ground war that would ravage the land and the people. Still, his power and wisdom were often useful to Tawa and the Itiwana.

Pinga remained alone in the Cliff Palace. She felt useless as she paced. Her faded powers were too weak to be useful against a creature like Spear-Finger, and she was not a trained warrior. Pahana had insisted that his mother stay safely out of danger. *This One wishes she could help. If only she could have her divine powers once more. How can she contribute?*

She glanced over her shoulder to see Black Crow perched on the chieftain's seat of power. His presence gave Pinga an idea. She tore off a handy piece of decorative animal skin and then used the slight remains of her abilities to manifest an icicle. She dirtied the tip of the icicle and scribbled a message on the back of the animal skin, using an ancient language that few people knew, but which Pinga had taught her daughter. She held it in front of Black Crow.

"Kia," she said urgently. "Find Kia. Go! Go to Kia."

The crow seemed to understand the message. It took the animal skin in its beak and flapped its wings. Pinga watched it fly off out of a smoke opening heading for Kolhu.

Masewa kept a safe distance from Spear-Finger, forcing himself to refrain from attacking the creature. He hated to admit to himself that he was powerless against the monster but was smart enough to refrain from doing something suicidal. Spear-Finger continued walking toward Shipapa-Lina and cackled at Masewa. He hated the sound of that mocking laugh but assumed the creature was doing it to get him angry enough to attack. His mount was already hurt, with some blood coming from its wound.

"Who sent you?" he asked. Unsurprisingly, he got no answer. "If the Enemy Way is listening, the Itiwana will not fall. Not today or any other day."

Spear-Finger looked up when it saw the large eagle circling above it. The monster's expression changed, and it hesitated. It recognized the enemy, even when it was transformed into an innocuous form.

"Maaaa-naaaa-baaaa-zoh!" she croaked with a voice that crackled like burning wood.

The shape-shifting Elder answered, "Above you and your evil, I soar, observing a creature I abhor. I proclaim that the Itiwana will prevail. Your fruitless attack will surely fail."

She pointed one of her spear-like fingers at Manabazo, and it suddenly jettisoned from her hand, firing into the air like an arrow. The small spear didn't score a direct hit on Manabazo although it pierced his wing. The Elder yelped as his limb was skewered, and he could no longer maintain his flight. He went into a spiral, flapping his good wing to slow his descent.

"Manabazo!" Masewa yelled, amazed that an Elder could be injured by this creature.

The wounded eagle landed on Lightning Charger, just behind Masewa. "I am harmed, but don't be alarmed. The blood is real, but I will heal. Forget my damaged wing because protecting the tribe is the important thing."

"I had thought it was forbidden for you two to fight," Masewa said.

"You are correct again. Such a conflict is forbidden," Manabazo said. "I am concerned. The situation has turned. Awona'Wilona has spoken, but the rules are broken. This is most worrisome. I fear the days to come."

Spear-Finger laughed maniacally, proud of her attack. She held up her hand and new spear-like fingers grew to replace the ones she had jettisoned. She continued walking toward Masewa and Shapapa-Lina.

Masewa directed his bison to back off, trotting back to Shipapa-Lina. He created more distance between himself and the creature. Masewa felt immense relief when he saw the rest of the Two Horn Riders and Faw-Faw guarding the village.

He saw Pahana at the forefront of the warriors. Masewa raced to him and pointed to Manabazo. "The Elder is injured."

"Manabazo, what happened?" Pahana asked, very concerned about the ramifications of an injury to an Elder, even one born on Earth.

The wounded Elder covered his bloodied wing with his good one. "Do not be concerned about me. I will heal, as you will see. The real danger is coming near. It is Spear-Finger you should fear. She defies even Awona'Wilona's mandate. You must defeat her before it's too late."

"But how?" Pahana asked.

"In this instance, I am not sure," Manabazo said. "I must ruminate to determine more."

"Then we must deal with this creature in the most direct way possible," Pahana said. "Brave and decisive action is called for. Even without any divine knowledge, we are blessed with the courage of our forefathers. Courage is from the soul. It can't be taught. Now this monster will learn what happens when it dares oppose those for whom courage is our power."

The Two Horn Riders all howled a unified war cry, signaling their willingness to fight, even against the most horrific of monsters. While Manabazo transformed into a snake and slithered away, intending to recover and think, Masewa took his place between O'Yewa and Calian.

The fearsome Spear-Finger came into view, marching at a steady pace toward the warriors, smiling the whole time. Her presence produced a feeling of dread that most of the younger warriors had never felt before. Even the most experienced warriors, such as Aholi, could not deny that this was the most frightening thing that had threatened Shipapa-Lina in many years, even more so than the Witch of the Whirlwind.

Responding to Pahana's gesture, the Two Horn Riders moved toward Spear-Finger. The bison circled around the creature, surrounding the intruder. However, being surrounded did not seem to intimidate Spear-Finger. The sinister smile never left her stony face as she looked over her adversaries. She continued walking, directly targeting Pahana and Mountain Fury. The big bison snorted and grunted as if reacting to some memory.

"Whatever your intentions, monster, don't expect to gain any satisfaction from the Itiwana!" Pahana yelled. "We've made a habit of thwarting the Enemy Way. They send witches and Vykans and skinwalkers against us, but here we stand. Unconquered and unafraid. We graciously allow you to retreat. Go now."

Spear-Finger only laughed in response. She pointed a long finger at Pahana. Masewa realized what the monster was about to do. Urging his bison forward, Masewa leaped off his mount, just as Spear-Finger launched a lethal projectile. Masewa tackled Pahana off Mountain Fury as the spike sailed past, missing them by inches.

As they fell to the ground, Calian and O'Yewa rode forward and placed themselves protectively between the stunned Pahana and Spear-Finger. Faw-Faw reflexively followed close behind Calian.

Aholi the War Chief took over while Pahana was stunned. "Arrows now!"

The Two Horn Riders began firing shafts at the stone beast, but their arrows bounced harmlessly off the cackling creature. Aholi lobbed his own spear at the invading monster, but the weapon was equally useless.

Still chortling, Spear-Finger unleashed more harpoons, killing or wounding a half-dozen of the Two Horn Riders. Aghast, Aholi charged forward on Brave Horn. He hoped the bison's inbred ability to harm supernatural beasts would damage or destroy the attacker. However, the impact barely staggered the laughing invader.

Spear-Finger slashed at the bison with long, rock claws. Brave Horn staggered as the wound was inflicted. Aholi retreated before his mount could be killed.

Pahana, who was back on his feet, paused to consider their situation. What was the best strategy to deal with this seemingly unstoppable creature? As he mused, Calian also charged at Spear-Finger, but the rock monster knocked the bison aside with a clubbing blow to the side of the head. The animal teetered, dazed by the impact. Calian jabbed his spear at the enemy, but it did no good at all.

Pahana reacted to give Calian a chance to escape. He used his power as the son of a northern Winter Elder to attack. Pointing, he manifested a half-dozen sharp icicles, which he launched at the monster. This attack also failed to do any harm.

Faw-Faw, who had always protected Calian, rushed forward, swinging the metal hammer he had taken from the Vykan, Iron Forge, years ago. Spear-Finger raised her arm to strike him, but Faw-Faw hit her in the wrist with the hammer. Although he did not completely detach the hand, Faw-Faw did take a chunk out of her upper arm and wrist.

For the first time, Spear-Finger looked concerned and yanked her arm back, inspecting the damage. Anger replaced the mocking smile. Faw-Faw drew back the ax to strike again, but Spear-Finger beat him to the punch, hitting him in the face. Faw-Faw fell, staggered by the impact. The creature aimed her long, sharp fingers at Faw-Faw.

Pahana realized that the creature was going to impale Faw-Faw with her javelin weapons. Pahana jumped protectively over him, simultaneously willing an ice shield into existence. The young Itiwana held up his hand, which now held a circular shield composed of thick ice. The creature's lances became embedded in the ice.

Mountain Fury ran forward, impacting against Spear-Finger, knocking her off balance. Spear-Finger tried to slice the big bison, but Pahana protected him with the ice shield although it shattered under the force of the monster's attack.

Calian and Masewa pulled the still-disoriented Faw-Faw away from Spear-Finger, while Pahana hopped onto Mountain Fury, ordering him to retreat from the stone monster.

He signaled for his people to stop their attack. "Stay back! We need to take the measure of this demon."

Everyone present moved backward, creating more distance from Spear-Finger. As for the rock monster, she looked at her damaged wrist with sneering rage, then continued walking toward Shipapa-Lina.

In another field, close by, stood a relic of a past Itiwana victory. It had remained alone in this field like a statue, a constant reminder of both the danger that constantly faced them and also what miracles they could accomplish.

The immobile form of Stone Coat cast its shadow on the ravaged field where the Itiwana had once fought the Salt Witch and her Tunerak Destroyers, along with their towering stone slave. Pogum and Tawa had managed to slay the witch and neutralize Stone Coat, leaving him as a warning to the enemy.

A swirl of pinkish-red mist materialized near Stone Coat. The strange mist formed into the transparent, spirit form of Kia, daughter of Tawa. The ghostly girl floated in front of Stone Coat, looking at the unmoving figure.

My father defeated this thing before I was born, she thought. *Now my mother has asked for my help in defeating a similar monster. I will not fail my family and my people.*

The ethereal form of the young girl passed into the body of Stone Coat like a spirit. Moments later, the body of Stone Coat moved for the first time in 22 summers.

The vision quest ritual had begun in the House of Many Hands. The Breathing Shaman whispered an ancient chant and blew into her numinous bone tube. Blue smoke blew from the tube, enveloping the cairn of crystals. She blew into it again, which produced an "om" sound that traveled to the four black onyx crystals, balanced upon the obsidian stone, glowing their eerie glow. The stones were now powered by the negative energy of her soul, which was transformed into a magical fuel.

The smoke from the tube began to form into an image, like a portal to another place. The Breathing Shaman got her first look at the Land of Everlasting Summer. *I'll observe these strangers, and they had best pray I like what I see.*

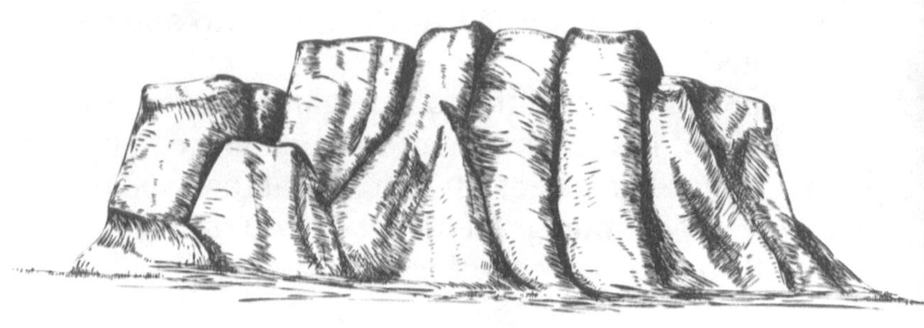

CHAPTER NINE

The monstrous Spear-Finger lumbered ever closer to Shipapa-Lina. Atira ordered the women of the Bow Sisterhood to fire, and they pelted the intruder with arrows. Spear-Finger ignored the attack, intent on destroying the Itiwana for the glory of Malsumis and the Winter Elders. Spear-Finger easily tore through a net that the Itiwana had prepared as a deterrent. Pahana attempted to utilize his divine frost abilities to create a frozen barrier to halt Spear-Finger's march, but once again, the effort ended in failure.

The Wood Man, Faw-Faw, mostly recovered from his earlier blow, leaped onto Spear-Finger's back, pounding furiously on the monster and roaring a primal yawp. Spear-Finger seemed unbothered by the attack. She grabbed Faw-Faw, lifting the large man up above her head and tossing him away as if he were a small squirrel or bunny. Faw-Faw crashed to the ground, roaring in pain.

Since everyone's attention was focused on Spear-Finger, no one immediately noticed the tall, slow-moving figure coming their way. It was Calian who first caught sight of the unexpected arrival.

"Look there!" Calian shouted, pointing in the distance.

The Itiwana all stared in horror as the legendary Stone Coat stomped toward Shipapa-Lina. Aholi, who had been there all those years ago when Stone Coat first attacked, was brought back to the horror of that original attack, where Tawa was almost killed. Pogum had saved the day, but neither Pogum nor Tawa were here now.

Even the monstrous Spear-Finger paused at the sight of the unexpected arrival. She turned toward him, although it was unclear whether she was going to greet Stone Coat as an ally or an enemy.

"Fall back!" Pahana yelled. "We need to reorganize for this new enemy!"

As the Two Horn Riders began to retreat, Pinga arrived on the scene. She needed to communicate with Pahana, but it was not going to be easy getting word to him during the chaos. Bison galloped everywhere, kicking up billowing dust. Pahana was in the middle of it all, trying to maintain order.

A bird with a bloodied wing walked toward her. "Stay back, sweet Lady Fair. These monsters will kill you without a care. They are a deadly pair. Danger is everywhere."

"Manabazo, are you hurt?" she asked.

He lifted his bloodied wing. "I heal quite quick. It is a useful trick. Do not worry. I will be healthy in a hurry."

"Listen to me," she said. "I must tell you something. It's about Stone Coat."

Nearby, the Itiwana all spread out, allowing Stone Coat to lumber unhindered toward the perplexed Spear-Finger. The two terrifying rock creatures came nose-to-nose, staring coldly at each other.

What's happening? Pahana wondered.

Everyone was stunned when Stone Coat swung its slab of an arm, striking Spear-Finger in the face. The surprised Spear-Finger staggered backward. She put a petrified hand to her petrified face, realizing there was now a crack on her stone visage. Stone Coat struck again, knocking her back several feet with the second blow.

Spear-Finger quickly regrouped and hit back, knocking Stone Coat off-balance. The young mind of Kia hesitated after the powerful attack. Spear-Finger slashed at Stone Coat with her claws, cutting gashes into its rocky torso.

Just when Spear-Finger was getting the upper hand, a massive snake appeared abruptly, pouncing from out of nowhere. It wrapped itself tightly around Spear-Finger, pinning her arms at her sides.

"You tried to kill me, but I am still here," Manabazo said, in his serpent form. "I oppose you, and I have no fear. You defy the divine rules, and now so do I. I will resist you 'til the day I die."

Taking advantage of Spear-Finger's momentary immobility, Stone Coat landed several more blows on Spear-Finger's head, eventually knocking it off. Spear-Finger's head flew from her shoulders with a gurgle. It rolled across the ground, stopping at Pahana's feet. Spear-Finger's body toppled.

Manabazo unwrapped himself from the creature. "This is justice, plain and true. I am glad to assist in destroying you. You dare to disobey the divine laws. You were not saved by your sharp claws. Spear-Finger is dead. I will make a decoration of her head."

The rest of the Itiwana slowly surrounded Stone-Coat, unsure of what to make of the creature. This legendarily dangerous monster had just saved them from another creature. Would it attack them now, or was it an ally?

They watched as a pinkish-red mist formed in the air above the petrified corpse, manifesting into the astral form of Kia, who smiled at her brother. "Hello, Pahana. Once again, you find yourself in need of my particular talents."

Pahana could scarcely believe what he was seeing. "Once again, Little Sister, you amaze me."

Pinga came jogging into view. "This One is pleased to see you received her message in time."

"You are the mind behind this, Mother?" Pahana asked.

"This One sent Black Crow to Kolhu with a message," Pinga said. "Such a useful bird."

"So, it appears," Pahana said. "My father knew how to choose his animals."

Pinga beamed affectionately at her daughter. "This One is proud of her daughter. You are a marvel, Kia. Thank you."

"I will always be here when you need me, Mother," Kia said. "But I must go now. Molowia will be furious with me. Goodbye, Mother. Be careful, Brother."

Kia vanished, leaving the Itiwana stunned. Most of them had not been aware of the power young Kia now possessed. When, they wondered, had the adorable daughter of the chief who used to pick flowers in the fields become such a powerful mystic? She was only the age of 14 summers old.

"I am highly confused about what I just witnessed," O'Yewa said.

"I share your befuddlement," Masewa added.

Pinga used her zen-like calming influence on the group. "Everyone be at peace. The danger is over. I will explain everything soon. Let the Shakowin convene at the Cliff Palace because we have much to discuss."

Yoki appeared, carrying the body of an Itiwana warrior named Tiponi. "Tell T'Soona that we have five injured braves who need his services. It is too late for Tiponi, however."

Everyone lowered their heads in honor of the fallen warrior. Pinga said a blessing over his body and the entire tribe let out a chant, telling the Holy Hunting Ground that an Itiwana warrior was coming.

"We'll bury Tiponi first," Pahana said. "And then we need to plan. The Enemy Way will regret this day ever occurred."

Opening her eyes, Kia found herself back in the Sun Dagger House. She was proud of herself for what she'd accomplished. No one else could have done what she just did. No one other than Pinga was aware that Kia possessed the ability. Despite the momentary panic she'd felt when Spear-Finger was pummeling her, she experienced a thrill at having defeated the enemy.

Soon enough, Molowia would realize what Kia had done, and she would be furious. There was already a tense rift between the two, with Molowia insistent that Kolhu never get directly involved in the war. Kia had been scolded previously for repeatedly intervening on behalf of her family, and Molowia had recently refused to teach Kia any further because of Kia's defiance.

Kia developed a slight headache from the exertion and needed to relax her muscles and meditate in order to ease the discomfort. She took some deep breaths, trying to release the tension from her petite body.

Then the whispering started. The soft voice seemed to be speaking into her left ear. Kia initially thought it was Shula-Witsa, the fire elemental who had been teaching Kia skills, such as the one she utilized today. However, this voice was softer. It didn't have the forceful and intimidating tone of Shula-Witsa.

"Who is this?" she asked aloud. "Who's speaking?"

"You are impressive," a female voice clearly said.

"But who are you?"

"I am a shaman, like yourself," the voice answered. "I reside in the Valley of the Blue Mists. We have been watching. You have great power. Where did you learn such abilities?"

Kia was suspicious. Despite being young, she had learned enough not to be naïve. She knew there were many cunning beings who would like to manipulate her. Even Shula-Witsa, who had been teaching her, was not to be completely trusted.

"I choose not to answer," Kia replied. "Identify yourself."

"I am called the Breathing Shaman," the voice said. "Your powers are worrisome to us. No one, except those trained by the Great Shaman, should possess such power. Especially not one so youthful. This power is difficult to master, even for the most wizened of us. We fear your childlike efforts to control potent forces you have no call to be tampering with."

Kia became angry. This person, whoever she was, had the same view of her as Molowia did.

Neither one seemed to have any faith that Kia could become the greatest of shaman. It appeared that only Shula-Witsa had any confidence in her.

"My training is most certainly not your affair," Kia responded. "I do not answer to you, whoever you are."

"You are willful," the Breathing Shaman said. "This is very concerning. Humility is necessary for a novice shaman. For one of such immense power, that makes you dangerous. Therefore, we give you the opportunity to come study with us. Otherwise, you will become a menace."

Kia was taken aback by this sudden offer from strangers. "But I don't even know you."

"Talk to Molowia," the Breathing Shaman said. "She knows of the valley. She was a student of the Great Shaman. She will advise you. Talk to her ... or answer to us!"

Kia began to protest but quickly realized that the unseen spirit had gone. She was left with a plethora of questions. *Who are these people? Why are they watching us? Why do they feel I am such a threat? Why are they so willing to train me? Should I even consider that? Should I talk to Molowia about this? What did they mean when they said she would answer to them?*

Kia wished she had someone to talk to about this. Her first instinct was to communicate with her mother. Surely Pinga could advise her. However, she reconsidered. If these strangers were monitoring her somehow, they might be able to overhear any astral communication Kia might attempt with Pinga. She did not want to directly involve the Itiwana and endanger her family any further. Her parents had enough to deal with. Kia chose to handle this without her parents' input. *I defeated Spear-Finger. Surely, I can manage this problem on my own.*

Pahana and the Shakowin had gathered in the Cliff Palace to discuss the current situation. Pinga, Atira, and Manabazo were present. T'Soona was occupied attending to the five wounded warriors.

"I had no idea Kia was capable of such a feat," Atira said. "But you seemed to know, Pinga."

"This One has been in contact with her daughter," Pinga said. "The girl first reached out to This One in dreams, in her astral form. After that, This One sent Black Crow to deliver messages to her. She assured This One that her powers had increased substantially. This One hoped that the girl could do what This One asked of her, even being able to send Wishpoosh to help Tawa. She succeeded quite well, wouldn't you say?"

"Quite well, indeed," Atira said. "She must surely have changed since I last saw her. I may not even recognize her when I see her again."

"We will need such power in this dire hour," Manabazo said. "Fist and spear and magical skill will aid us against those we must fight and kill."

"Or be killed," Pahana said tersely. "Ask Tiponi."

"We won't forget those who died for the cause," Atira said. "Don't let despair defeat you."

Pahana was pacing. Atira noted that his grandfather, Yana-Luha, often did the same thing when the situation was tense. Despite some early missteps in his temporary stewardship of the tribe, she felt he was guiding the Itiwana in a manner worthy of Tawa.

"Why did Spear-Finger attack you, Manabazo?" Pahana asked. "I thought direct combat between divine beings was forbidden by Awona'Wilona?"

Manabazo, now in raccoon form, caressed his sore but mostly healed paw. "It is forbidden, that's a fact. This is a worrisome and defiant act. To openly defy the most powerful god of all, means they must now be confident that we will fall."

"So, something has changed," Pahana said. "Do you think they've managed to free Malsumis? Is that why they're being so bold?"

"About this, I do not know, but I hope it is not so," Manabazo answered. "I must find out why, by communicating with those in the sky."

"Do so," Pahana said. "Let us know as soon as you learn something. As for the rest of us, we must contrive a better defense. I want no more of my people to join Tiponi."

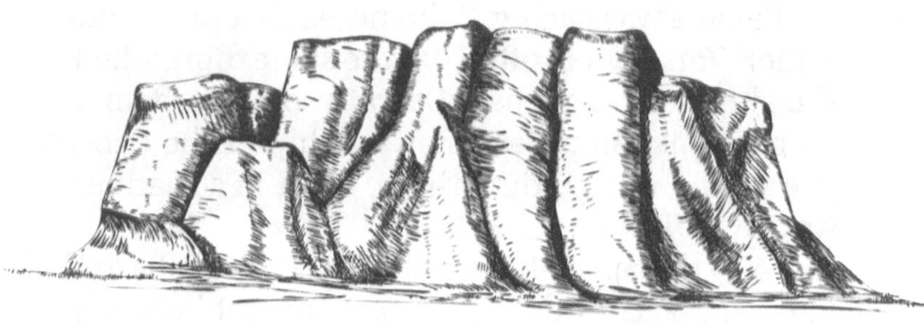

CHAPTER TEN

My man's missing, Dagwona thought, worriedly. *Tardy traveler. Whirlwind Witch worries.*

She sat upright in the cabin, looking a little stronger. She had become accustomed to Hayoka being at her side, catering to her needs. Dagwona had become emotionally attached to Hayoka and enjoyed his ministrations. Now, however, he had been gone for days. The Burned-Faced Man still looked after her, but she was both apprehensive and angry that Hayoka was not there.

She took a sip of the hot soup that the Burned-Faced Man had left for her. *Dagwona despairs.*

"Returned has your appetite," a voice in the dark said. "Good, this is."

The surprised witch turned her head, trying to sit up. "Who's here? Speak soundly."

In the flickering candlelight, Dagwona saw the furred form of Agwara the Snow Fox, seated comfortably near the door to the hut. He smirked with his sharp teeth. "Agwara arrives," she said. "Cunning creature comes."

"You might miss me, I feared," Agwara said. "To see me, you must be glad. Snow foxes and soup both soothe the soul."

"Taunting trickster," she said, agitated. "Mischievous mockery."

"Apologize, I do," the snow fox said. "Trying to lift your spirits, I was."

"Do Dagwona decently," she said. "Locate lover. Haul Hayoka here."

"Ah, missing your sweet northern darling, are you?" Agwara asked, glibly. "Touching, it is. But worry not. Know where he is, I do."

Agwara explained how he sent Hayoka to the Valley of the Blue Mists, hoping to incite a conflict between the shaman and the Itiwana. "Allies, he may find."

Dagwona seemed unhappy with this revelation. "Or others. Sinister shamanic sisters stalk site. Mystics may menace my man."

"Underestimate Hayoka, you should not," Agwara answered. "Sent him, I would not have, if capable, he was not."

"Bring beguiling brave back," she insisted. "Deliver Dagwona's dearest."

The snow fox raised his paw, grinning. "Ask again, you do not need to. Going, I am. Find

Hayoka, I will. Return him to his infatuated witch, I will."

"Greatly grateful," she said, laying her head back down.

"Always of service, I am," Agwara said, as he slipped out of the hut without the Burned-Faced Man seeing him.

Dagwona sometimes wondered if she should fully trust Agwara, despite their mutual loyalty vow to destroy the Itiwana. For now, she needed him. *Hoping Hayoka's healthy.*

I need for him to remove his helmet, Hayoka thought.

He and Red Rolf sat on the ground, tethered by the string. Red Rolf was sharpening his sword with a stone. He watched Hayoka out of the corner of his eye.

The son of Hobomok had managed to covertly grab a stone in his hand, while the Vykan was looking for his own sharpening stone. He was waiting for an opportunity to smash Red Rolf over the head but had to wait until the Vykan removed his metal skull cap.

Hayoka sat innocently. *Perhaps if I strike him on the back of the neck, or on the ear, I can stun him enough to have time to pull his helmet off. Then I can break his thick skull open with my rock.*

"Don't be unwise," the Vykan said, as if he could read Hayoka's intentions. "Gunnar seems to want you alive. I don't agree, but I serve. So don't make me cut your head off."

"I share Gunnar's wise desire not to have my head cut off," Hayoka said. "Very sage."

Unnoticed by either man, Agwara had sniffed them out and was watching from afar. His keen senses studied the situation. He deduced that Hayoka was a prisoner. This put Agwara in an awkward position. He needed to rescue Hayoka, but he did not want to hurt the Vykans or make enemies of them. He needed them to trust him in order for his plans to come to fruition.

Agwara crept stealthily toward the duo from behind. He was an expert at being unseen. When he got close enough, he blew outward with his otherworldly breath, causing a cloud of dirt to surround the two men. Red Rolf coughed as the dust cloud engulfed him.

Hayoka saw an opportunity to escape. Gripping the rock tightly, he lunged at Red Rolf, but the Vykan was expecting this. Red Rolf was too experienced a warrior to let some dust disorient him. He swung his hefty fist and landed a glancing blow on his captive. Hayoka was stunned, but the blow was not a direct hit, so he was still on his feet. Red Rolf reached out into the dust to restrain his captive, but at that moment, someone, or something, pulled the metal cap off his head.

Red Rolf paused, alarmed at the possibility of a hidden attacker. "Who in Odin's name...?"

Hayoka, who had refocused his thoughts, homed in on the sound of Red Rolf's voice. With all the strength he could muster, he slammed the rock into the Vykan's face. Red Rolf was staggered by the unexpectedly sturdy blow. As Hayoka was attacking, something bit through the binding that tethered him to Red Rolf. Hayoka had his chance. He knew he was faster than Red Rolf and more familiar with the terrain. While the Vykan was disoriented and blinded by dirt, it was time for Hayoka to flee.

Dashing with desperate rapidity, bounding over rocks, and leaping over small streams, Hayoka moved as he never had before. He wouldn't even slow down enough to look over his shoulder to determine whether Red Rolf was chasing him. He simply ran like a rabbit escaping a wolf, straining every muscle in his legs. His heart and lungs strained with remarkable energy as the long minutes passed. In his mind, he imagined Red Rolf running several steps behind him, brandishing his sword for a lethal swipe. *Can't stop! Can't stop!*

He lost track of time. His legs became heavy and stiff. He was struggling for breath. Finally, he slowed to a jog and took the risk of looking back. He turned his head in trepidation and dread.

No one was there. Red Rolf was nowhere in sight. He scanned the landscape, but not a living soul was present. *Safe! I'm safe!*

He dropped to the ground, allowing his tense body to relax. He breathed deeply as his heartbeat slowed. "Calm down. It's over," he muttered to himself.

"Over, it is not," a voice said.

He was only startled for a moment, but he recognized the voice. "Agwara. Do I have you to thank for my fortunate escape?"

"Helped you, I did," Agwara said. "Your ally, I am."

Hayoka turned to look at the white fox. Despite Agwara's assistance in his escape, Hayoka was beginning to feel uneasy around the manipulative creature. He knew he was just a pawn and that he couldn't trust Agwara. He was glad to be forming an alliance with the shamans of the Valley of the Blue Mists because he may need them if he chose to confront Agwara.

"To what do I owe this timely visitation?" Hayoka asked.

"Worried about you, Dagwona is," Agwara said. "Attend to her, you should."

"I'll do so, thank you," Hayoka said politely but coldly.

"Succeed, did you, in the valley?" Agwara asked, glaring expectantly at Hayoka. "Allies, do we have?"

Hayoka decided to play his own game with Agwara, making him wait for the answer. "I would love to speak with you on this matter, but as you say, Dagwona is waiting for me. I am consumed with concern for her. I will discuss the valley shamans with you after I attend to her."

Agwara narrowed his eyes, displeased. "A mere yes or no, I ask for. Simple and quick, such an answer is. No time, does it take."

"Time is not to be wasted," Hayoka said. "It's up to each of us to decide how much of it we can spare. At this moment, I can spare none for further conversation. Thank you for your assistance, Agwara. I will speak with you further after I see Dagwona."

Hayoka began to walk away. Agwara watched him silently for a few moments and then laughed. "Learning, you are. A game, we play. Patient, I will be. Soon, will we speak again."

The snow fox scurried away. Hayoka had hoped to get a psychological advantage over the wily fox, but apparently, he failed. He would have to deal with Agwara's mind games again later. For now, Dagwona was waiting.

I hope I didn't make a mistake leaving Tawa with Eithinoa and her ilk, Naya-Nazgani thought.

Night had fallen and the monster slayer was using celestial navigation to make his way south. He had promised Tawa that he would contact the dying man's family while he still clung to life. Tawa had given Naya-Nazgani directions as accurately as possible to the Land of Everlasting Summer. Having traveled as much as he had over the centuries, Naya-Nazgani was certain he'd passed through that area before and could find it again.

He worried about leaving Tawa alone with the enigmatic Earthmother and her giants. The monster hunter was not completely convinced of her sincerity, mostly because of the company she kept. He was not disposed to trust Cheenooks and other such creatures. Anyone who was allied with such creatures became untrustworthy in his eyes.

Still, something about the woman, Eithinoa, seemed so compassionate and kind that Naya-Nazgani was moved to ignore his suspicious instincts and leave the wounded man to her mystic ministrations.

I hope I haven't been cuckolded like a fool, he thought. *If I return and find they've killed Tawa, I will slay them all. I must find a method or weapon to deal with those giants. I've fought giants before, but none this large. I must devise a more formidable weapon to use when I return. If Eithinoa and her oversized allies are sinister, I'll make them pay. My first priority, however, is to find Shipapa-Lina.*

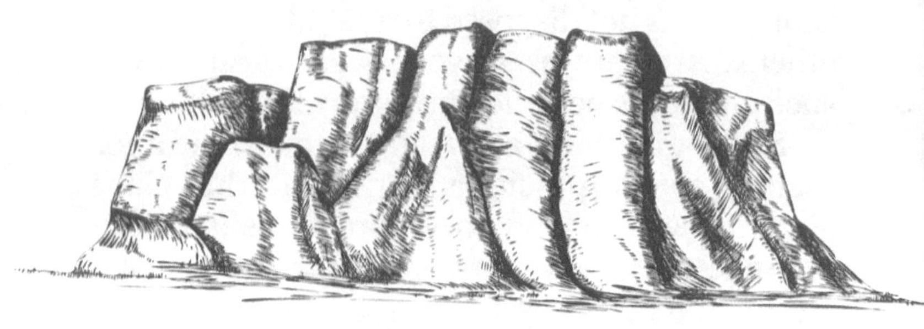

CHAPTER ELEVEN

The sound of chopping wood greeted Hayoka as he returned to the isolated cabin of the Burned-Faced Man. The disfigured monk was swinging his makeshift stone ax and piling up wood for the fire. The Burned-Faced Man saw Hayoka coming and took a break from chopping to greet his returning guest.

"You've been gone some considerable time," the monk said. "Dagwona has been concerned about you."

"My absence was unavoidable," Hayoka said. "How is Dagwona?"

"Stronger now," the monk said. "You'll be pleased at her progress."

"Excellent news. Excuse me while I look in on her."

Hayoka entered the cabin and was delighted to find Dagwona on her feet. She was standing, putting on her tree-bark body armor. He watched her thinly toned muscles sliding the garments over her beige skin. At first, she didn't turn to look at whoever had come into the room. She apparently assumed it was just the Burned-Faced Man checking on her.

"I'd forgotten what a divine sight you are when in motion," Hayoka said.

Dagwona spun to see Hayoka standing in the doorway. For a moment, she smiled. Then the smile switched to an aloof, accusing frown. "He's here. Lagging late. Missing many moons."

Hayoka folded his hands and assumed a remorseful posture. "I apologize for my extended absence. I didn't want to be separated from you for so long. Allow me to explain."

"Please proceed. Explain everything exactly."

Hayoka explained in detail how Agwara had sent him to the Valley of the Blue Mists and his encounter with the shamans who reside within. He described their powers and their crystals. Hayoka talked of the Keeper's willingness to form an alliance. He talked about his encounter with the Vykans and sending them to the valley. He assumed the Breathing Shaman and the Keeper would be able to handle them. "I may have to do some clever talking to the Keeper later."

Dagwona's tone was surprisingly harsh. "Tender talk? Keeper comely? Finds female favorable?"

Hayoka had not considered that Dagwona could be jealous of a mortal. "No, not in the slightest. She's barely a shadow of you. However, she is a useful ally. I must be nice to her."

"Not notably nice!" she insisted. "Stay surly."

"Of course," he answered with a charming smile. "Though all women stand under the same moon, some are illuminated like goddesses. You are one such."

She grinned slightly, for a brief moment, and then resumed her stern demeanor. "Worrisome women. Must manipulate magical matriarchs. Control crystals."

"I plan to," he said. "I'll see they dance to our tune."

"Sway stupid shaman," she cried. "Persuade powerful people. Dagwona demands debt."

"I remember your anger against the Itiwana," Hayoka said.

"Remember rightful revenge!" she snapped. "Punish Pahana. Squash Shipapa-Lina. Bury barbaric, bison-bestowed buffoons. Achieve avenging action!"

Hayoka could see that all Dagwona cared about was her revenge on the Itiwana. Hayoka, however, needed to leave his options open. "We need to be patient. We can't be so..."

"Whirlwind Witch won't wait!" Dagwona yelled. "Don't delay delivering devastating deathblow!"

Hayoka tried to calm her down. "You need to trust me. We must act slowly. Haste can ruin everything. We need careful contemplation and..."

"No, no, no!" she yelled. "Immediately incinerate Itiwana!"

"Let me handle this," he said calmly. "Trust me to do what needs to be done."

Dagwona sneered. "Hayoka hesitates. Witch wonders why. Suddenly suspicious."

Hayoka didn't want to face the wrath of an angry witch who controlled the wind. "I would never betray you, my sweet. You're just upset due to your injury."

He reached out to touch her, but she slapped his hand away. Hayoka backed up, alarmed. "Dagwona, please. I—"

"Stay silent!" the witch yelled. "Dagwona disappointed. I'm irate. Feeling fury!"

Hayoka could hear the wind outside starting to increase and knew he had to talk fast.

"What can I do to convince you I have your interests at heart?" Hayoka asked. "I despair at having lost your complete trust."

"Begin bloodbath!" she shouted. "Eradicate enemies. Slaughter Shipapa-Lina!"

"Dagwona, I—"

"Win Witch's worship," she demanded. "Prove profound passion. Elsewise, exit entirely!"

No sooner had she challenged him to prove his devotion by killing the Itiwana, she walked swiftly out of the cabin, with a healthy stride he didn't think she was capable of yet. Once outside, she raised her hands and a funnel of wind engulfed her. The wind began to lift her in the air.

"Dagwona, wait!" Hayoka yelled.

She ignored his pleas and floated high into the air. A jet stream yanked her to the north, and she jetted out of sight. Hayoka was quite sad to see her go. *I must hold her dearer than I thought because her departure breaks my cold heart.*

The Burned-Faced Man had witnessed Dagwona flying away. "Is she coming back?"

"I fear not," Hayoka said.

"I am sad for you both," the monk said.

Hayoka frowned at the clouds. "Don't be sad for me. Be sad for the world that has spit upon me once again. I'm becoming angry out of habit and others will soon know my displeasure. I intend to become disagreeable. Thank you for your assistance these past weeks, Monk. I suggest you avoid the rest of the world from this point on. Things are going to become unpleasant."

The Burned-Faced Man watched Hayoka walk away, hoping he hadn't made a mistake in helping these two strangers.

Molowia was beginning to feel her age. The decades of ruling Kolhu had been rewarding but sometimes difficult. For the most part, she had enjoyed the responsibility of guiding the Itiwana of Kolhu, despite the constant threat of the god war.

Lately, however, the stress was beginning to take its toll. It was the situation with Kia that was causing her such anxiety. While she loved her nephew's daughter with a motherly affection, she had become distrustful of the girl's rapidly growing power and even more rapidly growing rebelliousness. Young Kia had gone from becoming Molowia's intended successor to being a possible threat to Kolhu's continued safety.

I should contact her parents about this, Molowia thought. *I need to resolve this problem as soon as possible, for everyone's good.*

She had been unable to meditate, which had never happened to her before. Meditation had always been the one thing that calmed her mind. Frustrated, she sat by the fire in her private chamber, seeking some semblance of serenity.

A delicate footfall caught her attention, and she saw Kia standing in the entranceway to her chamber. Molowia was surprised at her own uneasiness with Kia's unexpected arrival. She would never have believed the sweet little girl she took in to train would one day make her uneasy.

"Can I speak to you, Cacique?" young Kia asked with polite deference.

Molowia was relieved to see this change in her. "Of course. Sit down."

Kia moved with the confident grace of a much older woman. She sat cross-legged, facing Molowia, who turned toward the young girl with trepidation. Kia smiled disarmingly.

"I need your advice, Cacique," Kia said.

Molowia was delighted to hear that Kia still respected her. "On which subject?"

"I have been contacted," Kia said. "By the Breathing Shaman of the Valley of the Blue Mists."

Molowia rarely displayed any surprise outwardly, but in this instance, she failed to hide her amazement. She quickly regained her Zen-like calm. "I see. This explains quite a bit. I have been of the opinion that another voice was whispering in your ear."

Young Kia was silent for a moment, as if she were considering revealing something further, but was hesitant. "She says my power is impressive and she would like to train me. This intimidating woman seems to feel the shamans of the valley can teach me better than you. She suggested I ask you about them."

Molowia gave a sigh. "I thank you for telling me this. It relieves my mind. I have been concerned about your increasing abilities. I assume that she was the reason for your recent spell and the purple light that enveloped the Sun Dagger house."

Kia hesitated again. "I have learned much lately, without your knowledge."

"Apparently," Molowia said, reproachfully. "I would have hoped you'd be as honest with me as I have always been with you. Our family strength has long been loyalty, honor, and wisdom. We don't deceive each other."

"Please accept my apologies, Cacique," Kia said contritely.

Molowia rubbed her hands together as she considered this new information. "Would you prefer to be taught by someone else?"

"I don't know very much about these shamanic women," Kia said. "Since they suggested I talk to you, that's what I'm doing."

"So you are," Molowia replied. "Since you are being honest, I'll tell you what I know of them. The Valley of the Blue Mists was the home of the Great Shaman, the most powerful mortal mystic who ever walked Ulah-Nane. It was he who trained me. Within the valley is the House of Many Hands. It is a mystic sanctuary, guarded by mystic totems and eldritch beings. When the Great Shaman vanished on his quest, he left the House of Many Hands under the stewardship of his best student. She is known today as the Breathing Shaman. She and her sister control the mystic crystals. They have several students whom they are training. The sisters locate those with great potential and induce them to become disciples. They fear any young shaman misusing their powers, as the Salt Witch did. They prefer to keep a watchful eye on the young generation of mystics. Apparently, the shaman sisters have their sights set on you."

"Yes, they seemed very eager for me to accept their offer."

"Were they threatening?"

"Implicitly."

"Of course," Molowia said. "I should have foreseen this, but I didn't expect the Breathing Shaman to attempt to steal my student Ent. She should have more respect for me."

As she spoke those words, Molowia felt the embarrassing realization that she had been losing control of Kia. Her young pupil had been lying to her and defying her edicts about involving herself in the war of the Sky Elders. Kia even utilized the mighty Wishpoosh as a weapon. Such a thing was highly dangerous and even Molowia handled that powerful creature with extreme care. Given what little influence she seemed to have over Kia, she could understand why the shaman sisters of the valley were doubting her abilities as a teacher. If they could monitor Kia with their powers, they knew that the girl was far too independent and willful for such a young person with unpredictable powers. *Perhaps their qualms about me are reasonable. Could they teach her better than I?*

"What should I do?" Kia asked.

Conflicted, Molowia ran a hand through her curly hair. "What would you like to do, child? Do you wish to remain here and continue your training with me?"

After a long, thoughtful pause, Kia responded. "I would like to meet these women before I make up my mind."

"Perhaps you should," Molowia commented. "I shall consider it."

"Of course, Cacique. As always, I await your instructions."

As the smiling Kia respectfully exited the chamber, Molowia bit her lip. For the first time in many, many years, she felt as though she was losing control of events in Kolhu.

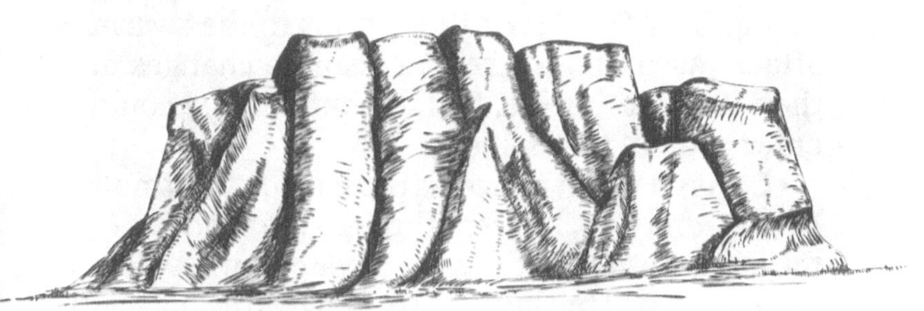

CHAPTER TWELVE

Now the hardest part begins, Hayoka thought, as he approached Shipapa-Lina. As he crossed the ravaged fields and the shadow of the mesa blocked out the sun, Hayoka wondered what he would say to Pahana, in order to manipulate the Itiwana to travel to the Valley of the Blue Mists.

He was surprised to find that the figure of Stone Coat was no longer standing in the field. *Clearly, something has occurred while I was away. No one can truthfully call Shipapa-Lina a dull place.*

Hayoka hoped to avoid the Two Horn Rider sentries because he wanted to be sure that he was alone when he approached the tribal chieftain. His plan was to slip in unnoticed and lurk covertly until he could get to Pahana without the rest of the Shakowin present. He knew the routine of the sentries since Pahana had begun training him to be a Two Horn Rider prior to the swarm attack. Assuming there had been no changes in their normal routine, he felt confident he could enter without harassment.

Covered in dirt as well as paint made from mud, berries, and clay, he crept through the shadows of the mesa, until he got close to Shipapa-Lina, where there were still bushes and trees. The Itiwana had chased off the swarm before they could destroy the flora of Shipapa-Lina, allowing Hayoka some cover to sneak closer to the Cliff Palace.

Passing the aqueduct, he saw a duck and wondered if the little fowl could be Manabazo, observing him. He warily watched the bird as he moved stealthily along. This distraction proved his undoing.

Something slammed into the back of his head, knocking him to his knees. His head ringing, he looked around, only to receive a knee to the face. He dropped to the dirt as another foot impacted against his ribs. Hayoka yelped in pain.

Laying in the dirt, he looked up to see the last face he wanted to see. Calian stood over him with a hateful sneer and clenched fists. "You're like a weed that keeps regrowing in the garden. Perpetually poisoning an otherwise pristine patch of earth."

Attempting to hide how much the attack had hurt him, Hayoka forced a tone of bravado into his voice. "You continually find very demonstrative ways to make your feelings about me clear."

"Pray to whatever demons you worship that I never demonstrate my true attitudes toward you," Calian said. "I could peel you like an apple, and the gods would call it justice."

"Would you ask the gods if I can rise back to my feet?" Hayoka asked.

"I doubt you'll ever rise above what you are," Calian said. "But get to your feet. In fact, I suggest you take good care of those feet, since you may need them for running."

Rising unsteadily, maintaining his bluster, Hayoka jutted out his jaw. "If you're going to hit me again, please do so now, so we can conclude this violent display. I have other things I should be doing, and I imagine you must have something planned for today. Such as chewing on bones and growling."

"I might begin with your bones."

"Must you always resort to threats, Calian?"

"Only when you're concerned, Hayoka."

Before Hayoka could come up with his next retort, the twins O'Yewa and Masewa came racing to the scene, having heard the commotion while on patrol.

"You two are late again," Calian said.

Grim Masewa pointed at Hayoka. "How did he come to be here? When did he return?"

Calian gave them his disapproving face. "He slipped past you. I'm disappointed in you."

O'Yewa was embarrassed but still upbeat. "Thankfully, we have you to correct our mistakes."

"I shouldn't need to nurse you like infants," Calian said. "Don't make jokes. Do better."

"We should take this weasel to Pahana," Masewa said.

"I have a feeling that's just what he wants," Calian said. "Let's take him to the Shakowin. They're less likely to be charmed by his honey tongue."

Masewa jabbed Hayoka in the rump with his spear. "Start moving."

Hayoka rubbed his rear. "Such a welcoming clan."

The trio led Hayoka toward the cliff housing. Hayoka was frustrated that his plan to reach Pahana had failed. *Calian is a problem I need to deal with. Ulah-Nane is not large enough to accommodate the two of us.*

Tipoli had been buried and there was a somber mood infecting Shipapa-Lina. The Itiwana were dreading what sort of dangerous creature would attack the village next. They were barely able to stop Spear-Finger, and that was only due to some magical help. Would they be so fortunate next time?

Atira and Pinga watched while the women of the Bow Sisterhood practiced shooting at small targets, while the men were building another defensive wall and deep pit as part of their preparation for future attacks.

"This One thinks the pit should be much deeper," Pinga commented.

"It will be," Atira answered. "The bottom of the pit will be lined with the sharpened horns of fallen bison. And the tips will be tinged with a poison T'Soona is creating. He who falls therein will not be climbing out."

"Effective," Pinga said.

"We have several ideas for new defensive measures," Atira said. "We want to—"

"Wait, we have company," Pinga said.

The two women watched Hayoka being led to them by Calian, O'Yewa, and Masewa. Atira was no happier to see Hayoka than Calian was. Every time she looked at him, she saw his father, Hobomok.

"What mischief has this little mosquito been committing now?" Atira asked.

"Sneaking into Shipapa-Lina without permission," Calian said. "He was avoiding the sentries by blending into the terrain with his camouflage paint. I discovered him creeping along near the aqueduct."

Atira glared fiercely at Hayoka. "Why didn't you announce yourself to the sentries?"

Hayoka pointed to his bruises. "The welcome I tend to receive when visiting your charming little village has not been the type I wish to relive. I find your hospitality dubious."

Atira folded her arms. "Perhaps you should consider not visiting us any further."

"A fine suggestion," Hayoka said. "But I have vital matters to discuss with your ill-disposed tribe, and I prefer to speak to a rational, reasonable man. I want to talk to Pahana."

"What is this vital subject you need to inform us of?" Atira asked.

"I'll tell that to Pahana," Hayoka said. "He's the only one open-minded enough to listen."

Calian stepped forward. "I'd gladly beat the information out of him!"

Atira gestured for him to calm down. "We're not savages, Calian. We either let him have his say or we send him away."

"I approve of sending him far away!" Calian said.

Hayoka emitted an exaggerated sigh. "This is exactly what I meant about not being open-minded."

"I could open your skull!" Calian replied.

Pinga interrupted Hayoka's next quip. "Such quarrels accomplish nothing for us. This One thinks we should allow Pahana to hear what our wily visitor has come to tell us."

"Thank you, wise lady," Hayoka said with a slight bow.

"Oh, very well," Atira said, uncertainly. "O'Yewa, go and fetch him."

"Immediately, I fly!" O'Yewa answered, running to retrieve the acting chieftain.

Finally, Hayoka thought. *This farce was getting tiring. Now I need to convince Pahana.*

Minutes later, Pahana arrived, with O'Yewa chattering in his ear. Hayoka hoped Pahana's welcome would be more benign than what he had received so far.

Pahana appeared sad when he locked eyes with Hayoka. "It seems that no matter how many times I put my faith in you, I find myself looking foolish for it. Having trained with the Two Horned Riders, you know that we must be cautious. When you sneak into our home like a snake in the weeds, it causes distrust. Don't you realize that the people here already distrust you enough? The last thing we need from you is to cause further unease among my people while Tawa is away. This was a stupid act for a seemingly intelligent man. Or do I overestimate you?"

"I will let you decide how foolish I am when you hear the information I have to trade," Hayoka stated.

"Go on," Pahana said. "Impress me with your knowledge. What do I need to hear?"

"You need to hear about an unexpected new factor in this whole, absurd war," Hayoka said. "People of great power. The power to be great allies or great enemies. The power to tilt the balance in your favor, or against you."

Pahana and Atira exchanged glances, unsettled by this information. Hayoka could tell they were eager to listen now. *I've caught their interest, like fish in a net. Now to pull them in.*

Hayoka described his visit with the shamans of the Valley of the Blue Mists. He described the powerful crystals with their numerous, unpredictable abilities. He mentioned the monster who guarded the House of Many Hands. "Now that they've decided to end their isolation and enter the fray, you can't afford to ignore them. You can't risk them joining forces with the Enemy Way. I can help you negotiate with them. They trust me and only me. The next step is yours. Shall I take you to them or will you chase me away from Shipapa-Lina, as Calian would have you do?"

"Can we believe any of this?" Calian asked. "This man is not to be trusted. It may be a trap."

Hayoka smirked. "You needn't believe me. Ask Molowia. She learned her craft there."

"So, that's it," Atira said. "When I was very young and newly wed to Yana-Luha, he told me that his sister Molowia once studied magic in a secret location, hidden in a valley somewhere. This hidden place was the home of—"

"Of the Great Shaman," Hayoka said. "He created it. That's what they told me in the valley."

Everyone was quiet for a moment, forced to believe Hayoka, despite their distrust. Hayoka could see that he had them in the palm of his hand.

"This One believes he speaks the truth," Pinga said.

"I agree, Mother," Pahana replied. "We must meet these shamanic women. We dare not miss the opportunity to form such an alliance. Very well, Hayoka. I accept your offer. You may lead us to the Valley of the Blue Mists and introduce us to your new friends. If this works as you suggest it will, you will win our trust."

"I'll lead you there with pleasure," Hayoka said, winking mockingly at the angry Calian. "With infinite pleasure."

The Vykans had no fear of the valley or the strange, blue mist that swirled. Gunnar, Grimhilt, and Drengar looked down at the sapphire blue haze, thinking only of the potential power to be gained.

"The mist, at least, seems to be true," Gunnar said. "A good portent for the rest of it."

"Could there be monsters within?" Grimhilt asked. "Beasts for us to slay?"

"I hope so," Gunnar said with an eager chuckle.

Drengar let out a boisterous laugh and raised his ax. "The Valley of the Blue Mists shall run red with blood!"

They descended into the mist, seeking both power and action. Once at the bottom, they wandered, unable to see beyond an arm's length. After a long time wandering blindly in the mist, their eager glee began to diminish. Their meager patience faded as they wondered if they'd truly find crystals or creatures.

"If that skraeling lied to us, I'll—"

A hoarse, female voice echoed around them, startling the battle-hardened Vykans. "Intruders are forbidden here! Leave the valley while you can."

"Ha! Do you think you can frighten Vykans?" Gunnar yelled to the unseen speaker. "We are unlike anyone you have encountered before. We are the greatest warriors Odin has ever sent to terrify this world. We make men flee in terror and turn women into widows. We are the Vykans and we do not flee! We fight!"

"You have been warned once and now you are warned a second time," the voice said. "Do not expect a third. Expect us to repel you from our valley."

"Try your best, witch!" Gunnar yelled. "Whatever monsters you send will soon lay dead at our feet. We will ravage the young women and force the old to cook our meals. We dare you to stop us!"

"Challenge accepted!" the voice said.

Moments later, a rumbling sound and vibration alerted the Vykans that the shamans were beginning their defensive measures. They raised their weapons confidently.

"Let us make swift sport of whatever beast dares to be the first to confront us," Gunnar ordered.

From above, they heard a rumbling sound, which they thought was the beginning of a landslide. *I hadn't considered that possibility!* Gunnar thought fearfully.

The rumbling was followed by a loud growl and a massive roar. The Vykans froze, wondering what sort of beast created that terrifying howl. Whatever it was, the creature was big. The Vykans had never heard of the Slide Rock Bolter.

The horrifying Slide Rock Bolter was an immense creature, the magnitude of a sperm whale. It had a huge mouth, the size of a cave, with teeth like stalactites and stalagmites. The massive monster clung to the walls of the valley; its fin-like tail equipped with hooks that secured its voluminous weight to the top edge of the slope. It remained suspended there as its fisheyes looked through the blue mist, hoping to spot prey.

When the leviathan was alerted to the presence of the Vykans, via a mystical warning from the Breathing Shaman, it scanned the valley with its wide-angle vision until it spotted the trio of intruders. Salivating at the prospect of a meal, it drooled a greasy, slippery substance from its maw. The greasy slime dripped down the slope, creating a slippery slide for the monster.

The beast waited until the Vykans were in the proper position. It unhooked its tail from the cliff, and its tremendous weight caused the Slide Rock Bolter to slide down the slope. It roared, and the valley rumbled from its titanic bulk skimming downward.

The confused and frightened Vykans could only look around, trying to determine what threat was coming their way. The rumbling got louder and louder. *What in Odin's name?*

Gunar was the first to see the colossal silhouette appearing from the mist. Before he could even warn his fellow warriors, the monster's maw came clearly into view. Overcome with terror, he dived out of its path in an effort to evade the monstrosity but was not entirely successful. Although he avoided that nightmarish mouth, the beast's weight slammed into him before he could get clear. He was knocked several yards, smashed by the awesome weight of the monster.

Drengar was lucky enough to be out of the creature's direct path. He caught sight of it out of the corner of his eye but froze at the sight of it. The Slide Rock Bolter narrowly missed him. Only inches separated Drengar from serious injury or death. He almost fainted as the giant creature glided past him.

Grimhilt was not so lucky. He had not seen the creature until it was too late. He turned to see the giant mouth rushing toward him. Grimhilt screamed, but there was nothing he could do. That cavernous mouth gobbled him up as the Slide Rock Bolter continued skating along on its slimy underbelly. Its momentum brought it all the way to the far slope of the Valley of the Blue Mists. The force supplied by its weight helped push it up the far slope. Its momentum faded as it neared the top. Swinging its tail around behind it, the Slide Rock Bolter hooked itself to the cliff again as it chewed on its meal, spitting out the metal sword and shield.

Gunnar and Drengar trembled in the presence of the monster, fully aware it was still close by and could soon return. Drengar began running in a panic as the injured Gunnar tried to stand. The impact had severely injured him. He had multiple broken bones. He spotted Drengar running through the mist.

"Wait!" Gunnar shouted. "Help me! Stop!"

Drengar ran a few more steps before pausing. The large man hesitated, debating whether he should risk going back for his leader. His fear of the Slide Rock Bolter had turned his bravado to faint-heartedness.

"Please, help me!" Gunnar cried. "You're my countryman! Don't leave me!"

After a few more seconds of deliberation, Drengar returned to aid his leader. With his impressive strength, he scooped Gunnar up, cradling him in muscular arms. Gunnar moaned in pain as his broken bones were lifted roughly off the ground. Every movement was agony, but it was still preferable to remaining there, where that unspeakably horrific monster might return. Drengar moved as fast as he could while supporting the weight of Gunnar. The injured Gunnar tossed away his sword and helmet and everything metal to make himself lighter.

"Flee like the winged goats of Thor," Gunnar said, desperately.

As they escaped the valley, they heard the mocking voice of the Breathing Shaman yell tauntingly, "You were warned! Do not ever return!"

At that moment, neither Gunnar nor Drengar had any intention of ever returning to the Valley of the Blue Mists.

The feathery, ebony messenger of the Itiwana returned from Kolhu. Black Crow had been sent with a message to Molowia. Pinga had written to the leader of Kolhu to ask about the shamanic women of the Valley of the Blue Mists. Molowia wrote back, telling Pinga everything she knew about the House of Many Hands, and how they were attempting to recruit Kia. Pinga was upset to find that her daughter was a pawn in this strange game.

More than ever, This One is convinced we must talk to these shaman women and find out exactly what their intentions are.

CHAPTER THIRTEEN

The Itiwana gathered to give Pahana and his party a proper send-off. Assembled near the imposing figures of Stone Coat and Spear-Finger, the tribespeople showed their support for the leaders of the besieged village.

Pinga had informed Pahana, Atira, and T'Soona of what Molowia had told her about Kia. This made the situation even more personal and imperative for the ruling clan. They all agreed that, despite the doubts Calian had about trusting Hayoka, they needed to confront the Breathing Shaman and her fellow shamans.

It was agreed that Pahana would lead the chosen group of Itiwana to the Valley of the Blue Mists. Accompanying him was to be his mother, Pinga, Calian, the twins O'Yewa and Masewa, and Faw-Faw. Their escorts were four hand-picked members of the Two Horn Riders. Guiding this assemblage to their enigmatic objective was the polarizing figure of Hayoka.

The remaining members of the Shakowin—Atira and T'Soona—were left with the stewardship of Shipapa-Lina. Aholi, as usual, was trusted to oversee the Two Horn Riders, assisted by Yoki. Dour Evaki and Hani the Teacher were left to supervise the Bow Sisterhood.

"I hesitate to leave you now," Pahana said to his grandmother.

"Shipapa-Lina has survived your absence before," Atira answered, always quick to remind Pahana of his mistakes, lest he become too complacent. "Trust T'Soona and myself to care for Shipapa-Lina as my husband and son have done so well."

"I accept the rebuke," Pahana said. "And I pray to Awona'Wilona that nothing comes your way that the Shakowin is unable to deter. We will return as swiftly as possible."

"Do so," Atira said. "And I pray your father returns to us soon."

"As does This One," Pinga said. "Tawa is needed."

Pahana was once again reminded that no one had a fraction of the faith in him that they had in Tawa. Despite his success in defending the Tree of Life, he had still not gained the level of respect that he'd hoped for. *My father is a magnificent hero and deserves every accolade he receives, but why is there none left for me? Will I forever be in my father's shadow?*

"And while we're on the topic of absences, why hasn't Manabazo returned yet?" T'Soona asked. "Has he learned anything that can help us? Did he meet a female Elder and run off for a tryst? What could be delaying him?"

"We could certainly use his assistance now," Atira said. "He's always been here when we needed him. Have faith he'll return soon."

"It's not a question of faith, but of time," Pahana said. "It would be imprudent to hesitate. Still, I will do one final inspection of the sentries. When I return, we will be off, regardless of whether our shape-changing friend has returned."

Pahana rode off, clearly agitated by the delay. Calian began to follow behind him. "I should attend him in these matters," Calian said.

"Wait!" Atira said, grabbing his wrist. "I want a word."

"My ear is forever yours," Calian answered.

"Have I told you how much we cherish your loyalty?" Atira asked. "Our clan. The Shakowin. Myself most of all. You are so much like your father. My brother. He was a great man."

"Yes, I have so often been told," Calian answered. "And I have lived my life as a tribute to the amazing man I have never met."

"Pogum was the one we always sent on difficult and dangerous tasks," Atira told him.

"I know many of the stories," Calian said. "I am humbled to have his blood."

"Let me tell you one story you may not have heard," Atira said. "It happened in places far from Shipapa-Lina before the war of Sky Elders began. My brother told me of this adventure and asked me not to speak of it because he found it sad. Still, I will tell you because I want you to know how much trust we placed in your father and why yours is the most heroic of lineages. Listen to the story of Pogum and the Khagan and the Saint of Magic."

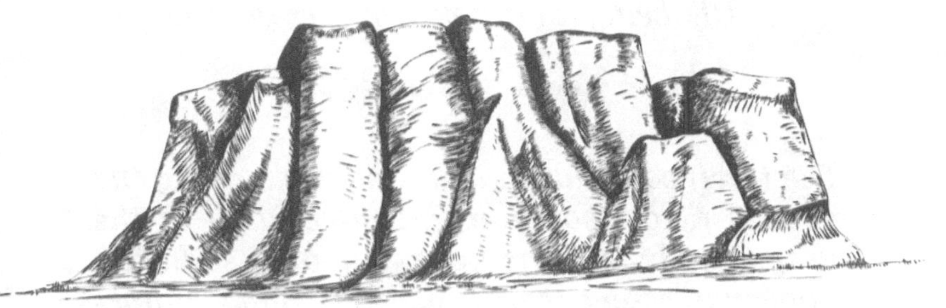

CHAPTER FOURTEEN

AD 1227—The Strong Debi-Kway
Season of the Great Turtle's Trek

There was panic in the village of the Taya people. The nomadic Aguacane tribe, formerly of the southern Taya people, frantically panicked. Women cried and men argued over what to do because their children were missing.

The Aguacane tribe were not warriors. They were roaming farmers, traveling according to the weather and avoiding hostile neighbors. Their attempt to remain peaceful by staying away from aggressors failed this time. They were invaded at night by a savage group. One man was killed and several more were injured.

But the worst part was that the children had been taken.

And the beings that took them were carnivores!

The terrified children were marched along the grassy fields, sobbing uncontrollably in the desperate hope their parents would suddenly appear to rescue them. Their terrifying captors roared for the young ones to remain silent and keep walking. The frightened children helplessly continued their trek to an unknown destination.

The horrific captors were known as the Puk-Wudjies. These rarely seen creatures were half humanoid and half porcupine. The swamp-dwelling Puk-Wudjies were bipeds with spikey spines projecting from their back. They were bipedal and walked on their hind legs but stood much smaller than humans. They were roughly the same height as the children they had stolen.

The Puk-Wudjies had canid noses and very large ears. A light coat of gray hair covered their silvery bodies, which would glow in the moonlight. The creatures had the ability to fade covertly into the darkness. This is why few humans ever saw them, and the few who encoun-tered them feared them.

Normally, the Puk-Wudjies remained in their swamps and caves. They mostly avoided humans because their numbers were small. They would usually wait for someone to come into their domain and then slay the intruder for a meal.

That changed on this day. For once, the Puk-Wudjies raided a local tribe and absconded with the smallest victims—the ones easy to steal away and least likely to resist. They captured the children of the Aguacane.

A rescue party had been raised by the Aguacane to save their missing children. The legion of rescuers was not experienced warriors, but one among them had had combat training and so rallied the Taya into an army. Every able-bodied male adult of the tribe formed a group designated to find their children. Many of them were hunters, so tracking the enemy would not be the problem. The difficulty would begin when they caught up to their foes. Even those who were too elderly to be going into battle joined in the hunt.

The leader of this motley attack force was a woman. Her name was Aqueena. Smart, athletic, and beautiful, Aqueena had been holding the tribe together while her father, Nacomah, the tribal leader, had been very ill. Most of the Aguacane had come to look at her as the interim chief of the traveling tribe.

Aqueena had started training with a spear and bow at a young age. Her father wanted her to be able to protect herself, so he taught her everything he knew about combat. He even took *her with him to battle a group of crop thieves who had been stealing their food. She learned well.*

Initially, her small size and loveliness made it difficult for her to establish herself as an equal among the men. It took her many years of hard work to perfect her skills as a hunter and fighter. However, it was only after Nacomah fell ill that she won the respect of her people by ruling so well during his convalescence.

The lovely warrior woman tossed her dark hair aside as she came out of her makeshift tent, where the men were waiting for her. She stood before the gathering of inexperienced soldiers, who waited to see how she would comport herself as their war chief. Aqueena knew there were doubters among them. Some thought the idea of a woman leading a war party was foolish. She wanted to prove them wrong, but that was secondary. The most important thing was saving the children.

Not knowing what else to say that would inspire her army, Aqueena simply yelled, "For the children!"

The Taya warriors yawped with vociferous verbal power, indicating their willingness to do anything for their children. Nothing would stop them from either rescuing their children or dying in the attempt.

The time came to leave on the mission, and everyone waited for Aqueena to lead the way. With a spear in one hand, a bow in the other, and a quiver over her slender shoulder, Aqueena marched forward followed by her determined tribesmen.

Pogum strode along the emerald fields of Ulah-Nane, ignoring the beauty of the scenic landscape and focused on his quarry. A party of raiders from the nearest tribe had snuck into the village of the Itiwana at night to steal their harvest. Pogum and a few alert Itiwana warriors drove the handful of thieves away, losing only a handful of their corn crop.

Pogum had been sent out by the Itiwana chieftain, Yana-Luha, to determine if there were still raiders nearby. Pogum was a great tracker and fighter as well as a fast runner if the need to chase or flee arose. He was unflinchingly loyal to his chieftain, Yana-Luha, and his people. Everyone respected his formidable abilities, so he was chosen to go on the scouting mission alone.

Pogum was a trim, wiry man of twenty-nine summers. He had an angular nose and a streak of white in his black hair. Pogum bore a small scar on his left cheek from an earlier raid. He had several other slight blemishes on his body, but to his mind, they were horrible disfigurements. His dysmorphic view of his own appearance led him to become a loner. He obsessed over his imagined hideousness and avoided company when he wasn't needed by his chieftain.

Pogum found some tracks, but a quick examination proved that these were not the footprints of the raiders he was hunting. This was a bigger party although the prints were very small. Who are they and why are they near the village of the Itiwana? Are they friend or threat? He decided he had to find out for the safety of his tribe. Pogum trailed the mysterious people—or whatever they might be.

The Khagan waited for the party of Puk-Wudjies he had sent out. Since he had been accepted into their ranks, he had worked his way into a position of authority. The Khagan had once been a general for the great Genghis Khan. He had shared many adventures and battles with the mighty Khan, but left China in 1227 after Khan died from an infection due to an arrow wound inflicted by the Western Xia.

He had come across the Puk-Wudjies when he accidentally entered their territory. A group of them attacked him, and he slayed their leader. He threatened to kill the beta leader named Mikum Wesu, but the fast-talking Puk-Wudjie promised to welcome the Khagan into their midst and to serve him for one year. Mikum Wesu had kept his promise and had been obedient to the Khagan for several seasons. The year was nearly over and Mikum Wesu looked forward to killing the

Khagan, but for now, he was bound to his vow and served the Asian warlord.

Mikum Wesu and his contingent of Puk-Wudjies returned to their cave, dragging the terrified children behind. The Khagan nodded in satisfaction. Perfect. I can use these children for slave labor until my project is completed. Then the Puk-Wudjies can devour them for all I care. Children don't have the will to resist the way adults do. And they will make good hostages should anyone attempt to attack me here. None of these soft local tribes has the spirit to sacrifice children to defeat an enemy.

The Puk-Wudjies chose the children of the Aguacane tribe because they had accidentally crossed paths once before. The Puk-Wudjies formerly lived in a swamp near a field where the Aguacane set up their temporary home. The Aguacane bribed the Maushop giant with plentiful food, urging the big man to drive the Puk-Wudjies from the swampland they inhabited. The giant agreed and stomped on several Puk-Wudjies. They did not forget that and so deliberately chose the Taya people when the Khagan told them to find children to steal.

Pogum was tracking the footprints, having come to realize that many of those he was following were children. The depths of their imprints showed their slight weight. Why are children being led through the Land of Endless Summer by a group of apparently tiny men? *He needed to know. Whatever happened in the Land of Everlasting Summer was of interest to the Itiwana, and Pogum was devoted to protecting the Itiwana.*

It wasn't long after that when he came across the rescue party of the Taya people, led by Aqueena. He knew these were not the people he was chasing. Yet another group is coming close to Shipapa-Lina. What's happening here?

He stood on the road, blocking their path. They saw him and immediately became nervous. They brandished their weapons clumsily. Pogum took note of this. These are no warriors. They seem frightened. And they are led by a woman.

"Who are you?" *Aqueena demanded, trying to sound aggressive.*

"I am Pogum of the Itiwana of Shipapa-Lina," *he said.* "You are crossing our land of Everlasting Summer. I would know the reason why."

"You're in no position to make demands, Pogum of the Itiwana," *Aqueena said.* "However, we have no malice toward you and apologize for treading upon your land. We have an important purpose here, and you are delaying us."

"Indeed?" *he asked.* "Perhaps I can assist you. No one knows this land better than I. What are you looking for?"

"Children," *she said.*

Aqueena explained the situation to Pogum, who now understood about the tracks and the reason the Aguacane seemed so fearful. Despite his mission to find the crop thieves, he knew he had to help these people.

"If these raiders you describe are who I think they are, you'll need help," he said. "I know of them. The Itiwana have fought these villains before. Let me assist you."

Aqueena was grateful for the assistance of an experienced warrior. "Very well, Pogum of the Itiwana. We welcome your aid. What advice do you have for me?"

"First of all," he said. "Remain downwind when you approach them. Their noses are as keen as any animal's you can name."

The Khagan monitored the progress on his machine. The vital part of the device needed to be placed deep inside the casing, which was too small for adult men and women to enter. While the Puk-Wudjies could fit inside the device, they might rebel at being used for such slave labor. The children, on the other hand, had proved quite useful.

The workforce of captive children they had procured was effectively moving the internal parts of the device. He would have preferred adults, but they didn't have enough metal to make a larger machine that would accommodate grown men. He had to settle for what he could build using the supplies he had brought from China as well as what he'd stolen from the pirates on the trip across the sea. Still, once properly motivated by fear, the children performed a good day's labor. They cried about being forced to climb inside the bizarre contraption, but that was a minor annoyance. The machine was being completed, and that was what was important.

The Khagan ordered his Puk-Wudjie servants to set up a defensive stance on the side of a hill near the cave mouth where he slept. He didn't want to be taken by surprise by anyone.

"See that they keep working," he told Mikum Wesu. "I want that device finished before my enemies can find me." The Khagan then went back into his cave to rest.

Pogum used his unparalleled tracking skills and knowledge of the area to guide the rag-tag rescue army of the Aguacane to their destination. They camped at a distance from the bottom of the hill. "Let's not bring a large party any closer. They'll hear and smell you. I should go alone."

"Not without me," Aqueena said. "This is my responsibility. I vowed to return the children to their parents."

"Come along, then," he said. "Tarrying is the act of people without courage. You have courage. Follow me."

Aqueena was impressed by Pogum. She followed him and had to strain in order to keep up.

He led her to a covert spot near the bottom of the hill. Pogum and Aqueena had not expected the Puk-Wudgjies to be out in force, having formed a defensive line.

"We can't charge them," Pogum said. "Not on that hill. We'll be suffering a severe disadvantage, fighting an uphill battle against creatures with unknown powers."

Pogum suggested they discuss the best strategy, and Aqueena agreed. As Pogum debated with Aqueena, the man from Shipapa-Lina had an idea.

"They seem to be over-confident," Pogum said. "And they've gathered on the hilltop. They don't know we're here. So, it's possible that they've left the children lightly guarded. I think I know a way to save the children without a battle."

"Tell me," Aqueena said, excitedly.

"I'll show you," Pogum answered.

Pogum and Aqueena stealthily made their way around the hill, using shrubs for cover. They got to a vantage point where they could see that the children were being held in a fenced-off area near the mine shaft now that they were done working. There were only two Puk-Wudjie guards. Clearly, they didn't consider the children capable of escaping or resisting.

One Puk-Wudjie had his back turned to Pogum, and the other was sitting on a rock dozing off. Pogum felt confident he could get to them quickly, before they knew he was there, and slay both before they could sound an alarm.

Then he could take the children to safety, and no one would die.

"This is perfect," Aqueena said. "Smartly done. I'm impressed."

"I'll impress you a bit more," Pogum said. "Wait here."

The next morning, the Khagan and Mikum Wesu walked with cocky arrogance toward the pen where the children were being held, intending to force them into another day's work. To the Khagan's shock, all he found when he arrived were two dead Puk-Wudjie guards. The pen was open, and the children were gone.

"No!" the Khagan shouted. "I needed those children! I need to complete my weapon! Who did this? Who dared do this to the warlord Khagan?"

Back with the rag-tag army of the Aguacane, the joyful fathers were embracing their returned children. Tears of joy flowed without embarrassment. Aqueena smiled a wide, toothy smile upon seeing the families reunited without a single casualty.

Aqueena kissed Pogum on the cheek. "Thank you, noble Pogum. You've done a wonderful thing this day."

Pogum touched his cheek where she'd kissed him. He wondered how such an attractive woman could bear to kiss a scarred mess like himself. I'm so ugly and she's so beautiful. Unsure what to say, he returned to the matter at hand.

"You should go now," Pogum said. "They'll be coming after us soon. They won't be happy to find out the children are gone. Hurry home."

"But won't they come after us?" Aqueena asked. "They'll track us."

"Don't you fret about that," Pogum said. "I'll see to the Puk-Wudjies. You see to the children. Go quickly."

Aqueena ordered her men to take the children home, and they immediately agreed without hesitation. As they trekked away, Aqueena returned to Pogum's side.

"You should be leading your people home," he said. "Hurry."

"I won't leave this burden to you alone," Aqueena said. "This is our fight. You've done us a service we cannot repay. I will stay and help you with this."

"You don't need to—" Pogum began.

"But I do," Aqueena said. "We'll work together. What do we do next?"

Pogum could see that she was going nowhere. "As you wish. Listen to me carefully. If we make a mistake, we'll be eaten. And I do not intend to be eaten today."

"I'm in agreement with that," Aqueena said. "I'm in your hands. What do we do?"

The Khagan led his army of Puk-Wudjies down a path, using his military experience to track the footprints of the children. Marching furiously down the road, the Khagan was surprised to see a man standing on the path, blocking their progress.

"Come no farther," Pogum ordered. "Return to your caves or face retaliation for your actions."

The Khagan was experienced enough to realize that there were no other armies hidden in the area. Pogum was alone. "You're a bold rascal. I declare it. Who are you, fool?"

"I am Pogum, and this is my home," he said. "You are intruders. Identify yourself."

The Khagan was both infuriated and amused. "Although I need not answer to you, I will tell you anyway. You speak to the noble warlord Khagan, one-time ally of the mighty Genghis Khan and one of China's greatest soldiers."

Pogum glared at him, unimpressed. "I don't know this Genghis Khan or this China you speak of, so forgive my lack of awe at your statement."

"Primitive!" the Khagan said. "You're a pathetic savage. You have the intelligence of a monkey."

"I don't know what a monkey is," Pogum said. "So your insult does not affect me in any way. But if you think I'm unintelligent, then how do you explain the ease with which I stole the children away from you?"

"Ah, so that was you, was it?" the Khagan said. "I give you one chance to tell me where they are before I have these little flesh-eating dwarves rip into your flesh, swallow your genitals, and eat your tiny brain."

Pogum still showed no reaction. "Before your little friends eat me, there is something I would know. Why did you take the children? What were you doing with them? Puk-Wudjies don't normally do this. What's your plan?"

The Khagan admired Pogum's bravery and liked to brag, so he decided to talk. "My plan? A savage like you could never understand. How could you comprehend my special field cannon? How could you conceive of gunpowder? This device will make it simple to conquer this backward, animalistic, primitive land of yours. No one here can stop me."

"Oh?" Pogum said. "You're forgetting one thing."

"Really?" the Khagan said mockingly. "Please enlighten me as to what that may be."

"The Puk-Wudjies have many enemies," he said.

As he spoke, a volley of two arrows and several stones came out of the woods, landing at the feet of the Puk-Wudjies. The dwarves jumped back in alarm. Numerous voices murmured from the tree line. The Khagan was confused.

"The Apache don't like your little friends," Pogum said. "I contacted them. You're surrounded. At my signal, they'll cut all of you down."

The Khagan was uncharacteristically lost for words. This was utterly unexpected. The Puk-Wudjies were clearly afraid of these Apache, and Pogum spoke with confidence.

"Still, the Itiwana don't want to start a war," Pogum said. "We get no joy from streams of blood. I would prefer not one person to die. A battle of champions. I'm one champion."

The Khagan gritted his teeth but couldn't help but admire Pogum's cunning. "And I'm the other, eh? A battle between us alone."

"That's my challenge," Pogum said. "Have you the courage to accept?"

The Khagan laughed and stepped forward. "Of course I do. The day a warlord of the Khan cannot defeat a primitive such as yourself, I may as well take my own life. Come forward, Pogum. Try to defeat the Khagan!"

Pogum did not falter. He rushed into the fight, where the Khagan was eager to lock up with him. The Khagan had protective layers of clothes, whereas Pogum was mostly bare, except for his knee-length breechcloth kilt. The Khagan had a metal sword, while Pogum had a wooden spear and a tomahawk. The advantage would seem to have been all in the favor of the Khagan.

But the Khagan did not know the speed and agility of wiry Pogum. The Itiwana leaped, dodged, rolled on the ground, and generally outmaneuvered the slower, heavier Khagan. The Khagan's sword sliced toward Pogum, but the Itiwana hunter used his stone tomahawk to parry the metal blade. The sword did make a few minor cuts, but nothing serious.

The battle raged for several long minutes until the Khagan began to get tired. He wasn't used to fighting at this pace, and he was getting older. He didn't have the energy to continue the fight. In his desperation, he leaped at Pogum, hoping he could grab the Itiwana and immobilize him enough to use his sword.

The strategy was his final mistake. Thrown off-balance by his own lunge, he left himself open to counterattack. Pogum buried his tomahawk in the Khagan's throat.

The warlord gurgled, as blood spit from his neck. The Khagan fell to the ground, as the blood left his body. He died when Pogum stabbed his spear into his fallen body.

As Pogum stood over the body of the Khagan, he looked at the Puk-Wudjies. "You should leave before the Apache lose their reserve."

"We shall," Mikum Wesu said. "We hated him anyway. We would have killed him, eventually. You spared us a few months of his rancid presence. We're leaving."

The Puk-Wudjies retreated down the path and out of sight. Pogum breathed heavily and looked at the several small wounds he had gotten. Oh no! More scars. I'll be more hideous than ever!

Several people came out of the bushes, where they had been watching the fight. But they were not Apache. One was the lovely Aqueena. The other three were friends of Pogum, whom he sometimes shared adventures with.

"Your friends were very helpful," Aqueena said.

Pogum forced a smile onto his exhausted visage. "Thank you for coming, my friends. I was hoping some of you would be at the Burned-Faced Man's cabin, but I dared not hope it would be all of you."

"A merry coincidence indeed that we were all there," the Burned-Faced Man said. "Awona'Wilona smiled upon you."

The man carrying a flute pointed to Aqueena. "Could we refuse such a pretty messenger? When this lovely girl came to tell us you were in danger, would we say no to her?"

"I'm glad you didn't," Pogum said. "I owe you, my friends."

"We're old friends, Pogum," one of the men said. "We were glad we were able to be of help. We enjoyed another victory in your company. And your attractive companion was an extra pleasure."

"We have a lot to catch up on, old friends," Pogum said.

Pogum looked over his companions. The first of these old friends and allies was a man from the southern lands called the Aztec. He was clad all in a protective battle suit called an ichca-huipilli, made from animal hide, leather, and cotton, with a cloak covering him. He walked with a swagger, armed with a wooden sword, embedded with rocks and crystals to make it *cut better. The Aztec was one of the world's best and most fearless fighters. He had encountered Pogum a few years earlier, and the pair joined forces, becoming frequent brothers in adventure. The Aztec often stayed at the cabin of the Burned-Faced Man when he was in Ulah-Nane, but often traveled back to his home region. His people were mostly extinct, but he held onto their traditions.*

The second member of the group was known as the Burned Monk, and also as the Burned-Faced Man. Once young and handsome, he came from a place across the waters he called Europe. His strange accent was unfamiliar to Pogum, but he had learned to speak the local language well. The Burned-Faced Man carried a heavy staff and some gold crosses. His face had been badly burned years earlier, and he preferred to spend time alone. He liked the company of Pogum and the Aztec, who sometimes stayed at his cabin.

The next of the teammates was the Piper. Pogum knew very little about this small, slim man, except that he traveled the world, even venturing outside Ulah-Nane. The Piper didn't talk about his past or why he kept moving so frequently. The Piper wore some strange green garments that Pogum had never seen before. The musical imp loved a good, exciting adventure and never backed down from a challenge. His flute seemed to have charmed, mystical abilities. Whenever he was near the Land of Everlasting Summer, he stopped to visit his friend, the

Burned-Faced man, whom he had apparently met across the sea.

The final member of this odd crew was known only as the Fisherman. He seemed, on the surface, to be the unexceptional member of the group. He was a round fellow, with no combat experience or fighting skill. He dressed in clothing made from the skin of several sea animals, which he had caught. The Fisherman had been abandoned in Ulah-Nane after being captured by people he called pirates and dumped ashore years ago. He was adopted by a local tribe and repaid them by using his incredible fishing skills to supply food when hunting was scarce. He was known as the finest fisherman in Ulah-Nane and did not seem formidable at all. Yet, he was considered a dangerous man.

As his friends watched, Aqueena decided to show her gratitude and her interest in Pogum. She hugged him affectionately and gave him another kiss, but this time, it was on his lips. Pogum paused, more scared by the kiss than by fright.

"You're quite a man, Pogum of the Itiwana," she said. "I like you. I'd like to stay and know your mind, but I must return to my people who need a leader, and to my ailing father. Still, I wish I could know you better."

"I've never been better," Pogum said, walking away with a satisfied smile. "This day was not what I expected. Perhaps you'd allow me to accompany you home?"

"I'd love nothing more," she said. "Walk with me."

His friends laughed and gave him gestures of approval. They were happy to see the normally shy and introspective Pogum getting some female attention.

"You're all invited, of course," Aqueena said. "My people will want to reward you all."

"Gladly," the Piper said.

Pogum and the others escorted Aqueena back to her normally peaceful village. Pogum knew her tribe would surely get back to their families without incident, but he'd come to feel protective of them. Also, he enjoyed the presence of Aqueena. They talked on the way back, and Pogum couldn't recall the last time he had enjoyed anyone's company that much. The Fisherman, the Aztec, the Burned-Faced Man, and the Piper all walked along with them, enjoying jovial conversations.

The group dallied and stopped to fish for dinner, taking their blessed time on the casual outing. Night fell and they camped out until morning. Aqueena knew her fellow Tayans would no doubt be back home by now, but she was having too much fun with this group of mighty misfits.

The following day, the group got back to Aqueena's village. She expected a grand welcome, or at least the sight of happy families reunited and celebrating. Instead, she found nothing.

"My people?" she asked in panic. "Where are they?"

Aqueena ran into each of the temporary, nomadic huts, but no one was present. "What's happened? Where is everyone?"

"Spread out and look around," Pogum said to his friends.

The clever and courageous Itiwana known as Pogum stood in the center of the nomad encampment, listening to the ominous silence and sniffing for the scent of death. He didn't detect even the merest whiff of blood or decay. Pogum lowered his head to the ground to better listen for any sounds. Although he was attuned to the slightest noise, there was nothing to hear except the wind and the footsteps of his allies.

Pogum and his friends were too experienced in odd and dangerous matters to be unnerved by this cryptic enigma. The most important thing was to find out if the missing population was alive, and if so, where were they being held? To do that, he had to track them. How do we track these people if they left no footprints or hoof prints?

The Burned Monk shared the same thought with Pogum. "Whoever's been inflicting their devilry on this village is maddeningly clever. I can't find a single trace that identifies the bloody attackers at all."

The Aztec, who was within earshot, made a gesture to indicate that he'd found nothing, either. Pogum could tell by the look on the face of the Piper that he was similarly frustrated. And while Aqueena was in shock, she didn't seem to have anything to report. The Fisherman merely stood close by, watching the others work. He waited quietly until it was his time to contribute the one thing he had to offer.

The exasperated Pogum would not accept failure when people were in danger. He looked up, seeking inspiration in the skies. He then noticed a black buzzard flying overhead. This wasn't unusual, but watching the bird caused a thought to stir in his brain... What if something swooped down here and carried the townspeople off? *It seemed insane, but it would explain the lack of footprints or hoof prints.* Could some sort of aerial creatures have attacked the town? If so, where did they fly away to?

Wherever they went, it wouldn't be into the region of a large tribe because the villains most likely wouldn't want someone spotting flying beasts carrying humans overhead. Certainly, Pogum and none of his companions saw anything in the sky. Therefore, the stolen villagers were probably nearby, in an isolated location. If the creatures responsible were supernatural or demonic, as he feared, their lair would probably have some sort of magical or religious significance.

"How well do you know this area?" *Pogum asked the Burned-Faced Man.*

"Rather well, indeed," *the monk with the burned face answered with bravado.* "I've lived and hunted alone in this region, as you well know. There's not an acre in all this area I haven't traversed."

"If you traverse it, you'll clean it up," the Piper said.

Pogum often found the Piper's glib musings irritating, but he also had to admit the musical imp was frequently amusing. He turned his attention back to the Burned-Faced Man. "Do you know of any sites in the area that might be used for unholy ceremonies? Are there any sacred locations known for odd rituals?"

The Burned-Faced Monk thought for a minute. "No spot I know of in the region fits that description. However, there is the medicine wheel circle of the Great Shaman."

Pogum raised his eyebrows, surprised that he hadn't thought of that himself. The ancient medicine circle was the perfect place for a ceremony of dark magic, and it was only a few miles from here. At night, some flying creatures could have carried the townsfolk there without fear of being spotted. It was just a wild hunch, but his instincts were telling him this was the case. Since no other conceivable answers were presenting themselves, it was worth investigating.

"Everyone, gather around!" he shouted. "I have an idea. We have to embark on a little hike."

"To where are we headed?" asked the Aztec.

"Someplace holy where monsters dwell," he answered cryptically.

When the friends gathered, Pogum led the group along a grassy footpath toward the nearby *area where the Great Shaman once visited and where the sacred medicine circle was located.*

As they walked, Pogum was having trouble remembering the right direction, since he hadn't been to the spot in years. The Burned-Faced Man, realizing Pogum was lost, took the lead. He could envision every inch of these environs in his flawless memory.

The Aztec spoke to the Piper as they hiked while Aqueena walked distractedly alone, worried about her people. The others guessed from experience that she was not in the mood to talk. As for the Fisherman, he lagged at the rear, not eager to be involved in this, fearing he'd have to use his special ability. He was more terrified of his own power than he was of whoever or whatever might be behind these disappearances.

After a lengthy walk, Pogum and the group of oddities reached the medicine circle. Some of the totems had fallen over due to the ravages of time and weather. Most of them were cracked and worn. A few still stood defiantly, daring the universe to destroy them. The totems of the medicine circle oozed an aura of something otherworldly.

"What are we looking for, precisely?" the Piper asked.

Pogum wasn't exactly sure himself. All he could think to say was, "Clues."

The Burned Monk, the Aztec, and the Piper exchanged annoyed glances, having hoped for something more substantive than that. Regardless, they cooperated and began looking around. Aqueena stood with her arms folded, frowning with a despondent look that said, "We're just chasing our own tails."

Aqueena was unfocused but forced herself to join the search. Pogum stepped into the circle to help her look for unspecified clues, which may or may not exist. As usual, the Fisherman did nothing. He remained outside the circle, hoping that he wouldn't be needed. He hated using his power.

The Aztec found a strange, webbed-foot print. It was far too big and deep to be a duck or any known creature with such a foot. "Over here, friends."

The allies gathered around, and the Aztec pointed with his wooden sword. The assembled group studied the odd print. Pogum kneeled to inspect it closer. "Judging by the print, whatever made this must be larger and heavier than a normal human."

"What could make such a print?" asked the Piper.

"I think I know," answered Pogum, remembering stories of a long-ago encounter Morning Star had with creatures he preferred to forget. "If I'm right, these things hide underground during the day."

"I see no way to gain underground access," the Aztec said, kicking some dirt with his sandaled foot.

"And they used to call me private," the Burned-Faced Man commented. "Quite the dilemma."

Pogum contemplated for a moment and looked at the fallen totems, particularly those lying exceptionally closest to the strange footprints. Impulsively, he lifted one of the large totems off the ground but found nothing unusual underneath. However, when he lifted the second, he found the hole in the ground.

"Success," the Aztec cried. "You were right, my friend."

The hole was large enough for a corpulent man to crawl down into the unseen depths. The edges were embedded with claw marks that indicated a living creature had dug its way down there with no tools. Whatever had done it, was probably not alone. One lone creature hadn't captured an entire town by itself.

"Oh, dear!" the Piper said. "I imagine we'll be crawling into that dark, dismal abyss."

Pogum silently nodded. He didn't know what he'd find down there, but if the townspeople were still alive under the ground, there was nothing else he could do except descend into the darkness.

"In his hands are the deepest places of the Earth," the Burned Monk said, quoting the Bible. "The good Lord will see us through."

Aqueena's only answer was to pull an arrow from her quiver. She was ready for a fight, even if it was against underground monsters. Everyone took a cue from her and began to prepare their own weapons. Only the Fisherman stood apart, looking sad and nervous. He was only a tiny bit afraid of what he would find underground. On the other hand, he was utterly terrified of what he might have to do.

Pogum climbed down into the hole. "Whoever is coming, follow me. No time to waste."

The Burned-Faced Man took a deep breath and whispered, "Angels and ministers of grace defend us!" He then jumped down into the hole.

Next, it was the Aztec's turn to climb down. "For the glory of the Aztecs!" he shouted, as he leaped into the unknown.

The Piper sighed. "The things I do for friends." Winking at Aqueena, he jumped.

Aqueena and the Fisherman were the only ones left. The Fisherman gestured for her to go first. Without a word, Aqueena jumped in.

"Must I do this?" the Fisherman murmured to himself, but reluctantly followed his allies inside.

The entire group vanished into the shadowy tunnel, their minds filled with equal parts foreboding and courage.

CHAPTER FIFTEEN

After what seemed like an endlessly long drop into the ill-omened blackness, Pogum hit the hard, inflexible ground. It was so dark, he wasn't prepared for the impact when he struck bottom. His toned body crashed with a solid thud. "Ugh!"

He heard nearby sounds and saw a crimson-tinged light coming from farther along the tunnel. He reflected the reddish light off the crystals on his tomahawk, providing some illumination in the consuming blackness. This slight, but welcome, sliver of light allowed the rest of the group to see the ground coming at them, so they were able to brace for the landing without taking the same painful bump Pogum suffered.

Aqueena tumbled into view and barely evaded the Fisherman, who dropped down seconds later.

Aqueena landed better than the men of the group who had preceded her. Immediately, she raised her bow and arrow, ready to fire at the slightest sign of an attacker. The rest of the group feared she would shoot one of them in the darkness.

"Stay behind me," Pogum adamantly instructed his friends. He felt very protective of his allies, having gotten them into this. Pogum walked toward the faint rubicund light and ever-loudening sounds; his battle spear and tomahawk at the ready.

At the end of the narrow tunnel, the friends found an expansive, hollowed-out chamber. They knew at once that this was not a naturally formed cavity. Someone had dug it out. The cave roof was held up by thick wooden planks, and the place was illuminated by multiple torches and glassy crystals.

Most significantly of all, the cavern was inhabited. When the odd group of friends saw what was happening within the cavern, even the experienced members of the group were taken aback. It was the kind of sight sane people never expect to see.

The group spied the captured Taya villagers. Or at least, the ones who were left alive. The terrified tribespeople were all bound with some sort of gangly, lime-colored vine. Laid out on the cave floor like chunks of meat, the horrified people cried, screamed, and begged their monstrous captors for release but received not a crumb of *pity. The bodies of the ones who had already been slain were piled up like cordwood.*

The gruesome creatures who had taken the human populace of the Tayan encampment were beasts that would normally only be seen in nightmares. They were seven feet tall, shaggy, and black, with sharp beaks. The beasts were birdlike beings although the long torso area was vaguely human. The monstrous beings had short legs, webbed feet, and clawed hands. They possessed bulging, lidless, obsidian eyes and made a frightening, squealing caw sound. More than 20 of them were present, each equally hideous.

"The Bool'bories!" Pogum whispered as feelings of revulsion and fury filled his mortal brain. He had so strongly hoped to never see these grotesque monsters ever again. Pogum had convinced himself they were extinct. Sadly for Aqueena and her people, his wishful thinking was wrong.

"Demons from hell!" the Burned Monk gasped.

"Demons indeed," said Pogum. "They're carrion eaters."

The Bool'bories were dragging one of the terrified humans to a primitive wooden altar and tying her down. There was some sort of tube and vase combination set up to catch the blood of the victim. The woman screamed in horrified, panicked terror as she was bound. Pogum found it strange that the Bool'bories were wasting time with altars. They're flesh-eaters. Why are some of these people still alive after a whole day and night? What are the Bool'bories waiting for?

From out of a heavily shadowed corner of the cavern, stepped a man. This was seemingly just a normal man. He was not a young man, but he had an aura of authority. He wore white monk's robes, similar to those of the Burned-Faced Man, and possessed a well-trimmed white beard. He carried an old, yellowed scroll. The Bool'bories all stepped aside to allow him a clear path to the altar. The woman begged him for release, but he simply shook his head with a lack of sympathy and opened his discolored scroll.

The Piper tried his best to keep up his con-fidence but was failing. "Never in my most drunken nightmares have I ever imagined such things! I thought I'd seen everything during my years of travel!"

"This is worse than I ever conceived of," the Aztec said. "And that man is working with them!"

Pogum assumed that whoever this person turned out to be, he was the reason that the Bool'bories delayed in their meal. What is he planning?

Pogum squinted to get a better look at the man who was performing the ceremony. Nothing about him looked familiar, but Pogum felt like he'd seen that old scroll before, many years ago, but he couldn't place it. "Does anyone recognize that worm of a man?"

"I'm fairly sure he's a friar," the Burned-Faced Man answered. "If I remember correctly, he calls himself the Saint of Magic."

"What is he planning to do to those poor people?" asked the Aztec.

Pogum finally recognized the scroll. "That's one of the ancient scrolls stolen from the Sun Temple. Pekwin showed them to me once."

"If I recall correctly," the Burned-Faced Man said. "The Saint of Magic was obsessed with the part of the Bible that said the world will end in ice."

"He must be trying to raise Malsumis!" Pogum deduced. "To create a new age of ice. I won't allow it. And I certainly know what the Bool'bories are going to do if we don't stop them. I won't let them devour anyone else!"

Pogum seriously thought about sending his friends back to the surface because he knew how deadly the Bool'bories were. On the other hand, he knew he'd need their help in freeing the tribes-folk. He had to weigh the good of his friends against the innocent lives of the Tayan people. It was a hard choice, even for a man accustomed to battle and adventure.

The nervous Fisherman meekly muttered, "What shall we do now?"

Aqueena raised her arrow. "We kill them all!"

"Don't..." Pogum started to say, to no avail.

Before Pogum could stop her, she fired her arrow and hit the old magician in the back. The Saint of Magic fell with a sickening scream of *agony. Pogum knew that any chance of a covert rescue was impossible now.*

Aqueena shouted, "Let them hold their unholy ceremony now!"

The Bool'bories had become aware of the presence of the invaders. Baying their frightening squeals, the beasts moved toward Pogum and his friends. Some took to the air while others lumbered on their webbed feet. Intruders had attacked their master, and they were not happy about it.

Pogum raised his tomahawk with one hand and his spear in the other, realizing there was no other option now except to fight. His decision had been made for him. "Follow me! Go for their hearts!"

While he'd come to prefer less violent solutions in recent years, he actually had no qualms about killing Bool'bories. Having seen what the beasts were doing to the locals of the village, he had become so maddened with fury that he felt the same bloodlust that Aqueena probably felt upon seeing her people used this way. When it came to killing men, he no longer enjoyed it, but when it came to slaying such monsters, brutality erupted from the recesses of his soul and screamed for blood.

Followed by the Aztec and Aqueena, Pogum dove headfirst into combat. Aqueena fired her weapon, and the Aztec charged forward brandishing his wooden blade thinking of his warrior heritage the whole time. He would willingly die at the hands of monsters before he would run scared.

As the Burned-Faced Man struck monsters with his heavy staff, he glanced at the Fisherman. "It's time, old fellow. Do what you do."

The Fisherman frowned morosely, asking, "Must I do this?"

"You know the answer to that, my friend," replied the Burned Monk. "Do what needs to be done."

The Burned Monk rushed farther into the fray, leaving the Fisherman alone and conflicted. Dare he do what he needed to do? He hated to unleash his power.

Pogum cut a crimson swath of blood through the Bool'bories. Using his powerful arms, he swung his tomahawk with skill and stabbed outward with his spear. He slew several of the beasts. He knew they were resilient and decapitation was one of the few ways to destroy them. Another was to go for their cold hearts.

Behind him, the Aztec utilized his special wooden sword, which had charmed jewels embedded in it, fit for killing monsters. Its power took many of the Bool'bories by surprise. The blade swung and damaged their wings, causing them to drop to the ground, where he quickly stabbed them in the heart. These beasts were not easy to kill, but he wounded a few of them. The Aztec was glad to see some of the creatures pause, frightened by his skill and his weapon.

However, not all of them were intimidated. Some renewed their attack, crazed with anger at seeing their brethren fall. The Piper used his flute to unleash a sonic attack that was both hypnotic and painful to the beasts. His friends were spared this by some trick of his. He and the Burned-Faced Man flanked the Aztec, adding his wooden blade to their attack, hoping that cumulative wounds could do enough damage to kill the beasts.

Aqueena, having no time to reload her bow with a new shaft, began using her bow as a club. She quickly discovered that this was useless against the monsters. Still, she refused to back down. Blinded by rage, she fought on. Instead of joining the others, she attacked solo.

On her own, she ran headlong toward one of the creatures, and she paid for her mistake. The monster swung its large, clawed hand, ripping Aqueena's abdomen open. She stopped, looking down at her fatal wound. The realization hit her that her life had just come to an end. She dropped her bow, took one last look at Pogum, and collapsed.

"No!" Pogum yelled, seeing his new friend fall in battle.

A maelstrom of rage, the likes of which he hadn't felt in many years, swirled in his fevered brain. The sight of the woman he liked so much being killed so violently triggered his blood-lust, which exploded inside him. He let out an enraged, anguished cry and unleashed another lethal spear attack. Nothing was going to stop him from killing every single Bool'borie in sight!

The Aztec, the Piper, and the Burned-Faced Monk also felt intense anger at seeing Aqueena fall, yet they were too badly under siege by the beasts surrounding them to begin the offensive they would have liked to have. At that moment, they had to focus on surviving. It was the most dangerous situation any of the three veteran adventurers had been in.

The Fisherman had seen enough. Although he didn't know Aqueena very well, she was pretty and brave, and he liked her. Seeing her gutted by a monster was too much for him to tolerate. He could no longer stand idly by. It was time to unleash his secret power!

The Fisherman closed his eyes and clenched his fists with gritted teeth. He concentrated for a few seconds... and he began to change! His entire body began to blur into a haze of fog. A nauseating stench, like that of rotting fish, was emitted as the obscured figure reconfigured into a solid form. When he rematerialized, he was no longer the Fisherman. He was no longer human.

His body had grown and changed, and he had become a green, amphibious creature. He now had a fishlike face and finned ears, as well as dark gills on the side of his head. He had grown razor-sharp claws on his fingers and had shark teeth. Two long, prehensile toes had burst out of his sandals. Thick, protective scales covered his skin. He immediately started laughing *a maniacal, inhuman laugh that echoed hauntingly throughout the cavern. He was no longer a simple fisherman. He was the macabre creature called N'Dam-Keno, the bestial merman.*

CHAPTER SIXTEEN

*efore the Fisherman had come to Ulah-
Nane unwillingly after being captured by
pirates, he'd been on a simple fishing trip in his
native Scotland. While fishing, he had accidentally caught a mermaid. To induce him to free her,
she had made love to him. He did so, unaware
that she had put a curse on him.*

*It was only after he had been taken in by
the local tribe in Ulah-Nane that he realized
he periodically transformed into the merman,
N'Dam-Keno. At first, he was an uncontrollable,
murderous beast when he transformed. Luckily,
he had gotten help from the Great Shaman to
learn to control his ability. Now he was able to
restrain his amphibious form, to an extent.*

*However, when he let the beast out, N'Dam-
Keno showed no mercy to any foe. The merman*

enjoyed chaos and violence. He was useful in a fight, but even his allies knew that having such a living weapon on their side could often be as much a problem as an advantage.

The Fisherman was perpetually locked in a struggle to keep the evil spirit under control. The eldritch pressure of the primal entity endlessly tried to induce the Fisherman to release him. The villagers understood this and were compassionate toward the Fisherman. Whenever he was unable to keep control of the creature any longer, they had ways to restrain him. There and then, he was unrestrained.

Pogum and the Burned-Faced Man had discovered the Fisherman and his power years ago. He liked to keep the Fisherman close by when they worked together in order to make sure that the merman didn't get completely out of control. Renaming him N'Dam-Keno, after an old myth from the days of Morning Star, he often recruited the Fisherman to join him in his travels as a way of helping the Fisherman release all those violent urges in a useful way, where he could be supervised. The rest of his friends were terrified of the transformed N'Dam-Keno. Pogum himself was wary of the amphibious beast. The Fisherman sometimes went to the cabin of the Burned-Faced Man to learn prayer and meditation. He was there when Aqueena had come asking for help.

Cackling wildly, N'Dam-Keno leaped into the air, covering several meters with ease. This laugh drew the attention of everyone in the cavern, including the Bool'bories. They were surprised and alarmed by the sudden appearance of a more dangerous beast than themselves. The Aztec and the Piper were also nervous at the sight of the fishlike beast because they could never predict what he was going to do. They prayed his aggressions would be limited to the monsters.

Chortling and hooting, the nefarious N'Dam-Keno jabbed his claws into the chest of one of the creatures. With a yank, he removed the green heart of the Bool'borie. N'Dam-Keno laughed crazily as the Bool'borie collapsed to the floor.

"You're a heartless one!" screamed N'Dam-Keno, with violent mirth, as he threw the still-beating heart to the ground and continued his insane laughter. "Now I think I will have some fun!"

When one of the vengeful Bool'bories lunged at N'Dam-Keno, shrieking in primal rage, the leaping fish man revealed another of his powers. N'Dam-Keno spit a green poison-like substance at the Bool'borie while emitting squid-like ink. The two substances engulfed the raging Bool'borie, debilitating the creature in seconds. All the while, the unnatural laughter of N'Dam-Keno echoed throughout the cavern, chilling the hearts of everyone who heard it.

Between Pogum, N'Dam-Keno, and the rest of the group, they managed to turn the tide and gain the upper hand in the conflict. The bird-like creatures were put on the defensive. The combined power, rage, and skill of the heroic fighters was *unlike anything the ambush-minded Bool'bories had ever experienced.*

While momentum was on their side and the Bool'bories were distracted, the Aztec signaled to a pair of his allies, indicating they should assist the captured visitors. "Our main priority is to help these people. Come along, friends!"

The Piper and the Burned Monk followed the Aztec's lead and began freeing the captured villagers, leaving Pogum and N'Dam-Keno to deal with the monsters. The Aztec pointed to the tunnel with his wooden sword.

"This way," he said. "Stay close to us. Move quickly!"

Once freed from their bonds, the Taya people sprinted in horrified panic toward the tunnel leading to the surface. They stampeded in such fear that they almost trampled each other and their rescuers. The Aztec led the way and his two companions brought up the rear, trying to ensure they all got out safely.

"Go!" Pogum yelled. "Aztec, Piper, and Monk! You three get out! The Fisherman and I can hold them."

Pogum knew these three men would normally not leave a comrade in danger, but there were only a few of the Bool'bories left at this point and the beasts seemed no match for the combination of Pogum and N'Dam-Keno. Therefore, the man of the Aztecs reluctantly decided that he should obey Pogum's command.

One of the Bool'bories noticed the fleeing people and wasn't pleased to see their future meal leaving. It swooped down to reclaim some of the humans before they could escape. With a fierce caw, the creature dove swiftly, with murderous intent. It caught the Aztec, ripping him open.

N'Dam-Keno grabbed the monster and avenged his friend in a permanent way, but it was too late for the Aztec.

Pogum shouted in fury and continued his attack. He hadn't felt such hatred before. All he could think about was killing his foes.

The villagers escaped as the Burned-Faced Man and Piper covered their escape. The Bool'bories were busy battling Pogum and N'Dam-Keno, and not faring well. The Piper and the Monk saw to it that the surviving people of the town escaped unharmed.

The Burned-Faced Monk led the townspeople along the tunnel, guiding them to a rope ladder they had spotted earlier, which the Saint of Magic had no doubt used to get in and out of the pit. The Burned Monk swiftly climbed to the top of the ladder to assist the Taya folk, while the Piper stayed at the bottom, guarding the rear. The villagers climbed up one-by-one.

Pogum decided it was a good time to get out of harm's way before there were any other casualties. Two deaths were more than enough. N'Dam-Keno, however, had other ideas. With his mortal teammates safe, he completely cut loose.

N'Dam-Keno needed no inspiration to fight with savage abandon.

The fight in the cavern was coming to an end. N'Dam-Keno was easily wiping out their monstrous foes. Spear and tomahawk and claw and poison struck out at the remaining Bool'bories, dismembering limbs and removing their emerald hearts. Not one of the monsters was alive when the violence stopped.

N'Dam-Keno cackled with wild, ferocious glee. "Are there no more? Not even three or four? Alas, I was just beginning to enjoy my day! It was a glorious battle. Is there nothing else I can kill?"

The crazed being heard a soft moan and realized that the man in the priest's robes was still alive. "Ah, I am not deprived. A small bonus remains alive."

As N'Dam-Keno hopped toward the wounded man, eager for another kill, Pogum gestured for him to halt because he wanted to ask the man questions about Malsumis. N'Dam-Keno, however, was too quick to the kill. The fish man tore the Saint of Magic in half.

The frightful sound of N'Dam-Keno's gleeful laughter so infuriated Pogum that he let loose a strong blow to the fish-man's scaley face. Hit so unexpectedly, N'Dam-Keno was staggered, but not hurt.

"Never strike me!" the merman shouted.

"I do not fear you, N'Dam-Keno," Pogum said. "Will you attack me? Fight me?"

However, just as Pogum was preparing for retaliation from the fish beast, the soul of the Fisherman took over and N'Dam-Keno transformed back into his human form. Pogum's rage lessened as he witnessed the change.

"I didn't want him to hurt you," the Fisherman said.

Pogum calmed himself and lowered his head sadly, looking at the slain Taya people.

Nothing good happened here today.

Pogum and the Fisherman walked out of the tunnel, glancing sadly at the slain Aqueena and the Aztec, as well as the other bodies. Pogum found his remaining two friends safely waiting for him in the medicine circle. The Burned-Faced Man noticed that the Fisherman looked guilty about something.

"What happened?" he asked Pogum.

"It's of no matter," Pogum answered quickly. "N'Dam-Keno just got out of control."

"As usual," the Burned-Faced Man quipped.

"And what of the Aztec and Aqueena?" the Piper asked. "We shan't leave them where they lay, I assume."

Pogum shook his head. "I'll get my Itiwana friends, and we'll retrieve the bodies, then block up this tunnel. Seal it off forever. Let's put this nightmare in the past. I hope to never see a day like this one again."

"I don't wish to see anything like this again either," the Piper said. He held out his flute, offering it to Pogum. "I'm done with such things.

I no longer find it charming or challenging. Take this instrument of mine. It tempts me into situations such as this. No more. Take it. Give it as a gift to someone."

Pogum took the flute. "Very well. I understand your decision. I will give this to my sister, Atira. She so enjoys music. As for me, I am tired. I just want to go home. I have no heart for fighting another battle anytime soon."

Pogum had no idea that a greater adventure soon awaited him.

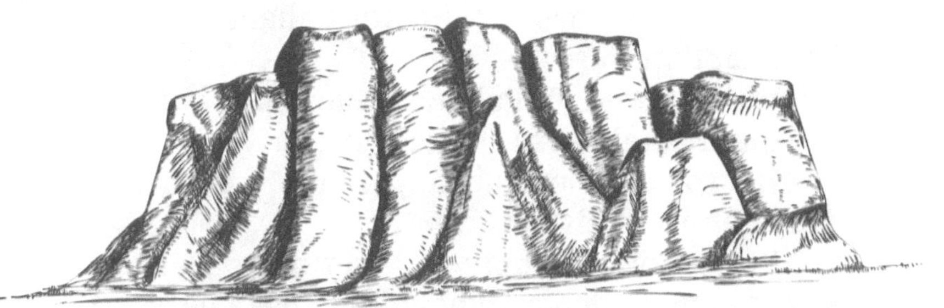

CHAPTER SEVENTEEN

Atira finished her tale, and Calian, who had listened in rapt attention and admiration of his father's heroism, felt simultaneously like smiling and weeping. His father's valor and compassion were inspiring but also intimidating. And the sad end of the story made him doubt his own ability. If even Pogum couldn't protect the lives of his allies, could Calian guarantee the safety of Pahana?

"I tell you this because I want you to know that, even in the face of the greatest hardship and loss, Pogum never faltered. He risked his life many times and ultimately sacrificed his life for us all. I have no doubt he passed that nobility on to you. We are all relying on you to be as true and reliable as the brightest star that guides us. Be like your father, Pogum, and do your destiny much honor."

"I thank you very much," Calian said. "I prize your faith in me greater than any riches. I will not hesitate to lay down my life for Pahana and the Itiwana. I promise."

At that moment, Pahana came riding back. "I see that Manabazo has not returned."

"His travels continue, apparently," Atira said. "He'll return in his own time."

"But I won't be here to greet him," Pahana said. "Time to depart. Should you need us, send Black Crow with a message. And now... where is Hayoka?"

Hayoka, who had been lurking unobtrusively behind the immobile figure of Stone Coat, stepped forward. "Here."

"Our trek relies on you," Pahana ordered. "This is your opportunity for honor. Don't waste the occasion."

Hayoka lowered his head in a respectful bow. "I surely won't waste this opportunity."

Pinga joined Pahana on the back of Mountain Fury. They all rode out of the village on their mounts with Pahana in the lead. Hayoka rode on a young, small bison named Bold Flower, who was rejected as a steed for a warrior. This was a reprieve for the animal, who would otherwise have ended up as meat for the tribe. Faw-Faw walked along on his own overlarge feet.

Hayoka noticed that Calian persistently kept a watchful eye on him. *I won't waste this opportunity... the opportunity to deal with Calian, among other things.*

I feel both apprehensive and exhilarated! Kia thought as she paced in circles around her flickering fire pit.

She considered what these mysterious shamanic women could teach her. Kia was consumed with gaining more mystical knowledge and increasing her power. However, the not-so-subtle threats made by the Breathing Shaman were troublesome to her. Kia had no hint regarding what sort of punishment these unseen women would unleash, but she did not recognize their authority to do so. Kia did not like threats.

She deliberated the positives and negatives of training with the shamans of the Valley of the Blue Mists. *Can I trust them? Should I risk joining strangers who have threatened me? Do they have anything to teach me that Molowia can't?* Kia already felt she had moved beyond Molowia. If these women were trained by the same teacher as Molowia, would they know anything Molowia didn't?

Of course, Molowia had admitted that she was withholding her teachings as punishment for disobedience and for acting to help her family without permission. Kia strongly felt that the ruling was unfair.

Abruptly, the small flame of the fire pit spit upward volcanically. Kia was startled by the blazing eruption, wondering if she was under attack. She ducked into a defensive crouch, holding her hands above her head, preparing to cast a defensive spell.

"Do not fear. Do not," the familiar but intimidating voice said. "It's your teacher. Your mentor."

Kia lowered her hands although she wasn't totally comfortable with the new arrival. "Shula-Witsa. Once again, you come when you're not called."

"You need me. You do," Shula-Witsa said, as his fiery face materialized in the chamber.

"Why do I need you just now?" Kia asked.

"The valley shamans. Those women," Shula-Witsa said. "They vex you. They do. You need advice. You do."

Kia's interest was immediately piqued. "You're right. Go on then."

"Go to them. Join them," Shula-Witsa answered.

"Why?" she asked, eager for any information that would help inform her decision.

"Find the crystals. Use them," the flaming spirit said.

Kia approached the Elder, her face revealing a youthful neediness. "What crystals? I don't understand."

"You will know. You will," Shula-Witsa said. "They have power. Great power. They'll enhance you. Empower you. You'll grow stronger. You will."

Kia began to stammer an answer, but no discernible words came out. She was confused enough without all this talk of magical crystals.

But if they could make her more powerful, why not take the opportunity to get hold of them?

"But what of Molowia?" Kia asked. "She hasn't given her permission to go to the Valley of the Blue Mists yet."

"Then persuade her. Convince her," Shula-Witsa insisted.

"I don't know if I can," Kia said. "She doesn't fully trust me. How can I talk her into it?"

"Not with words. No words," the Fire Elder said. "You know how. You know."

It took Kia a moment to understand what the Elder was saying. When she realized the implications of the suggestion, she gasped. "No. I couldn't do that to Molowia!"

"You must, Kia! You must!" Shula-Witsa insisted. "It is necessary. It is."

"But to betray Molowia in such a way!" Kia protested. "I mustn't!"

"Think of Tawa. Of Pinga," Shula-Witsa replied. "Think of Pahana. Your family. They need you. They do. They're in danger. They are. They need you. They do."

Kia thought about Molowia's mandate that Kia could not involve herself in the Elder war and therefore could not help her family. This rule enraged Kia. She would do anything for her family.

"I'm not sure," Kia meekly said. "I want to help them, but..."

"Don't fail them! Don't fail!" the blazing face said. "Save your family. Save them!"

Kia paced for a minute and then spun toward Shula-Witsa with fierce determination on her youthful face. "You're right. I must do it for them. May the gods forgive me!"

Kia sat and crossed her legs and arms. Closing her eyes, she chanted the forbidden spell Shula-Witsa had taught her.

Molowia had fallen asleep, torn with indecision about whether to send Kia to study with the shamans of the House of Many Hands. As she drifted into overdue slumber, she considered unburdening herself of Kia's rebellion and frightening power. Still, her affection for Kia and familial responsibility induced her to keep the girl close, hoping to regain the devoted relationship the pair had once had.

Pinga had asked Molowia to wait until the delegation from Shipapa-Lina had the chance to meet the women and determine their real intentions. Molowia agreed to do so although she feared what any further contamination this Breathing Shaman could do to Kia should she continue to pressure the young girl. All this stress had affected her ability to sleep. After several days of fitful naps, she finally fell into a comfortable sleep.

Then the voices came in her dreams. Persuasive, enticing, and compelling voices sang to her snoozing brain. She was serenaded by seductive tones, manipulating her resting mind.

These whispers influenced the thoughts and judgments of the sleeping shaman. These silent words spoke to her and altered her thoughts.

Molowia woke as if some unseen hand had shaken her back to wakefulness. The first thought that struck her as she opened her eyes was to send Kia to the Valley of the Blue Mists.

It's the best thing to do. She belongs in the House of Many Hands. The Breathing Shaman can teach her better than I, and it will free me to attend to other matters in Kolhu. It's the right thing to do.

The rain tapered off, and the only sound was that of bison hooves in the mud. The Itiwana delegation was soaked by the brief but heavy downpour. When the sun finally made its reappearance, a scorching heat quickly dried the damp travelers.

As they neared the valley, Calian was wary. He didn't trust Hayoka for even a moment. He suspected they were being led into a trap, but since he couldn't deter Pahana from following Hayoka to this unfamiliar valley, all he could do was remain prepared for treachery.

Pinga was sitting on Mountain Fury, just behind Pahana. She was holding him around the waist to keep balanced. "This One senses your trepidation, my son."

"A good leader should be alert to danger at all times, wouldn't you agree?" Pahana said.

"This One agrees," Pinga replied. "But she senses a specific apprehension now. Are you regretting your willingness to trust Hayoka?"

"I have hope Hayoka will prove to be a faithful friend," Pahana answered. "But I don't confuse my hopes with the reality of the world around us. These women have designs on Kia, which may or may not be benign, and it's possible we're being led into an ambush. However, this trip should answer a multitude of questions. When this is over, I will know whether I can trust Hayoka and whether we have new allies to help us in our cause."

"You are wise, Son," Pinga said, affectionately. "Tawa will be proud when he returns. This One hopes he is safe and well."

"I'm confident he is," Pahana said. "My father can survive anything."

In the lead, Hayoka was keenly aware that the people following him would quickly put a spear in his back if they spotted even a hint of deceit. Calian, in particular, would take great glee in stomping vigorously on his dead body.

When the valley came into view, Hayoka suddenly became more nervous than he had been the entire trip. *And now it begins. I must win the trust of both parties, or one of them will surely remove my head and dangle the rest of me from a tree for the wolves to devour.*

Hayoka held up his hand. "Hold, all of you. Wait here, I'll go down myself to let them know that friends have come to visit."

"Why alone?" Calian asked, suspiciously.

Hayoka expected this from Calian. "Haven't I told you they have defenses which you do not want to confront? Perhaps I confused you. I apologize for the intelligence of my words."

"Clever words, indeed," Calian said. "Perhaps I should collect your clever tongue to marvel at it daily."

"Enough venom spewing," Pahana said. "Go Hayoka, but be wise. Think carefully about what you do next."

No one else among the Itiwana could make Hayoka feel such anguish with a simple accusation. Hayoka simply nodded and, without a word, rode little Bold Flower toward the valley.

The young bison hesitated at the edge, spooked by the strange, swirling mists. "Go on, little fellow. Be as bold as your name."

Bold Flower would not move. Annoyed, Hayoka hopped off the animal. "Fine, then. Your name should be Timid Flower. I have two perfectly good feet."

Calian shouted, "Even bison don't want your company!"

Pahana gestured for Calian to be silent. "Cease your mockery. Now is not the time for pettiness."

"As you wish."

Hayoka ignored this taunting, walking down a path into the cobalt haze. The insults made him more apt to enact Agwara's plan to use the shaman of the valley to destroy the Itiwana of Shipapa-Lina.

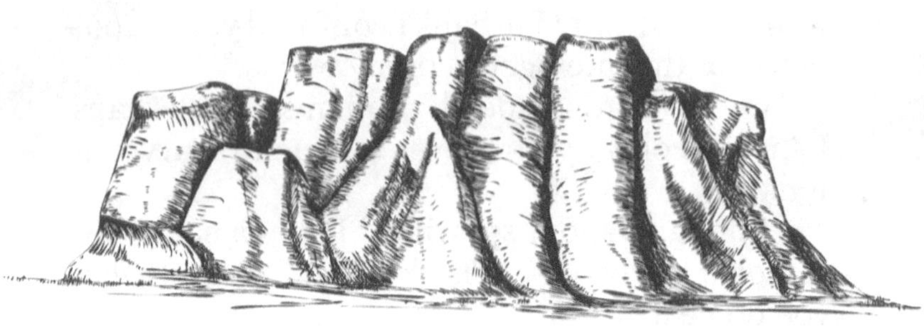

CHAPTER EIGHTEEN

"**I**'m here!" Hayoka shouted into the azure fog of the valley. "I've come back, as promised."

Hayoka waited to hear a response from either the Keeper or the Breathing Shaman. *I hope it's the Keeper who responds. I'm not certain the Breathing Shaman won't unleash the Guardian on me.*

He walked randomly, calling out to the women of the House of Many Hands. Hayoka was oblivious to the fact that the Slide Rock Bolter hung on a cliff not far from where he wandered. His voice roused the hungry giant, who scanned the mist with its piercing vision, isolating the visitor.

The behemoth waited for Hayoka to step into the proper spot, at which point it would unhook itself from its perch and devour another small meal. However, someone had other ideas.

The dulcet whispers of the Keeper impelled the giant to remain where it was. Despite its appetite, it obeyed the Keeper's command to spare the stranger. The massive beast grunted but surrendered to the melodic sounds and drifted back to sleep.

Hayoka knew nothing of this as he strolled blindly in the mists. "Can you hear me, Keeper?" he shouted.

"I can," the voice of the unseen Keeper replied. "I'm delighted to see that you've returned. But I do not see any of the Itiwana. Have you failed?"

"Would I disappoint you?" Hayoka said mirthfully. "Of course, I brought them. They're waiting just outside the valley. I didn't want to alarm you. Shall I summon them?"

"Have you warned them of the consequences of violence against us?" she asked.

"I have," Hayoka said. "I believe they will be reasonable. I will do my best to see that they act responsibly and peacefully."

"I accept your word," the Keeper said.

"All but one," Hayoka added in an overly dramatic voice. "There's one among us named Calian. He's a dour young snake with a streak in his hair. Calian is full of hate, and he doesn't trust you or myself. I fear he may try to sabotage our plans. I tried to induce Pahana to leave him behind, but the man has an unwise soft spot for Calian. I would advise you to use whatever force you deem necessary to control him. Even lethal force."

"Thank you for the warning," the Keeper said. "We will make certain this Calian understands what real power is, and how easily we can crush someone so insignificant."

"Well said and wisely decided," Hayoka replied. "Now I will summon my companions."

Tawa could barely muster the strength to moan. Sweat poured from every inch of his skin and he floated in and out of consciousness. His life was near its end, and all he could think of, in his delirium, was seeing his family one more time.

In the divine grass house, the Earthmother, Eithinoa, continued to place hands on the half-dead Tawa, filling him with as much life energy as she could spare. She knew she couldn't keep the dying man alive for much longer.

"In exhaustion, I say I cannot maintain your life much longer," Eithinoa admitted, unsure if he could understand her at this point. "In sorrow, I say I wish I could save you. In hope, I say I will do my best to keep you with us until your family arrives."

Eithinoa wondered where Tawa's family was. She assumed he was wondering the same thing.

"Tread carefully and slowly," Hayoka said to the Itiwana. "Don't do anything to startle our hosts.

Otherwise, you'll meet creatures that will make you feel most unwelcome."

The Itiwana had abandoned their bison and their weapons, leaving them in the care of the four escorts and Faw-Faw. Only Pahana, Pinga, O'Yewa, Masewa, Calian, and Hayoka descended into the valley.

"I can't see a cursed thing!" Masewa said. "I hope there are no pits or crevasses or fissures."

"If you fall into one, I promise to come back and feed you," O'Yewa replied playfully.

"I'll toss you into one of them if you don't stop being irritating," Masewa said.

"I'm never irritating," O'Yewa said. "I'm engaging."

"Stop that!" Pahana ordered. "You two gibbering gophers could annoy a stone."

"Remain alert," Pinga said. "This One senses powerful forces nearby. She sees spirits, spirits in this very place. This One may be archaic, but that doesn't mean she is not right."

"Spirits?" Pahana asked. "Good or evil?"

"Can there ever be one without the other?" Pinga replied. "Prepare for either one."

Hayoka spoke with blustering self-assurance. "Don't fear. I've arranged for our safe passage. Be assured that you're under my protection. You're welcome."

Calian gritted his teeth, seething with the urge to pummel Hayoka vigorously. *One day, Pahana is going to see through this rancid skunk, and when he does, I will savor the feel of my fists battering him.*

The Itiwana stopped, alarmed, at the sound of heavy footsteps and hefty breathing. Something large was nearby in the mists.

"Stay calm," Pahana commanded. "It may not attack. Whatever it may be."

"I suddenly wish we had brought Faw-Faw down with us," O'Yewa said.

"This is exactly why I did not bring him," Pahana said. "We don't want any needless fighting."

"Everyone, be calm," Hayoka said loudly. "I told you about the Guardian. It will only attack if the Breathing Shaman or the Keeper tells it to. And I have their word they won't do any such thing unless we attack first."

"I hope so," Masewa said. "But I fear we may regret leaving our weapons behind."

"Brave hearts, all of you," Pahana said. "Do not give these mystics the impression of cowardice."

"You heard our leader," Calian said. "We walk fearlessly into the alien darkness others dread, confident that we can survive whatever lurks within. We have endured much, and we will endure further, but we will never submit to fright."

"Nicely said," Pahana added, never having been very adept at the kind of inspiring speeches that Tawa could so readily extemporize. He was a planner, not a talker.

The group was emboldened by the brave words. Moments later, the group heard the heavy footsteps of the Guardian move away. Its loud breathing could no longer be heard. Hayoka chose to take credit for this.

"You see," Hayoka said. "I told you I'd bring you safely through. Just trust in me."

"Then where is this House of Many Hands?" Calian said.

Hayoka looked around, clueless as to where he should lead them. He was unconscious when he was brought to the shamanic sanctuary. "Don't be scared. I'll get you there."

"I am not scared!" Calian said. "I'm angry."

"That's not unusual," Hayoka said.

"Just get us there, Hayoka," Pahana ordered.

Hayoka looked around, perplexed, and then saw the swarm of fireflies. They hovered in front of the Itiwana as if trying to get the visitors' attention. Hayoka realized this was a sign from the Keeper. "We follow the lights. It's just like following the stars, only closer."

The fireflies began drifting away, leaving just enough of them to create a trail in the air. Hayoka quickly followed their path. "Hurry, then. Let us not keep our hosts waiting."

"We've come this far, so I am disposed to trust him now," Pahana said.

The Itiwana followed him although Calian paused, wishing he could find some proof of deceit. With a frustrated grumble, he joined his people, counting the seconds before the expected trap ensnared them.

The insects seemed to be leading them on a deliberately confusing zig-zag route through the mist, designed to prevent the visitors from memorizing the footpath to the House of Many Hands. After a long, winding walk, they saw the ingress point underneath the Full Moon Arch.

Hayoka marched boldly into the House of Many Hands, acting as if he lived there. Pahana was prepared to be the second man in, but Calian leaped ahead of him, ready to take the hit of whatever peril might be waiting beyond that door. Pahana was a bit surprised to see Calian jump into his path, which was disrespectful, but he quickly deduced what Calian was thinking. *Such a devoted warrior.*

Pahana entered, with his mother inches behind, clutching his biceps. The twins guarded the rear. O'Yewa gestured for Masewa to go in first. Grim Masewa shook his head in annoyance but entered before his brother. O'Yewa heard the breathing of the Guardian again and rushed to join his family.

Awaiting them inside were a half-dozen women dressed in silk and cotton with snakeskin belts. The shortest, eldest woman stood in the front, holding a bone tube. She pointed the tube at the Itiwana visitors.

"Against my best judgment, you now walk in the hallowed place built by the Great Shaman," the woman with the bone tube said. "All who walk into this place must act in accordance with our rules, or they will answer to me personally. And my answers to those who disrespect this place will not be to your liking."

"I will vouch for my companions," Hayoka said. "Let me introduce you to my friend Pahana, son of the Itiwana Chieftain. Pahana, this is the Breathing Shaman."

"It's an honor to be invited to this sacred place," Pahana said. "Molowia has spoken of it in reverence. I only regret that my father could not be here himself, but he has been away for two full moons, at the behest of the gods. Still, I carry his authority and I hope that when he returns, he will find that we have new allies in the House of Many Hands."

"We will judge your sincerity," the Breathing Shaman said. "I hope for your safety that Hayoka's words of praise regarding you are justified."

One of the other women stepped forward, gently pushing the Breathing Shaman's arm down. "The endeavor of hospitality has not improved your humor one bit, I see. Calm your icy rage. I've known you great and majestic and fierce. Now let me know you as a peacemaker."

Hayoka offered a slight bow. "Thank you. Let me introduce you to the Itiwana. This is the Keeper."

"You are welcome here," the Keeper said.

"Permitted might be a better word," the Breathing Shaman said, as the Keeper nudged her into silence.

Pahana stepped forward. "Your trepidation is clear, and I don't blame you for it. We, also, are at our most cautious. Let's hope none of us will feel that same way after we have a chance to speak to each other.”

“We do hope so,” the Keeper said. “Come along. Let's withdraw to the room of the talking stick.”

The six women led the Itiwana down an adobe passageway adorned with pictographs. The Keeper glided gracefully, while the Breathing Shaman shuffled with feet that seemed too small for her thickset body. The shaman sisters turned into a spherical chamber, where twelve bushes of hay were arranged in a circle around a pile of stones and crystals.

The six mystic women sat in a semi-circle on the hay bales on the far side of the room. The Keeper gestured for the visitors to be seated. The Itiwana all looked at Pahana, who calmly took a seat opposite the Breathing Shaman. Pinga sat next to him, and the twins joined them. Calian began to sit but noticed Hayoka loitering near the entrance.

“Will you be joining us?” Calian asked, looking askance at Hayoka.

“I think not,” Hayoka said. “This is between the Itiwana and the sisterhood of the House of Many Hands. I've done my part to bring you together. I leave the rest to your wisdom.”

Calian was apprehensive as Hayoka walked off unattended. *What's he planning now?*

The Breathing Shaman and the Keeper both looked at Pinga. “You once walked among the Sky Elders, did you not?” the elder sister asked.

"This One did," Pinga answered. "She has been happier as a mortal woman."

"Still, it is an honor to have you here," the Keeper said. "I look forward to hearing your thoughts."

"We will speak of many things," Pinga said. "But This One would prefer to begin with your true intentions toward her daughter. Why have you contacted Kia?"

"We do what we must," the Breathing Shaman said.

"That sounds ominous," Pahana said. "Care to clarify?"

"We understand your concern for the girl," the Keeper said. "But you must understand our concerns."

"Which are?" Pahana asked.

"She is too powerful!" the Breathing Shaman said sharply. "We have seen and sensed incredible gifts possessed by her, yet her mind is that of an immature child. She does not have the years to contain such power. At this moment in time when gods and demons are bringing war to the mortal realm, such capabilities cannot be allowed to run rampant."

"Run rampant?" Pinga asked. "You speak of This One's daughter as if Kia were a wild boar rampaging across a field of baby chicks."

"She could become just that should her power continue to grow unabated," the Breathing Shaman said.

Pahana brushed his mother's shoulder to calm her. He knew that her family was the one thing that caused the serene goddess to lose her composure. "And you shaman women are maintaining that only you can prevent my sister from becoming a menace to us all?"

"We do maintain this," the eldest sister said. "Only the teachings of the Great Shaman can teach a mortal to control such power."

"Molowia was taught by the Great Shaman," Pahana said. "Why not leave Kia's teachings to her?"

The Breathing Shaman was becoming increasingly defensive. "Molowia has failed. Kia is in contact with fantastic forces, to which Molowia is oblivious."

"Which forces?" Pinga asked, concerned.

"Shula-Witsa," the Keeper replied.

If Pinga were not already an albino, she would have turned pale. "Shula-Witsa? The fiery schemer!"

"What's wrong, Mother?" Pahana asked.

"Kia may indeed be involved with forces she cannot comprehend," Pinga responded.

"Indeed," the Breathing Shaman said. "And we can help her."

Pinga became suddenly angry. "This One will ensure the safety of her daughter!"

"It seems you do not trust us," the Keeper said.

"Nor you, us," Pinga replied.

Pahana breathed a weary sigh of both impatience and disappointment. "It seems we are quite far apart."

"So it seems," the Breathing Shaman answered sternly.

Calian had been looking at the door since Hayoka left, while the leaders debated. Finally, he got up and exited the room. "If you'll permit me to a brief absence, my clan chief."

This did not escape the Keeper's notice. "Who is that man?"

"That's Calian," Pahana said. "The most loyal of men."

Calian! the Keeper thought. *He's the one Hayoka warned us of. Where is he going?*

I regret doing it, but it needed doing, Kia thought, as she rode across the field.

The youthful mystic sat cross-legged upon a small pink cloud, which supported her like an unseen, floating horse. Accompanying her were the adventurous hunter brothers Paquan-Hoya and Bolon-Hoya. Paquan-Hoya carried a wooden shield and a slingshot, while Bolon-Hoya had a bow and arrow. They had been chosen by Molowia as Kia's escorts to the Valley of the Blue Mists. Not that Kia needed protection, considering her formidable powers, but Molowia felt such a young girl should not travel cross-country alone.

That decision, at least, was genuinely made by Molowia. The choice to allow Kia to go to the valley, however, was furtively swayed.

I hate manipulating Molowia's mind, Kia thought forlornly. *She's my teacher and my kin. She'd no doubt hate me if she was aware of what I did. Still, it's all for the best. She's taught me all she could teach me. I am beyond her. I hope these women of the valley will be adequate teachers. Or perhaps I'll teach them something.*

They took a pause in their trip so that Paquan-Hoya and Bolon-Hoya, who were both on foot, could rest and drink some water from a stream. Kia sat calmly on her cloud, hoping her guides were leading her in the right direction. *Perhaps I should be sure we're not lost.*

Kia shut her eyes and reached out with her senses, scanning Ulah-Nane for mystic energy, which she suspected would be the Valley of the Blue Mists. She was getting more and more proficient at using her astral senses to peer across great distances.

"Kia!" she heard, surprising her. "Kia!"

Kia looked around, although it seemed like the voice was inside her head, rather than someone nearby. "Who's speaking?"

"My time is running out," a familiar voice said, desperately. "My thoughts are like mud. My body fails me."

"Father?" Kia asked, afraid of the answer.

"It's me, Sweet Daughter," Tawa's distant mind said. "Time is short. I'm at the northern mountain called Kuwahi. It is home to the White Bear, king of all bears. The situation is dire. I need..."

Tawa's voice faded, and Kia shouted, "Father? Father!"

The brothers came in response to her shouts.

"What's wrong?" they both asked.

Kia stared into space, panic in her adolescent eyes, as she tried to regain contact with her father, but could not do so. "Perhaps the worst thing possible!"

The shining pile of crystals beckoned to Hayoka. He stared in fascination at the beautiful stones, feeling the aura of their power. No one else was present in the chamber. It seemed that everyone who resided within this odd adobe dwelling was occupied with the Itiwana inside that spherical room.

Dare I take them? he mused. *No, not now. It will surely be obvious who the thief is if I'm the only one without a plausible excuse to exculpate me.*

Tantalized, he reached out to touch the gleaming gems. As his fingertips made contact, he felt a galvanic jolt and staggered against the wall, trying to regain his equilibrium. He was unprepared for the power of those stones.

"Excellent!" a harsh, feral voice said. "The human is weak and soft but does the deed well."

Hayoka's focus was brought back to the room, apprehensively inspecting the chamber. The voice was very familiar. He had heard it inside his head since he was a small child. He couldn't remember a time when that voice was not whispering to him furtively.

"Show yourself!" Hayoka demanded.

A canine silhouette seemed to appear in the corner of the room. The animal's eyes glowed in the shadows, gazing into Hayoka's soul, as if it knew that soul intimately. Which it did.

"It's you, at last," Hayoka said, in an awed voice. "The Coyote!"

"Coyote walks once more," the canine spirit said. "Long has Coyote lived inside weak, soft human. Useful has the weak human been. Just as his father was."

Hayoka walked physically closer to the being, who had mentally and spiritually been closer to him than any other living being. "I feel like I know you."

"Human does know Coyote," the canine replied. "Has Coyote not been the friend who counsels soft human? Your constant companion, Coyote has been. When human was alone, Coyote was there. The human knows Coyote, and Coyote knows the human."

Gingerly, Hayoka touched Coyote's fur. "I often wondered if I was insane. Whenever I heard your voice in my head, I wondered if my mind was addled. Seeing you now is both comforting and terrifying. It's as if I'm seeing part of my own mind."

"Coyote has always been part of human's mind," the animal spirit said. "Hayoka is Coyote. Coyote is Hayoka. Always one."

Hayoka looked at the crystals. "Are the gems the reason I can see you? Was it because I touched them?"

"Indeed, human," Coyote said. "Short will be the duration, but for these moments, Coyote and the soft human are separate. Ask Coyote your questions."

Hayoka stammered, struggling to decide what to ask first. "Why me? Why did you choose to live inside me? Why am I special?"

The Coyote made a sound that could have been a chuckle or a growl. "The human's father was important. The mortal named Hobomok was the ideal vessel, who came to Coyote at the perfect time. The human's father, Hobomok, served Coyote well. When the mortal Hobomok was slain by the hated Itiwana, his wife was with child."

"Yes, my mother was carrying me when my father died," Hayoka said.

"And thus, the human was a flesh link to your mortal sire," Coyote said. "The Coyote needed a healthy new body when the mortal Hobomok died. And so, the Coyote's spirit fled from the dead form of Hobomok, into the unborn form of Hayoka. Coyote was with the human in your mother's belly. When the human born, Coyote was reborn. Coyote has been the one guiding the human ever since the human was suckling your mortal mother's teat."

Hayoka stepped back and paced a bit, trying to sort out his feelings. Nothing had ever prepared him for this conversation. "Why have you taken physical form? I'm guessing you must have a purpose, other than talking to me."

Coyote snorted and nodded simultaneously. "Indeed so, human. Coyote has come to help with a problem that vexes us. Something must be done about Calian."

Hayoka liked the sound of that. "On this, we agree. He's become my nemesis. I was hoping to convince the Keeper that he was an enemy and persuade them to eliminate the suspicious swine."

"The Coyote concurs," the canid creature said. "And the Coyote knows just the way. Trust the Coyote. Has the Coyote ever misled the human?"

Hayoka didn't know how to answer that since he was unsure which of his past thoughts were his own and which were placed into his brain by Coyote. "I'll trust you. Do what needs to be done. How can I help?"

The Coyote suddenly sniffed the air and showed his fangs in a frightening grin. "The Coyote smells the enemy now. The accursed Calian is approaching. The Coyote must act now."

The Coyote seemed to blend into the shadows and become invisible. Hayoka turned to see Calian arriving, clearly looking for him. *There's the swaggering swine. Well, I may be rid of him very soon.*

Calian locked accusing eyes with Hayoka and asked, "What are you doing here?"

"Nothing to concern you," Hayoka said. "Shouldn't you be with your tribesmen?"

"I should be where I'm needed," Calian said. "And at the moment, I am best utilized keeping a watchful eye on anyone or anything that may endanger our purpose for being here."

"But it was I who brought you here, you mistrustful buffoon," Hayoka said loudly, showing no fear of Calian, due to the coyote's presence. "I would suggest you left your brain in Shipapa-Lina, but I'm doubting you ever had one, since you've never impressed anyone with your feeble attempts at thinking."

Calian approached Hayoka threateningly. "I could easily knock the scheming brain out of your deceitful head and then bury it in the cornfield as fertilizer. Insult me again."

A fierce growl resounded throughout the chamber, causing Calian to instinctively crouch into a defensive stance. Calian spotted the glowing eyes of the coyote staring at him, snarling.

"What in Awona'Wilona's holy name?" Calian asked.

Calian backed away, toward the entrance, and walked into the Keeper who was entering. "What are you doing in here?" she asked angrily.

With a roar, the Coyote leaped. A dark silhouette slammed into Hayoka, knocking him to the ground. The shadow kept moving, leaping toward the Keeper and Hayoka.

The Keeper spotted the dark form. "What evil have you brought here, Calian?" she shouted.

As the Coyote sprung toward them, Calian dodged the attack, and the animal spirit pounced on the Keeper, pinning her to the ground. "For Calian!" Coyote said, as it bit her, sinking its fangs into her shoulder.

The woman screamed in pain as a chunk of her flesh was torn off. She went into shock from the agony as the animal spirit went for her throat. She wasn't coherent enough to see Calian coming to her rescue. With no other weapons available, he grabbed one of the charmed stones and flung it at the beast. It struck Coyote in the eye. Being an enchanted jewel, it caused a sharp jolt of pain in the beast's panoptic orb. Coyote howled, as much in rage as in pain.

"Cursed, weak human dares strike Coyote!" the creature shouted furiously. "Weak, foolish human must suffer slowly!"

The Coyote forgot about the Keeper and stalked toward Calian, who was backed into a corner. Calian grabbed Hayoka, who was stunned and semi-conscious after being knocked over by Coyote.

"Stop, or I'll snap this pathetic idiot's neck!" Calian cried desperately.

Coyote paused, needing the body of Hayoka. The standoff was ended when footsteps echoed down the hallway. Coyote became transparent and faded from view. At the same time, Hayoka jerked spasmodically. He opened his eyes and sat up, observing the situation.

Pahana and the rest of the Itiwana came rushing in, accompanied by the Breathing Shaman. They saw Calian leaning over the wounded Keeper.

"What evil have you perpetrated, Calian?" the Breathing Shaman shouted.

"I've done nothing," Calian said defensively. "There was a beast here. An animal."

The Breathing Shaman checked on the Keeper. "No beast or animal could enter here. The Guardian protects us."

The delirious Keeper muttered, "Calian. He's brought evil here. Evil!"

The Breathing Shaman pointed accusingly at Calian. "We were warned about you!"

Pahana stepped in front of Calian. "This man is a man of honor. If he says he has done nothing wrong, you can be sure it's factual."

Pinga added, "This One knows that Calian has no power to summon beasts out of the air."

Pahana looked to Hayoka for answers. "What did you see?"

Hayoka shrugged. "I was struck from behind. I recall nothing until moments ago."

The Breathing Shaman rose, furious, staring at Calian. "You will know the punishments that we can inflict. Be fearful, Calian!"

The Breathing Shaman blew her bone tube, and a ball of flaming vapor burst from it. Fortunately for Calian, Pahana was able to create an icy mist that neutralized the attack. As this was happening,

Masewa kicked the bone tube out of the Breathing Shaman's grasp. O'Yewa stood on it.

The Breathing Shaman glared defiantly. "And I expect you Itiwana swine will kill me now?"

"We've no wish to kill anyone," Pahana said. "There has been a misunderstanding."

"No, there is no misunderstanding between us," the shaman said. "I see you for what you are. You are Anasazi. The enemy! Go now! Leave my home. Return to your precious Shipapa-Lina. But know that I will not forget this."

Pinga grabbed Pahana by the arm. "This One senses discussion and explanation will do no good. We are in danger here. We must go."

Sadly, Pahana agreed. "I suppose you're right. We'll let the shaman tend to her sister. We hope that, after emotions have leveled like the tide, these women will see reason. Come along, everyone. Let's go home."

The Breathing Shaman sneered as they left. *The Guardian and the Bolter will avenge us.*

As the Itiwana fled the House of Many Hands, stepping into the mist outside, they heard the ferocious growl of the Guardian. Its heavy footsteps came closer.

"This is bound to be unpleasant," O'Yewa said.

Unable to see the beast that was coming toward them, Pahana had the idea of using his icy ability to create an icy slick on the ground. The ploy succeeded, and they heard the sound of the big, unseen protector of the valley slip.

They heard another, louder sound. It was coming closer with great rapidity. It sounded like a rockslide. Pinga knew what it was.

"Spread out quickly!" she yelled. "Disperse. The Slide Rock Bolter is coming!"

The Itiwana scattered in every direction. Moments later, a massive monstrosity slid past them. The leviathan was tremendous. It missed them by less than an arm's length.

"Come this way!" Pinga yelled.

"How do you know?" Masewa asked.

"This One left a sprinkle of ice crystals at the spot where we left the bison," Pinga said. "In case we got lost. She can sense it from here. Follow her."

Pinga led the Itiwana through the mist. They ran, hearing the thumping footsteps of the Guardian close behind. They rushed frantically up the path until they got to the light of day.

"Thank Awona'Wilona," O'Yewa said, relieved.

"We should depart this region as quickly as bison can travel," Pahana ordered.

Returning to Faw-Faw and the other Itiwana, Pahana and his companions leaped onto their mounts and rode off quickly, looking over their shoulders pensively.

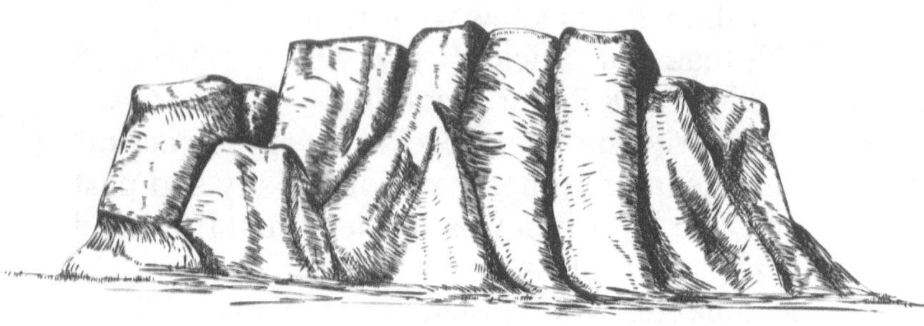

CHAPTER NINETEEN

I must help Father, Kia thought. As her two guides walked on either side of her, she floated along on her cloud, hoping to get another message from her father. Failing to reestablish contact, she continued onward to the Valley of the Blue Mists, hoping that the shamanic women there might be able to help her reach him psychically.

Scanning Ulah-Nane with her mind, she sensed someone else close by. Someone just as dead to her as her father. *Mother? Pahana?*

"We must go this way," Kia suddenly said, pointing south.

"Why?" Bolon-Hoya asked.

"Just trust me!" Kia said. "We must go that way. Hurry!"

The hunter brothers exchanged confused looks but knew that Kia could see around corners that most mortals could not. They decided to accept her intuition, however eerie they found it.

She led her two escorts across lush fields, anxious to see her family and inform them of the message she had received. It was less than an hour before they spotted the Itiwana party traveling toward home.

"Mother!" she shouted, delighted to be reunited.

"Kia?" Pinga said, surprised.

They waited as Kia and the brothers rushed to meet them. Pinga hugged her daughter.

"What are you doing here?" Pahana asked.

"I have much to tell you," Kia said.

Kia painstakingly detailed everything that had happened to her over the past few days. Most importantly, she told them about Tawa.

"This One must get to Kuwahi!" Pinga cried. "If her man is in danger, she must be there!"

"And I will go with you," Pahana said. "We must find Tawa."

"But what of the danger?" O'Yewa said. "Those shamans will follow us to Shipapa-Lina to find Calian."

"Then I should not return to Shipapa-Lina," Calian said. "I should lure these women far from our home."

"Excellent idea," Pahana said. "You will come with my mother and me as we go to Kuwahi. The rest of you will return to Shipapa-Lina to warn Atira. In case the misguided women of the valley attack our home before we return."

"But shouldn't you come—" O'Yewa began to say.

"I've no time to repeat myself!" Pahana yelled. "Why must I waste time telling you twice? Go now. Tell Atira we will return with Tawa. He will know how to deal with these shamanic fools."

"And what of me?" Kia asked. "I want to go to Father, too."

Pinga petted her daughter's hair. "Oh, sweet girl. You have done so much already. This One is proud of you. But if these women follow us, This One does not want them to find you. Please, go back to Shipapa-Lina."

"But I am not afraid," she announced courageously. "I have powers."

"Indeed, you do, Sister," Pahana said. "And you must use those powers to protect Shipapa-Lina. Father would want our people protected. Please, do as we ask. Use your magic to help our people. Leave it to us to find Tawa."

Kia frowned, but nodded. "Very well. I will do that. I promise."

"Good girl. Sweet girl," Pinga said as she kissed Kia.

"Let's proceed then," Pahana said. "We all have important work to do. Faw-Faw, you will come with us to defend my mother and to guard Calian if these women find us."

"Gug," Faw-Faw said, partly comprehending the command.

"The days to come will be mad, difficult, and dangerous," Pahana said. "But we are the Itiwana. We will walk through storms and fire and swarms, only to return victorious. We do not fail. Let our enemies be warned!"

Shipapa-Lina was quiet. It would not remain that way long. Death incarnate was approaching.

The wailing wind and the creaky, clinking of the skeleton were the only sounds that could be heard across the barren plain, which had once been fertile. The formerly living being, which currently displayed its yellowish-white bones, followed its master obediently.

Marching across the dirt and dust of the plain, the 8-foot-tall glowing skeleton known as Baykuk was an intimidating sight. Its substantial shine covered the face of the woman who trekked behind it with portentous purpose.

The woman following the skeleton held a leathery pouch tightly to her chest. She held it as if it were a beloved infant. Dressed in a wrap-around cloak, with a snakeskin belt covering her salt-and-pepper hair, the woman named Eototo sat atop a small elk. The wind blew dust and dirt in her face as she scanned the horizon until she spotted the mesa.

The ravaged terrain looked mostly the same for as far as she could see. The area beyond the village was a barely habitable wasteland, ruined by the fire locusts.

Then she saw it. She spotted the small but thriving agricultural village on the horizon. On the side cliff of the mesa was an oasis of hope. She saw that there were cottages and families and a semblance of normalcy. It all seemed bizarrely out of place in the desolate wastes.

Eototo was an acolyte of the House of Many Hands. She had been taught the majestic magics of the Great Shaman by the Breathing Shaman. She had not been present when the Itiwana arrived in the Valley of the Blue Mists and attacked the Keeper of the Sacred Objects. The Breathing Shaman had contacted Eototo via her astral form and instructed her to go to Shipapa-Lina. The Breathing Shaman wanted Pahana, Calian, and the Itiwana to find death and destruction when they returned home.

We of the House of Many Hands do not forgive such a sin, Eototo thought. To inflict her rightful revenge, she awoke the glowing skeleton, Baykuk, to punish the Itiwana.

As Eototo and Baykuk approached the village, they were spotted by the inhabitants. She could see the villagers milling around like angry bees when someone comes too close to their hive. Even their distant voices sounded like bees buzzing. This buzz wasn't angry, however. It sounded like fear. She wondered if they'd put up a fight. Regardless of whether they did or not, they were going to know how deadly Baykuk could be.

Atira, the acting leader and protector of the community, was awoken by T'Soona. He told her about the monster that was approaching. This news didn't surprise the village leader, but it did illicit trepidatious alarm. Atira hopped to her feet, snapping into the leader's mindset that she had learned from her husband and son.

"Let's see to this, T'Soona," she ordered. "Tell Aholi to assemble the Two Horn riders. Whatever this is, I won't let it destroy our home!"

I think I've found it, Naya-Nazgani said, as he spotted the mesa. The directions he'd gotten had proven accurate. He'd found Shipapa-Lina. *Finally.*

As he got closer, hoping he'd soon be able to rest, his instincts suddenly cried out, telling him that monsters were near. Centuries of battling monsters had helped him develop a sixth sense. In the distance, he was a glowing beast. His natural instinct to kill such beasts kicked in. *A monster to kill!*

In Shipapa-Lina, Aholi had organized the Two Horn Riders into a defensive line. Atira and T'Soona watched from the rear, studying the woman and her strange skeletal companion.

"What in the name of sanity is that ridiculous-looking thing?" T'Soona asked.

"Don't take it too lightly," Atira warned. "I suspect it wasn't sent here because it was meek and gentle. Prepare for more violence."

Aholi trotted on his bison, confronting the newcomers. "Who are you? We require explanations before you come one step closer."

The woman slid inelegantly off her elk. "My name is Eototo. I'm here on a personal matter that you, the Itiwana, have brought upon yourself. I imagine you don't know what happened in the valley yet, but that doesn't matter."

Aholi was about to question her when he spotted a man running in their direction carrying an ax. Aholi turned his bison so he could see the newest arrival while also monitoring the other two.

"Yet another enemy!" T'Soona said. "It's sad how a people who do not want to be enemies with anyone seem to collect so many foes."

"I'm not so sure," Atira said.

Naya-Nazgani leaped between the Itiwana and the minions of the House of Many Hands. He waved his ax threateningly. "I am Naya-Nazgani, slayer of monsters. I see my next victim."

"I know of you," Eototo said, annoyed and confused by the monster hunter's unexpected interference. "This is no concern of yours."

"Where monsters walk, I am drawn to the battle!" Naya-Nazgani said. "Before such creatures can bring death to humans, I bring death to the monsters."

"Do not involve yourself in this matter," Eototo ordered. "You will step aside while Baykuk ravages this village and everyone in it. Otherwise, you will lose your overlong life. No third option."

Naya-Nazgani raised his ax and narrowed his eyes. "I stand on the border of death and no monster may pass. I live for the fight. Monsters die when I fight."

"Again, I've no desire to fight you, but no one threatens me," Eototo said. "Believe me, I don't want to see you slew. Don't do this. Just walk away and save yourself a world of agony."

"I absolutely refuse and await your monstrous companion to attempt to carry out your threat. Don't make me wait until I'm bored."

"Believe me, you don't want to do this!" she stated.

"Oh, but I truly do!" Naya-Nazgani shouted, annoyed at the discussion. "Send in the monster."

"I've wasted enough time!" Eototo bellowed. "Are you going to do as I ask, or does the skeleton attack?"

"Here I stand," Naya-Nazgani said. "I itch for the fight."

"As you wish," she said, taking some gems out of her sack. "Baykuk... kill!"

CHAPTER TWENTY

The big, frightening skeleton, glowing with eldritch heat, stomped forward, rattling. Naya-Nazgani ran fearlessly toward it, swinging his thickset ax. The skeleton tossed a fireball at the monster hunter. The blazing ball struck the ax. Embers spread everywhere, due to the impact. Naya-Nazgani rammed his fist and knee into the skeleton, staggering it. Baykuk took a step back and focused its shimmering energy on the man with the ax. The skeleton gave Naya-Nazgani a backhanded slap, knocking him to the dirt.

The monster slayer rubbed his jaw, refocusing his mind as the skeletal giant hurled another fireball at him. Naya-Nazgani rapidly rolled aside and the flaming orb missed him by centimeters, taking a chunk out of the ground with the blazing blast. The monster slayer popped back to his feet.

However, the skeleton was immediately upon him again, pursuing with single-minded persistence.

Before the boney creature could strike once more, Naya-Nazgani swung his sword, hacking some of the exposed bone off Baykuk's left side. The skeleton convulsed for a moment, having received considerable damage, but it was not defeated yet.

The bony giant grabbed Naya-Nazgani's muscular arm with its gaunt fingers. Swinging the monster slayer effortlessly, Baykuk tossed Naya-Nazgani 50 yards across the field, down an incline, and into a hollow of dead, brown grass. As Naya-Nazgani rolled down the steep hill, he heard the tinkling sound of the skeleton coming toward him. Having no time to regroup, he rolled hastily back to his feet and watched as Baykuk appeared at the top of the incline. He rushed at it as it descended the hill. They continued their furious battle.

Back at Shipapa-Lina, everyone was moving closer to the hollow, hoping to see what was happening down the incline. Eototo genuinely hadn't expected Naya-Nazgani to put up such an effective defense against the supernatural power of Baykuk. Despite the stories she'd heard over the years, she had convinced himself that Naya-Nazgani was an over-rated pretender. Eototo refused to believe that the skeleton could possibly be defeated by any flesh-and-blood man. *I just have to be patient and wait until the battle is over.*

As she waited and paced pensively, reluctant to get too close to the battle, she was pierced by an arrow from behind. Yoki came riding in proudly atop his mount. "Rather foolish to get so distracted in the company of an enemy."

"Well done," Aholi said. "Now we need only hope our new friend can defeat this sizable, shining skeleton."

Not far away, Naya-Nazgani was still battling the jingly, glowing skeleton. With uncanny speed and skill, he ducked under the skeleton's slim arm as it attempted to knock his head off with a side-handed chop.

Instead, with a deft and forceful swipe of his weapon, he chopped the skeleton's arm off. The skeleton swayed, unbalanced and enraged; its arm fell to the ground with a tinkling bounce. This momentary pause gave Naya-Nazgani the opportunity he needed to swiftly chop the glowing monster's head completely off.

As the glowing head rolled onto the ground, Baykuk's body staggered, out of control. Naya-Nazgani proceeded to dismember the skeleton until he was nothing more than a pile of bones. The head was still glowing, so Naya-Nazgani smashed it into fragments. The glow stopped. The monster slayer's instincts told him the creature was dead.

Naya-Nazgani climbed the embankment and saw the assembled Itiwana waiting to greet him. In unison, they all cheered vociferously in gratitude. Atira came forward and greeted the warrior.

"Remarkably well done," Atira said. "You are a warrior without peers. Thank you very much for your assistance."

"It's what I live to do," the monster hunter said.

"What's your name, stranger?" she asked.

"I am Naya-Nazgani."

"I don't know the name, but that doesn't matter," Atira said. "You've done us a great service, and we thank you. Consider yourself a welcome guest of the Itiwana."

"I came with a purpose," Naya-Nazgani said.

"And what would that be?" she asked.

"It's about Tawa," he said.

CHAPTER TWENTY-ONE

Pahana, Pinga, and Calian rode throughout the entire day, accompanied by Faw-Faw. Before they knew it, night was beginning to fall, but Pinga was unwilling to stop because she feared for her husband. Kia's warning was frightening to her. From the moment Black Crow had returned, she had felt an omen of impending doom regarding Tawa. She didn't want to waste a minute getting to him. She urged the rest of them on.

Pahana was similarly anxious to find his father. Aside from his affection for his sire, he also wanted to tell his father of all the things he had accomplished while his father was away. He hoped to gain the praise of Tawa.

Just as the sun was going down, keen-eyed Calian spotted the mountain. "Could that be our destination? Is that Kuwahi, home of the great White Bear?"""

"I would assume so," Pahana said.

"This One's instincts are telling her it is so," Pinga said. "Come. Let us go with great speed. This One's husband may need us."

Pahana nudged Mountain Fury into the lead. The rest follow behind. Faw-Faw was confused about where they were going, but simply followed along, sticking close to Calian, who he was determined to protect, as he always had.

It was dark by the time they reached the foot of Kuwahi. Even in the dark, the observant Calian spotted the giant's footprints. "What in Awona'Wilona's name?"

"What have you spotted?" Pahana asked.

"Something large lurks that way," Calian said. "I don't know if your father is in that direction, but..."

"We'll look that way," Pahana said. "If there's trouble, my father will be deep in the midst of it."

The Itiwana group found themselves traversing the road up the mountain toward the pinnacle. The bright moonlight illuminated the steep path. Calian tracked the giant footprints. He became somewhat alarmed when he noticed there were other, smaller footprints, which were still significantly larger than a normal human's footprints.

More than one type of giant walks these mountain paths, he thought.

He'd heard the stories of the beasts of Kuwahi, but now he was getting a sense of how large they really were, judging by the size of their feet. He now knew why the tribes of Ulah-Nane often described the rumored locals as "Big Feet."

"Let's be cautious," Calian said. "I don't think we're alone."

"What do you—" Pahana began to ask.

A large, shaggy beast popped out of the darkness and blocked their path. Pahana prepared to defend his mother. Faw-Faw tensed for a fight.

Several moments later, a second beast appeared behind them, cutting off their retreat. Calian knew what they were. The creatures were commonly known as sasquatches. He did not know that one of them was male and one was female.

The male Sasquatch was nine feet tall and covered in black fur. The female was over eight feet and possessed dark brown hair. Both weighed over 500 pounds. The creatures were wide and thick. They had a pronounced brow ridge and a large, low-set forehead. The top of their heads were rounded and crested. Their faces were vaguely human but somewhat more simian looking. Their feet were particularly big. They gave off a powerful and rather unpleasant odor.

Strange sounds and stranger smells from the darkness indicated that there were many more of the big-footed creatures lurking just out of sight. It was likely they were all ready to attack. The original two beasts let out a warning cry, which sounded like a cross between a bear's roar and a human's scream. The strange sound was like nothing that the Itiwana men had ever heard before, but they would all have described it as very loud. And it seemed decidedly unfriendly.

"My father isn't the only one deep in the midst of trouble," Pahana said.

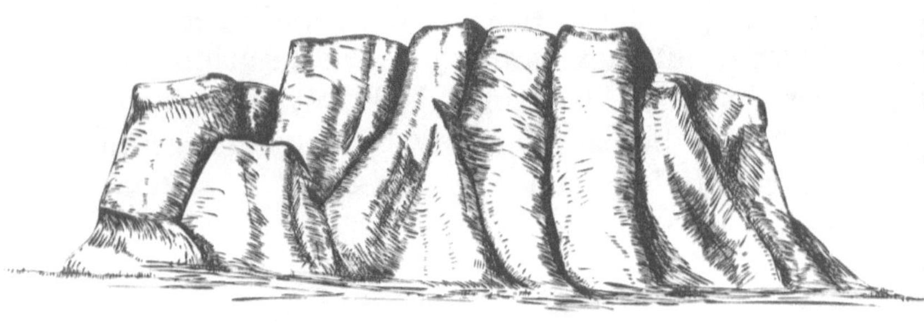

CHAPTER TWENTY-TWO

The Itiwana could see the sizable silhouettes belonging to dozens of towering sasquatches lurking in the darkness. The two sasquatches who flanked them were yowling their ferocious warning at the human who had dared to intrude upon their realm. The male sasquatch began to beat on his chest, to show his alpha male status. There was nowhere for the Itiwana to retreat to. Faw-Faw roared back, but Pahana patted him to silence the big, hairy man.

"Remain calm," Pahana said. "Don't do anything to make them attack. Perhaps we can ease our way out of this if everyone keeps a composed head."

Surprisingly, it was the normally obedient Faw-Faw who disobeyed the command. The hairy man stomped toward the male sasquatch.

"Stop!" Calian yelled to his friend and protector. "Come back here."

Faw-Faw, however, did not obey this time. He brazenly approached the sasquatch. The male bigfoot stared curiously at Faw-Faw, seemingly unworried about the hirsute man's approach. When Faw-Faw got close enough, they began to sniff each other. The sasquatch seemed to relax, as if recognizing a close kin. Like the hairy man tribe Faw-Faw came from, sasquatches were a variant of Cheenook giants. They were very similar in many ways and both sensed it, despite never having seen this distant breed of relative.

The two huge beings exchanged grunts, which did not seem hostile. This seemed to summon the big-footed brethren of the male sasquatch. The other sasquatches all came out of the darkness and began to examine Faw-Faw with great interest. Faw-Faw made his usual "Gug" sound, and the sasquatches responded with a whistling sound. This chorus continued for several minutes. Faw-Faw began to smile, seemingly enjoying the attention of creatures much like himself.

"Would anyone care to speculate about what's happening?" Pahana asked.

"I think this is a good omen," Calian said. "Faw-Faw seems relaxed and happy. I know him well, and he isn't alarmed. These creatures seem to have welcomed him."

"Let us pray that they welcome *us* as well," Pahana commented.

Calian nudged his mount forward, getting closer to the Cheenook crowd. "Faw-Faw. Do they know where Tawa is? Can they take us to the kik-mongwi?"

Faw-Faw began gesturing and "gugging" to the sasquatches, trying to relate Calian's message. It took some time, but the group of bigfeet finally got the gist of it. The alpha male sasquatch began to walk up the mountain, and the rest of the herd followed dutifully after him. Faw-Faw gestured for the Itiwana to follow him as he joined the sasquatch march.

"This One thinks we've been invited to visit their mountain," Pinga said, hiding that she was a bit nervous.

"Be wary," Calian cautioned. "These are wild creatures, and they could decide to attack us as quickly as they made friends with us."

"It may well be," Pahana said. "But it does not matter. If my father is with these brutes, then that's where I will be as well."

"Of course," Calian said. "And I, too. Into any darkness, against demons of fire and blood. There could be more foes than there are stars in the sky, and I will be at your side."

"Good. Come. We ride."

The three Itiwana and Faw-Faw followed after the large-footed giants. Pahana and Calian were ready to fight, if necessary, while Pinga was simply thinking of her husband. They rode along the eastern slope, which led to the pinnacle, which was known as the home of the mighty White Bear.

The herd of bigfeet and their new friends arrived at the temple of the Earthmother. The temple wasn't very big. As a temple, it was not impressive. From inside, there came a red, other-worldly glow. Calian spotted a familiar bison with a more familiar spear.

"Look, it's Brave Fire," Calian said. "And Dragonfly. Tawa is here!"

Pahana knew something was wrong if Tawa was separated from his sacred spear. Even more surprising than that was the sight of Gah-Oh, who stood in front of the dwelling, holding his humongous club, slapping it repeatedly into his free hand. Although they had seen Cheenook giants before, none of the Itiwana had ever seen one so imposingly massive as Gah-Oh. He was a giant among giants.

"Strange faces arrive unexpectedly, escorted by the trusted sasquatches," Gah-Oh stated matter-of-factly. "Immense Gah-Oh fervently hopes that yon intruders are here as benign friends, and not to do unnecessary harm. How is it possible that yon unknown travelers have successfully won the trust of the good sasquatches?"

"Perhaps they sense our inherent nobility and honor," Pahana answered.

"Perhaps yon tiny mortals are inherently noble and perhaps you stand as base deceivers," Gah-Oh replied. "Towering Gah-Oh is currently uncertain. Almighty Gah-Oh knows without doubt that this land of sublime peace is no place for wanton violence and brutal war. Any detestable villain who brings dire evil here will face the unbridled power of the great Gah-Oh."

"You have nothing to fear from us," Pahana said. "We have no desire to fight you. We've merely come seeking my father—Tawa, the kik-mongwi of the Itiwana. We have been led to believe that he may be here."

Gah-Oh cocked his head to the side, as if deep in thought. "The truth remains vexingly hidden. Gigantic Gah-Oh is maddeningly befuddled. Only the wise Earthmother has the pure clarity to determine the unquestionable veracity of yon human's unconfirmed words."

"Then let us meet this Earthmother," Pahana said. "The sooner you trust us, the sooner we can get directly to the task of finding my father."

"The sacred Earthmother is occupied," Gah-Oh said. "She will appear when her magnanimous act of kindness is completed."

Pahana did not want to wait, but he reluctantly held his tongue. Calian chimed in to speak for them. "Certainly, we of the Itiwana don't want to disrupt any act of kindness, good giant. We will wait."

Inside the temple, Eithinoa kneeled aside Tawa, who was still unconscious. He was floating on a pool of bubbling water. Tawa was so weak at this point that Eithinoa could feel the life force leaving him, drifting up to the blue ether like smoke rising from a burning fire. Her healing touch barely slowed the death process. The man was dying faster than she could heal him. She focused her efforts with all her will and even though his life force was slipping away by the moment, she managed to awaken him.

Tawa's eyes opened slowly. He was disoriented and confused about where he was. Then he noticed the woman kneeling beside him with her hand on his wound.

"It's ... almost over," he croaked in a faint voice.

"In compassion, I say that you are correct," Eithinoa answered. "In surprise, I say that I did not expect you to regain consciousness."

"I think ... I'm dying soon," Tawa groaned weakly.

"In honesty, I must tell you that your life force has mostly slipped away. In mercy, I say that I will do all I can to soothe your ailing body so that your passing will be peaceful."

"Thank you," Tawa said softly. "Did you ... get a message ... to my people? To the Itiwana?"

"In sympathy, I say that I have done what I can to see that your final words reach your people." She turned toward the temple opening. "Piasa. In haste, I call you."

Outside the temple, everyone heard the woman's voice calling. "Is that the Earth goddess?" Pahana asked.

"Yon melodious voice belongs to the beneficent Earthmother," Gah-Oh responded.

From out of a patch of grass came Piasa, the reptilian bird spirit of Ulah-Nane. It was a small dragon, half avian and half lizard. Piasa was the size of an iguana and his natural color changed to match his surroundings. At the moment, he was bright green. His eyes were large, black orbs. Piasa had been covertly watching the situation with the Itiwana visitors. But when he heard the call of the Earthmother, he unfolded his wings and flew to her side. The surprised visitors saw the large scaley feathered creature flying in the darkness and wondered what other strange sights they were going to see in this place.

Piasa flew into the temple and alighted on a stone near his mistress. He made a clucking sound. The dying Tawa wondered how this bizarre animal was going to deliver his message to the Itiwana.

"In earnestness, I say, I am glad you have arrived, good Piasa."

Piasa flapped his wings and, much to Tawa's incredulity, the words Eithinoa had spoken repeated like an echo, except that this time the sentence was more melodious, as if it was being sung. "In earnestness, I say, I am glad you have arrived, good Piasa," the musical echo reiterated.

Tawa actually managed a smile despite his pain. "It is good ... to know that ... in my final moments ... I am still witness to ... the marvels of the world."

"In goodwill, I say, speak your final words to Piasa and they will be echoed to the Itiwana."

"Itiwana," came the melodic echo from Piasa's wings. The lizard made a clucking sound that Eithinoa seemed to understand. "In astonishment, I find that you are not the only Itiwana here. Others have arrived."

Tawa tried to sit up but was far too weak. "Others? P...Please ... send them to me. I must ... see them. I must..."

"In pity, I will allow them to enter my temple," she said and then shouted to Gah-Oh. "In haste, giant one, send in the strangers."

Outside, Gah-Oh heard the call. "Vast Gah-Oh hears and happily complies, oh wondrous Eithinoa. Come ahead, yon mortal travelers. The magnanimous Earthmother grants the great honor of entering her sanctum."

"At long last," Pahana said and marched to the temple. Calian and Pinga followed him.

Calian looked back over his shoulder, wondering if the vengeance of the shaman women would find him at this vital moment. Pushing away such thoughts, he joined Pahana in the grass hut. Calian and Pahana entered cautiously, but Pinga was far too anxious to see her husband to bother with caution. They saw a woman sitting next to a pool of water, kneeling next to a man.

"Tawa," Pinga screamed, horrified, seeing his condition. She ran to him.

Pahana and Calian came closer to Tawa, stunned to see him so weak and pale. No one believed that Tawa could ever fall.

"Father," Pahana said, kneeling next to his mother.

Tawa had almost blacked out from the pain but refocused his mind when he saw his wife and son and his cousin kneeling over him. Pinga had taken his hand, tears in her eyes.

"My Pinga," he softly said. "Pahana. And Calian. My joy is as great as my surprise. My heart will be full when it stops beating."

"Father, what has happened?" Pahana asked with panicked concern. "How did you come to this?"

Tawa spoke in weak whispers. "I fought a poshayanki for a prize." Tawa reached into his belt and pulled out the prize he'd won. Eithinoa had brought it to him.

"The golden arrowhead of Awona'Wilona," Calian said, awed.

"You have reclaimed one of the two ancient weapons of our ancestors," Pahana said in reverence. "You are a warrior worthy of Morning Star, Father. Your accomplishments shame me. While you were away bringing glory to our clan, I tried to find the other lost weapon of Morning Star—the Tomahawk of Awona'Wilona. I failed, Father. But I will succeed next time."

"It ... does not matter," Tawa struggled to say. "All that is ... important now ... is that you are ... with me ... at the end."

"No, my love!" Pinga sobbed. "This cannot be the end. This One will find you a healer. We will..."

"No, my love," he said. "No healer can ... help me now. Even the Earthmother ... has failed. I accept that ... my time in this world ... is at an end. I am glad ... that my wife and son will be with me ... as I breathe my last breath."

Pinga couldn't accept this. "There must be something This One can do."

"You're doing it," Tawa said. "You ... are here. Let your beautiful face be ... the last thing I see. There can be no better way to die."

"Can I do nothing for you, Father?" Pahana asked.

"There is," Tawa spoke faintly. "Promise me ... that you will rule the Itiwana wisely."

"You are still the ruler," Pinga said. "You are..."

"Please, hush," Tawa said, barely audible. "Let me speak truth to my son."

"Speak to me, Father."

"Listen well, Son," Tawa said. "It falls to you now. You must be ... both a man and a chieftain. Neither is easy. You must leave ... your youthful recklessness ... behind. You must be wise. Swear to me ... that you will always ... think before you act. Swear that you will ... put the tribe before your own ... personal glory or honor. Swear it."

"I swear it, Father."

"Remember, my son. To be the kik-mongwi ... is to put duty before pride. Swear it again."

"I swear."

"Good," Tawa said. "Remember ... our people follow a man, not the headdress of the chieftain. And I leave you ... Dragonfly. It is ... tied to Brave Fire. I leave my mount to you, as well. Use them both ... to serve our people ... as best you can. And also ... see that you use the ... golden arrowhead ... to fulfill my vow ... to the Na-Ash-Jai."

"I will, Father."

Just then, the sound of hooves interrupted as a massive bison pushed its way into the grass hut.

It walked toward Tawa. The animal smelled its old master from outside. It lowered its head to lick Tawa's face. Tawa smiled.

"Mountain Fury, as well," Tawa said, weakly reaching out to pet the animal's nose. "All my most ... trusted ones are here. So good to see you, boy."

"Everyone loves you," Pinga said.

"So good to hear," Tawa said. "And there is one other who I trust. Good Calian?"

"I am here, Kik-Mongwi."

"Good cousin," Tawa said. "Always so loyal. You are ... so wise. Promise me you will ... always be vigilant. Be alert ... to danger to our tribe."

"I will always watch for danger to the Itiwana, Cousin."

"Good," Tawa said. "Pahana... Listen to Calian. Be wise in who you listen to and ... what company you keep. I want you ... to stay away from Hayoka. Do not heed him."

"As you wish, Father."

Tawa's voice could barely be heard by this point. "Pinga ... my last thoughts ... are of you. Of my family. You are ... the best of me."

"You were the greatest husband This One could have wished for," Pinga said, crying. "And the greatest leader for our people."

"Yes, you were," Pahana said.

"And you are all ... very welcome," he managed to murmur. "I was so honored. My life was ... so wonderful."

And then Tawa died.

CHAPTER TWENTY-THREE

Tawa was dead. Pinga cried as she embraced his pale body. She sobbed uncontrollably. Pahana and Calian bowed their heads. After a proper silence, they then let out a howl to the heavens, which told the Sky Elders that Tawa, the kik-mongwi of the Itiwana, was coming. Pahana folded his father's hands on his chest, where his heart beat no longer.

"In sadness, I grieve with you," Eithinoa said, putting a gentle hand on Pahana's shoulder.

"I thank you, Eithinoa," Pahana said quietly. "I am grateful that you cared for him in his final hours."

"It is a tragedy that even the Earthmother could do nothing for him," Calian said.

Eithinoa felt terrible for having failed to save Tawa, especially now that she'd seen the despair of his family. Still, all was not lost…

"In hope, I say there may be something I can do," Eithinoa said.

Pinga snapped to attention. "What is it? What can you do? Speak."

"In hesitation, I say that there is a power that can restore your father," the Earthmother said. "In warning, I say that it is a hostile spirit and not to be trifled with."

Pinga slammed his fist to the ground. "This is not a trifling matter. This One will face any spirit if it returns the great and noble Tawa to me. To all of us."

"Mother—" Pahana began to say.

"Evoke the spirit, This One demands," Pinga demanded of Eithinoa.

"In prudence, I must ask if you are certain," the Earthmother said. "In forewarning, I say that there will be repercussions because he will want something in return."

"Who will?" Pahana asked.

"Evoke the spirit!" Pinga shouted.

"In acquiescence, I agree," Eithinoa said, hesitantly.

Eithinoa stood next to the pool and waved her hands over it several times. She chanted something under her breath that the Itiwana couldn't quite make out. After a few minutes of this, the grass hut began to shake, and the Itiwana became rather apprehensive. A rumbling sound was heard.

The water began bubbling more than before, as if it were boiling.

Eithinoa sensed their concern. "In explanation, I tell you that the mighty spirit we seek has been trapped in a volcano in another part of Ulah-Nane. In fear, I say that he is dangerous to all the tribes, everywhere."

Calian was starting to put the pieces together, and he did not like what he was deducing. *A powerful, dangerous spirit trapped in a volcano? Oh, no.*

Before Calian could warn Pahana of his suspicions, a pillar of hot steam rose out of the pool and formed into a huge face. The scowling face spoke, and the voice echoed through the subterranean stone temple with painful volume. "I am Malsumis. I rise."

"Malsumis," Pahana repeated in alarm. "No. Not you."

"I am Malsumis. I demand to know who summoned me."

Eithinoa spread her arms. "In authority, I say that I am the sacred Earthmother, and I summoned you. In clarification, I tell you that these mortals wish to make a bargain with you."

"I am Malsumis. I will listen."

Pahana leaned closer to Pinga. "I know you didn't dream it would be Malsumis. Our enemy. We must abandon this."

"Indeed, we should stop this now!" Calian added.

Pinga hesitated, looking at her husband. "No. This One must try to bring him back."

Eithinoa was explaining the situation to Malsumis. "In essence, I conclude, these men will bargain for the life of this slain warrior."

The fiery face seemed to smile. "I am Malsumis. I reveal to you that this is within my power."

Pahana glanced over at Calian, who shook his head warningly. Pahana agreed but hesitated due to his mother's passionate desperation. How could he tell her no? Would she ever forgive him if he let this chance go by?

Pinga stood up and looked the face of Malsumis in the fiery eye. She never expected to be confronted by the master of the Enemy Way. "This One is called Pinga of the Itiwana, and this is her husband, Tawa. She wants him back."

"I am Malsumis. I know you."

"Yes, you do," Pinga said. "This One was once one of you. Awona'Wilona made me mortal."

"I am Malsumis. I recall now. I am Malsumis. I know that you are now with my enemies. I am Malsumis. I know that the Itiwana you love opposed me."

"This is true," Pinga said. "We have fought you and will continue to do so. But This One is willing to make a bargain with you now. Ask of her a boon and she will—"

"No!" Calian yelled forcefully. "Don't do this."

"This One must have her husband back," Pinga retorted. "Do not interfere."

"Mother, please, don't," Pahana said. "You mustn't—"

The spirit had no patience for this. He saw an opportunity and did not want to let the moment slip away without exploiting Pinga's weakness. "I am Malsumis. I forgive my enemies. I am Malsumis. I am magnanimous. I am Malsumis. I will show you how to save your husband—for a boon."

"And that boon is...?"

"I am Malsumis. I sense you possess the golden arrowhead of Awona'Wilona. I am Malsumis. I would have it for my own because it can free me."

Pinga looked at the golden arrowhead Pahana now held. "Give it to him!" she yelled.

Pahana paused. Should he give it to Malsumis? Could he crush his mother's heart a second time by keeping Tawa from her? The world still needed Tawa. And yet, this was Malsumis, the great enemy. How could he be trusted?

Calian could tell that Pahana was thinking about it. "You can't. You vowed to your father you'd carry out his debt of honor to the Na-Ash-Jai."

"And so I did," Pahana said. "Malsumis, I cannot give you the arrowhead. I intend to use it for the purpose my father promised it would serve."

"I am Malsumis. I say to go and fulfill your father's promise. I am Malsumis. I will await your return. I am Malsumis. I will accept the arrowhead when you are ready to give it to me."

Before Pahana could refuse, Pinga interrupted. "This One promises!"

Malsumis's grinning face vanished from sight. As it did, the pool stopped bubbling; however,

Tawa's body went into a sudden spasm, then became limp again. Eithinoa noticed but said nothing. She did not want to interfere in their family business.

Calian shook his head. "Tawa would not approve of this, Pinga. You've made a poor decision."

Pinga touched Tawa's face. "If a poor decision brings Tawa back to us, This One will make many more of them."

Pahana did not want to chastise his mother as she cradled the dead body of Tawa. She was not thinking clearly at the moment. "I will use the arrowhead as Tawa wished. I agree to nothing else."

"Good," Calian said.

Pahana ignored Pinga's accusing glare. "Let us take my father from here."

Calian and Pahana reverently lifted Tawa's body and placed it on Mountain Fury. They gently led the big bison out of the grass hut with their heads lowered in homage.

Eithinoa touched Pahana's shoulder. "In compassion, I say when you return I will be here to help you."

"Thank you," Pahana said. "But I don't think I'll ask anything further from you. You've done enough. We thank you."

"In empathy, I feel for your family," Eithinoa told him. "In patience, I say that I will be here when you need to return, to help you when you need it. In warning, I say you will."

Pahana was confused, but he was far too distracted to probe any further. He had to bring his father's body home, after which he would have to deal with the shamans of the valley and then carry out Tawa's promise to the Na-Ash-Jai. "I will be forever grateful for your kindness, Earthmother. I wish I could say more now, but I must go."

"In regret, I say goodbye to you."

"And to you, kind Eithinoa," he said.

Pahana took his mother by the hand and led her out of the hut. Calian hoped that when they got back to Shipapa-Lina, he could get help from Manabazo regarding Pinga's promise to Malsumis. There must be a way out of that insane deal.

Pahana seemed to guess what was on his mind. "You will say nothing about what my mother did. Not to anyone. Do you hear? I will deal with this matter. Only me."

Calian scowled, hating to agree to that, but he would never disobey his new chieftain. "As you will it, so it is."

Once outside, Faw-Faw spotted the men approaching with the kik-mongwi's body. It took him a moment to comprehend what had happened. When it finally dawned upon him, the big hairy man cried.

The sasquatches closed in around him, comforting him. Pahana noticed that Mountain Fury had laid on the ground, still holding Tawa on his back. Pahana tried to nudge the animal forward. "Let's go, big fellow."

The bison didn't move. Its eyes were closed. It lay on the ground, unmoving. Pahana examined the bison more carefully and realized it wasn't breathing. He felt for its heartbeat, but there was none.

Calian kneeled to examine it. "Is it...?"

"It is," Pahana said. "The poor brute hung on far past the limits of its years, just to see its master once more. It died carrying him one last time. Such a loyal animal. Amazing mount. Rest well, Mountain Fury."

Gah-Oh looked down at the bison. "Yon faithful creature breathes no more. Mighty Gah-Oh promises mourning mortals that he will attend to the body of the bold bison."

"Thank you," Pahana said. "This has been a sad day."

The Itiwana found Brave Fire grazing nearby. The animal recognized them and allowed them to place Tawa on its back. Pahana saw the Dragonfly lashed to the bison's side. He touched it lightly but did not clasp it because he did not wish to claim it yet. He knew it was his now, but he could not accept it at the moment. For now, it still belonged to his father.

"We should go now", Pahana said. "If the shaman women did not follow us here, they may have gone to Shipapa-Lina. Let's hurry home."

Pinga climbed onto Brave Fire behind her son. Her husband's body was behind her. In somber silence, they began to ride away. Faw-Faw reluctantly tore himself away from his new friends and followed the Itiwana. It was a mournful trip home.

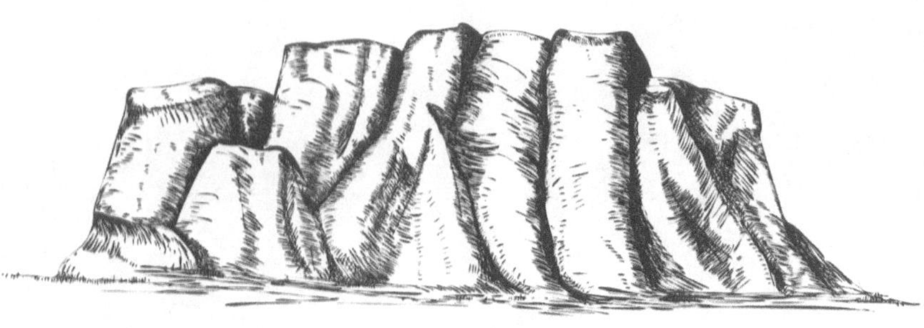

CHAPTER TWENTY-FOUR

"**I**'m glad to be home safely," O'Yewa said, as he saw the mesa come into view. He and his brother Masewa, along with young Kia, the hunter brothers from Kolhu, and the four Two Horn Riders who escorted them to the valley, had reached Shipapa-Lina. Trailing along behind them was Hayoka, who was clearly unwelcome in the group, so he kept to himself.

"Things seem quiet enough," Masewa said.

"Enjoy it now," O'Yewa said. "It's a certainty it won't last long."

Kia looked over Shipapa-Lina. She hadn't been home in two years, and seeing the mesa again brought a lump to her throat. *I've missed this special place so much. I'm home.*

A few sentinels of the Two Horn Riders guarding the perimeter greeted them upon their return. They explain how they had just been attacked by a skeleton monster. O'Yewa looked at his brother.

"You see," O'Yewa said. "It's never quiet in Shipapa-Lina."

Kia and her fellow travelers were led to the Cliff Palace, where the remainder of the Shakowin were meeting. Kia felt nostalgic joy at entering the majestic Cliff Palace again. She had grown up in the halls of that adobe edifice and now, despite the circumstances, she felt so comfortable being back again.

Hayoka stopped before entering the Cliff Palace. He knew that his face was not the one Atira wanted to see. He was, in fact, anticipating her suspicions about his involvement in the attack on the Keeper. *They'll blame me, somehow. And for once, they'll be right. I don't want to look Atira in the face just now. I should make myself scarce.*

In the Shakowin chamber, Kia, O'Yewa, and Masewa found Atira and T'Soona sitting cross-legged in conversation with a muscular man who was leaning against the wall with his arms crossed. A heavy, blood-stained ax was on the ground beside him.

"Kia!" Atira shouted with delight.

"Hello, Grandmother," Kia said, running to greet her family matriarch.

Kia embraced her grandmother lovingly. "I missed you very much."

"And I you," Atira said. "It's been too long. Welcome home, Child."

T'Soona put a friendly hand on O'Yewa's shoulder. "The brave and bold sons of Aholi have returned. Where is Pahana? How did you all fare in the Valley of the Blue Mists?"

The brothers again exchanged awkward glances. O'Yewa stammered, "Well..."

"Badly!" Masewa stated. "We must talk."

Masewa explained about the fiasco that occurred at the House of Many Hands and the threat by the Breathing Shaman. "She is convinced that Calian attacked the Keeper of Sacred Objects. We are uncertain what really happened, but Calian has been accused and no discussion seems likely to change that."

Atira considered for a moment. "Where was Hayoka at the time?"

"He was there," Masewa said. "In the room. He claims to have been unconscious, having been struck by someone."

Atira scowled with tight lips. "That is not a coincidence. Where is he now?"

"He's with us," O'Yewa said. "He's lurking somewhere like a fox outside a henhouse."

"We must keep him under observation," Atira said. "I must convince Pahana that the son of Hobomok is not to be trusted. You say he's gone to the mountain of the White Bear?"

Kia spoke now. "He has. I had a vision."

Kia explained her psychic vision. Atira slammed a fist on the ground.

"The young brat once again leaves Shipapa-Lina without its chieftain in a time of crisis. Does he ever learn? A leader must be present to lead."

"We'll handle it without him," T'Soona said.

Atira rose and pointed. "At least we have a powerful new ally to help us."

"Tawa only asked me to bring you a message," Naya-Nazgani said. "But now that I see a noble people besieged by monsters, I cannot leave. My life has been protecting tribes such as yours from monsters. As formidable as you are, I offer my aid."

"We thank you," Atira said. "We'll need you."

"And I'll help, too," young Kia said. "I have powers you don't know about."

"So I've heard," Atira said. "I'd recommend you be cautious with such power, but I fear we'll need whatever abilities you have. And now, we must make plans."

T'Soona grinned at Atira. "I love it when you make plans."

Atira found herself grinning, despite herself. T'Soona's ability to do this was why she cherished him. "I hope everyone will feel the same way when I'm done."

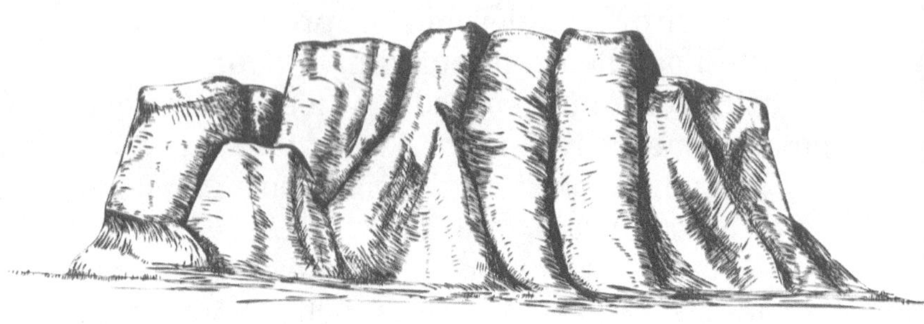

CHAPTER TWENTY-FIVE

I *should leave this place,* Hayoka thought. He saw Yoki following and watching him. *I feel their suspicious stares and I can guess that Atira told this young fool to observe me. My own kin. Infuriating. They won't be sorry to see me go. Of course, if I leave, won't they think I'm heading away to meet with their enemies? I must be cautious and sneak away when I have a chance.*

He saw Kia wandering across the village. *That girl will be important when matters come to a crisis point. What role will this child play?*

Kia strolled along, enjoying the feeling of being home again. She felt the urge to protect this place. *No one will destroy my home!*

She walked into the Sun Temple, where old Pekwin used to worship, and where she was taught to pray to Awona'Wilona. It was the most sacred spot in the Land of Everlasting Summer.

She sat down to meditate, lighting a small flame. She hoped to find some inner peace, but that did not happen. Only minutes after she began her quiet meditation, she heard the voices again. It was the voice of the woman who had contacted her before.

"Is that you?" she asked. "The Breathing Shaman?"

"It is," the shaman woman said.

"What could you want of me?" Kia asked scornfully.

"Your people have wronged us," the Breathing Shaman said. "There must be a reckoning, and there will be. Your tribe will be destroyed. I give you one chance to leave this evil, deceitful tribe. Join us and learn things that will delight and amaze you. Otherwise, we will battle you, and you must realize that, despite your natural power, you do not have the experience, skill, or intelligence to contend with our power. You will die along with them. Choose well or fall along with them."

"How dare you ask that?" Kia shouted. "Are you insane? I will never betray the Itiwana. I have no fear of dying along with my people and my family. Do not underestimate my power. Go from this place. It's a sacred place, and you do not deserve to be here."

"Very well, you were warned," the Breathing Shaman said. "Death is coming to you all."

Kia sensed that the Breathing Shaman was gone and wanted to calm herself, but her young mind swirled with anger and a bit of fear, despite her power. Although she boasted about her mystic might, she had clearly lost the last time she challenged a powerful foe. That floating head she'd fought in the nether realm was too much for her. Kia had doubts that she could defeat the more experienced shamanic women.

As if to prove her doubts were true, she tried to surprise the Breathing Shaman by contacting her, using the same method. Young Kia reached out with her thoughts, hoping to take the older shaman by surprise, to demonstrate her abilities. *If she wishes to be intrusive to my mind, I'll show her how it feels when someone invades your thoughts.*

She pushed her thoughts outward, hoping to reach her target, but something went wrong. She felt like her mind was suddenly caught, trapped in some void beyond the physical world. *What's happening?*

She heard the voice of the Breathing Shaman saying, *Did you think I wasn't prepared for this? You see why a child such as yourself has no business possessing such power. You have no idea what awaits beyond your home of Kolhu! Enjoy being trapped in this otherworldly spider web.*

Kia panicked and tried to retreat back to her body but could not escape. Her mind floated in a quiet, empty darkness. *No! No! Help me!*

Pahana, Pinga, Calian, and Faw-Faw were still heading back to Shipapa-Lina, disconsolate over the death of Tawa, whose body they were taking home to his people. No one spoke because they didn't have the spirit to speak. Tawa was gone, and the world was a worse place for his passing.

Pahana then saw something in the sky. It was large, and it flapped its wide wings as it descended toward them. "What is this now?"

Pinga and Calian looked up, now aware of the flying creature. As it came closer, it was revealed to be a bat of immense size. Its wingspan was longer than the length of a bison. It circled over them, making a frightful squeal of aggression.

"Camazotz!" Pinga said. "The death bat. It devours all blood from its victims."

"It will not devour us," Pahana said, leaping from his mount.

Calian shot an arrow at the bat, but the flying beast swatted it away with ease. It swooped at them, targeting Pinga. Calian yanked her from the bison, barely in time to save her from the bite of the beast. The creature circled for a second attack. Brave Fire snorted and bucked. Faw-Faw roared in challenge.

Pahana saw the sacred Dragonfly latched to the bison's side. He had been reluctant to take it, but if he was ever to be the bearer of his father's mighty spear, it must be now. He pulled the spear from its binding.

Father said the spear was mine now, Pahana thought. *He left it to me. I can only hope to control its power. Will it serve me as it served him? Am I truly its master?*

As the bat swooped to attack again, Pahana shouted. "Back, all of you. Even you, Faw-Faw. I must know if I am worthy of carrying Dragonfly into battle. I must face this monster alone!"

Pahana stood his ground as the huge bat flew toward him, bearing its fangs with murderous intent. Pahana raised his spear.

CHAPTER TWENTY-SIX

Kia was desperately trying to extricate herself from the lonely, empty void she was trapped in. She was terrified at the prospect of being trapped there forever. *Must escape! I have to get out of this place!*

Suddenly, she heard another voice. A female voice. *I am Ghigau, the fist of the House of Many Hands.*

Let me out of here! Kai cried.

You don't like it here, child? Hmmm. Perhaps you will prefer this...

Kia felt a yank, as if she were caught in a riptide. Abruptly, she found herself in another unfamiliar place. *Where am I?*

She found herself in something that seemed like an underground tunnel, but there was an unseen light source coming from somewhere. *What is this place?*

Kia saw that she had a body, but it didn't seem like a real body. She had been in an astral form before, so she was not fazed by finding herself in a spirit body in the spirit realm. She adjusted to the new body quicker this time than she had on previous occasions.

Kia squinted and raised her arms, attempting to use her powers to escape this place. To her horror, nothing happened. She tried again, but nothing happened. *Oh, no! My power is gone!*

The voice of Ghigau echoed through the cave. "You have no power here, little girl. You will remain here, powerless, until you agree to join us."

"Please let me go!" Kia pleaded.

"Will you join us?"

Kia paused before answering. "No."

"You'll change your mind," Ghigau said. "After a few years."

"No!" Kia yelled, fear chilling her soul.

Ghigau did not respond. Kia looked around at the barren walls of the caves. She walked a few steps but found that moving this new body was not as easy as it had been on other occasions.

"Having some difficulty?" Ghigau asked. "We created this astral body you now inhabit. Don't expect us to make it easy on you."

Kia defiantly continued to walk, determined to master this astral body. She moved slowly as if climbing out of the water with wet clothes. She felt as heavy as she would if carrying a pile of stones. Still, she pushed onward. "So heavy!"

She staggered on a few more steps, but then fell to her knees. It felt as if a giant hand was pushing her down. She shouted in angst as she failed to get back to her feet. She was on her hands and knees, and then down on her chest. She forced herself to roll over, but she was still pinned to the floor by the weight of her own body. *Can't move! Can't even lift my arms! So heavy! So horrible!'*

Kia lay helplessly on the cold floor of the cave, weeping in despair. She couldn't stand, roll over, or wriggle across the floor in any way. She was trapped in this simulated underground. She didn't know where she was and neither did anyone else. *Is this where it will end? Will I expire here, alone, in this desolate, gods-forsaken cave? Will anyone find me here, or is this my final fate?*

She feared for herself, and for the fact that the shamans of the Valley of the Blue Mists were trying to kill her people and there was no way she could warn them or help them at all. She hated being unable to act. She'd become so accustomed to being powerful that she couldn't accept that she was powerless to save herself. She lay there, immobile and defenseless.

She could only hope that Shula-Witsa was watching or some other deity among the Sky Elders would send a rescuer to extricate her from her peril. *I can only pray that someone comes to help me before it's too late!*

After an hour of lying helplessly on the ground, Kia's attention was drawn to a hissing sound. Managing to slightly turn her head, she saw a glowing, crimson snake slithering directly toward her.

"No!" she screamed as her terror of snakes filled her mind until the slithering creature was all she could see. "No, no! Go away! Stay away! Someone help me!"

She watched in blind dread as the large serpent came closer and closer. So great was her fear of snakes, combined with the stress of everything she'd been through that young Kia—age 14—fainted.

The snake continued to slide across the cave floor until it was distracted by a noise. A digging noise. From out of a non-solid patch of dirt and soil that covered an opening in the far wall came a dwarf Trog, whose body was covered with sheep-like wool. This small man was known as Fleecy Breast. He had once lived among mortal men but had been allowed by majestic Manitou to live unmolested in this secret, otherworldly place. Fleecy Breast had been living alone in this world-between-worlds for the longest time and was not used to having company. He was comfortable with solitude in the dark realm.

Fleecy Breast spotted the unconscious Kia and examined her more closely. He kicked aggressively at the snake, which slid away. Fleecy Breast was fascinated by the petite, innocent-looking child. After all this time alone... finally, a friend!

He gripped Kia under her arms and lifted her, dragging her to his lair.

Monsters were converging on Shipapa-Lina. The Itiwana tribe had been alerted by the sentries that another attack was coming. The Two Horn Riders were assembled, and the non-combatants were in their chambers on the cliff face.

Atira, T'Soona, and the twins hurried to take stock of the situation. Naya-Nazgani was with them, clutching his spear. *Whatever monstrous foe threatens these good people, they'll regret finding my ax here.*

The village was under siege by bear-like creatures, possessing thick elephant-like gray skin. They were as tall as a giraffe. They walked with a stiff-legged gait, which was why they were often called the stiff-legged bears although others simply called them the big man-eaters. Their carnivorous nature was well known. They had been common in the days of the legendary Morning Star but had been seen less and less over the centuries. Their appearances were so rare now, most thought they were extinct. Sightings were seen as mere fables; mistaken sightings of normal bears, obscured by darkness or blinding sunlight.

But they still existed. Wherever they had been, they had been summoned back by the Breathing Shaman, the Keeper, and the other women of the House of Many Hands. Their roar was like a savage trumpet of impending death. The strange animals salivated at the thought of the taste of flesh and blood. They would not leave until they had fed.

"The valley women are persistence incarnate," Atira said.

"They don't seem to care much about forgiveness and conversation," T'Soona said.

Naya-Nazgani held up his formidable ax. "Then why should we? If they want bloody battle, then let's not leave their desire unsatisfied. I have fought these creatures before, and I do not fear doing so again despite their number. Excuse me, dear Atira. I have monsters to slay. It's what I live for!"

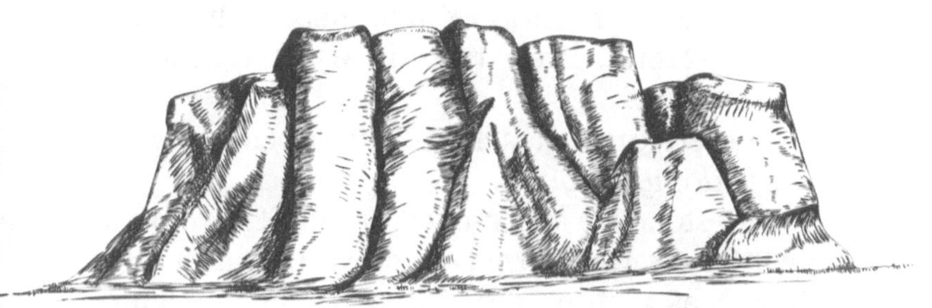

CHAPTER TWENTY-SEVEN

Kia woke still in the caves. She found she could now move and sat up. She looked around and discovered that she was in some sort of stone chamber carved into the deep reaches of the mountains in this unearthly realm. *Someone must dwell here.* It was bizarre to her that someone would choose to live in these caves, making living quarters out of cave formations.

Who brought me here? And why? And are they nearby?

Something moved in the corner. Kia looked and gasped when she saw the small, strange creature crouched, watching her. She had seen many unnatural beings since she began studying shamanism, so she was not afraid of its odd appearance. But she was curious. *What is that creature?*

She sat up, moving slowly and non-threateningly. Aware of her new powerlessness, she decided to be friendly. Kia smiled at the wooly dwarf. "Hello, little friend. My name is Kia. Who are you?"

The creature clearly did not speak English. *This is doing no good.*

She stood up and moved around the room as the little creature stared at her with great interest. There was a stone altar or panel in the center of the room, filled with multiple colorful little crystals. There was also a large opening, like a doorway. A nice, convenient way out.

Kia backed slowly toward the door. "Thank you for saving me from the snake. I hate those things. But it's time; I must go. I must return to my family. Goodbye, little friend."

As she attempted to exit the chamber, a thick cloud of silvery mist swirled in the entrance, and Kia was pushed back. *There's some sort of barrier here! I can't escape!*

Kia again attempted to talk to the child-like Fleecy Breast, but as before, it did her no good. The benign, but simple, little being did not understand a word.

She gave up on communicating. *I have to figure out how to get him out of the way so I can figure out how to open the portal!*

She made gestures to convince Fleecy Breast that she was hungry. The creature eventually understood. The little man walked to the panel, reached up, pressed the red, green, and blue crystals in a triangular configuration, and then walked out. Once outside, he touched the same pattern of crystals on a similar panel on the far tunnel wall. This action put the barrier back up.

Excellent! Kia thought. *I just have to press those colors in that sequence and I'm free!*

Once the wooly dwarf was gone, Kia rushed immediately to the panel, intending to press those crystals as the dwarf had done. However, there was a problem. Ghigau was still watching. As she reached out for the panel, the panel suddenly shined with incredible brightness, blinding Kia.

"Mustn't touch!" the voice of Ghigau said.

She took a step back, and the light stopped, but now she was too far away to reach the panel. She had to step closer to touch the crystals, but when she did, the crystals were illuminated again, obstructing her view of them.

Closing her eyes, she reached down and felt around, unable to see which crystals she was touching. *Dare I try this without being able to see? If I press the wrong crystals, what might happen? I know how powerful mystic objects can be. I don't know anything about these crystals. I might cause an earthquake or unleash monsters. I don't dare toy with these crystals without being able to see them, or I might end up summoning up something even worse! I might even destroy this chamber with me inside it! I mustn't risk it!*

She stepped back and closer a few times and was either too far away or unable to see the gems due to the lights. *Curse it all! Why is she torturing me like this? I don't even know her. How long will this go on?*

She paced furiously, scowling at the panel. It mocked her with its presence since she was unable to utilize this simple escape method. Occasionally she would step to the panel to give it another try, but each time she was reminded why that was not a practical idea when the overwhelming light blinded her. She didn't dare to randomly utilize the crystals by touch alone.

"There's nothing I can do right now," Kia muttered. "Unless my power comes back, I can't fight Ghigau!" She decided that she had to do something about the dwarf. *Even if I can't defeat her, maybe I can handle him.*

Soon after, Fleecy Breast returned, carrying that very snake that he had rescued her from before. It was now dead. The dwarf had apparently brought it here for her to eat. She winced at the sight of it. *I hate snakes.*

While he was gone, she started to enact another plan. The first thing she had to do was incapacitate him. She didn't want to hurt him because he had helped her and he didn't seem to be dangerous, but he was keeping her away from her family, and she had to get back to them. They needed her now more than ever.

She knew he'd be coming back soon, and she wanted to ambush him before he could prepare himself and create a defense. Since she was handicapped by her lack of power, she didn't dare fight him hand-to-hand without an advantage. She looked around for a weapon and found a stick that appeared to be a staff, or perhaps a club. She clutched it gratefully as her means of salvation. She would knock the dwarf out with it.

Kia peeked out the door, and she saw him coming. She hid in the corner and held up the stick so she could bring it down soundly on his head. She waited for the door to open. Young Kia was eager and ready to club him with the stick. But as she raised the stick over her head, Ghigau intervened again.

"No weapons, girl," Ghigau's voice said.

The club became heavy, just as had happened to her body before. Trying to support it, the sudden weight caused her to fall over backward. *Curse her! Why won't she leave me alone?*

There must be some way I can use this weapon against him, even with her sabotaging me, Kia contemplated.

The dwarf, Fleecy Breast, walked back in and saw Kia standing there, struggling to raise a stick. The little man made a surprised and angry grunt, apparently realizing what she had intended to do.

She had also lost her chance to take him by surprise. She still planned to use the stick, but he was ready for it now, and with the increased weight, it wouldn't be so easy. She lifted it up to waist level, which was the highest she could manage to support it. Then she lunged at him, trying to use the stick in any way she could. As she waved it clumsily, the quick little dwarf reached out and grabbed it. Kia tried to retain her weapon, but the tug of war caused her to lose her balance, making her topple forward. She let go of the stick to put her palms out, catching herself before her face hit the floor.

The dwarf now had the stick. He apparently had no trouble holding it with one hand. Ghigau's spell obviously only affected her. *He got my weapon from me, and he can use it!* Kia backed up nervously, expecting him to hit her with it, but instead, he tossed it aside.

He waved his hands in a bold, challenging manner as if to say, "I can beat you, girl. I don't need this little stick."

"I'll fight you without a stick," she said, trying to sound confident. But part of her was uncertain considering all her previous attempts to escape and how Ghigau was sabotaging her. Should she risk a fair fight with him, considering that shaman woman was ruining every plan she could think of?

She was slightly taller but clearly much lighter than Fleecy Breast was, so she wasn't overly confident she could out-wrestle him. But then again, what choice did she have? She felt she had to try.

Kia and Fleecy Breast faced each other unarmed. The dwarf looked much more confident than she felt. Kia wasn't a wrestler, and she didn't know much about her opponent. True, he'd disarmed her, but that was with help from Ghigau. Kia prayed she could defeat this small, unarmed being without her powers.

In desperate hope, she threw a punch at him. But as she swung her fist, some unseen force seemed to grab her arm, slowing her swing. The punch connected in slow motion, lacking any momentum or power. Kia knew it was Ghigau who had neutralized her blow. The punch had no force behind it at all. The dwarf stood there laughing at her, completely unharmed by the blow. He had barely even felt it. *I want to kill that woman, Ghigau!*

She tried once more. As before, the dwarf, Fleecy Breast, didn't feel it and grinned at her ineffectual attempts to fight. Neither blow had the slightest effect on him. She tried to kick Fleecy Breast, but that same force took hold of her legs and slowed them to a snail-like movement. Nothing she did seemed to have caused the slightest bit of harm to her opponent.

Kia trembled with helpless rage. She hated the Ghigau and wanted to kill her, and she wanted to take her frustrations out on this dwarf, but she was completely unable to do him any harm. As much as she wanted to knock that mocking smile off his face, she was utterly powerless against him.

"I hate you!" she screamed out in despair at Ghigau.

The unseen woman laughed. "I don't care. If you don't join us, the torment continues."

"If only I had a weapon!" Kia snapped.

The woman cackled as if she had an idea. "Want a weapon? All right, then."

Ghigau magically conjured up a large war club. Kia found it on the ground in front of her.

The young girl was confused by this. *What is she planning now?*

"Here, young one. Use this," Ghigau said.

Kia studied the mallet that lay at her feet. She suspected what Ghigau was doing. *She's just trying to torment me. I won't play along.*

Kia turned her back on the club, unwilling to be a pawn again. As for Fleecy Breast, he was confounded by the appearance of the club. He backed away from it, unsure of what was happening. He huddled in the corner and covered his face. Then he activated the crystals on the panel and ran out of the chamber.

Kia found herself alone and wondered if Ghigau was still watching. "Are you there?" she asked, but there was no answer.

As she paced, Kia moved near the far wall. As she turned, her elbow accidentally brushed against a large green stone embedded in the wall. The kinetic motion of the physical contact activated the mystic stone that happened to contain an ancient spirit. This timeless being was long since dead and yet still very much sentient and present. With a wisp of smoke, a man materialized in the room.

Kia was startled to see what appeared to be an ancient, withered man, with a white beard that nearly reached his knees. He wore an animal skin and leaned on a staff. "Greetings, young one," he said.

Kia overcame her surprise. Such miraculous happenings were becoming common to her, but she was unnerved regardless, not knowing what to expect from this inexplicable newcomer. *How did he even get in here?*

"Ummm... hello," she said. "I'm Kia. Who are you?"

"My name has been lost to time," he said, with a touch of sadness. "I am now known as the Old Man of the Mountain."

"I've heard the stories," Kia said. "I thought they were myths. I see I was wrong."

"I sense that you are in distress," the Old Man said. "And while the affairs of living mortals no longer concern me, I have not encountered so innocent a mortal in many centuries. And I would deem myself a fiend indeed if I did not assist you in any way possible. How may I serve you, young one?"

Kia was thankful that she had found an ally whom she could communicate with. "I thank you for your kindness, good sir. Can you help me return to my world? I cannot get past this unseen barrier, nor do I know the way back to the physical realm. Can you help me?"

"I can, and I will," the Old Man said waving his staff toward the door. The mist swirled and faded, and the barrier was gone. "You may pass now. And as for the way to the physical world, you must go right when you leave this chamber. Walk 100 paces until you see the oval tunnel with the green mold. That tunnel will lead you up to the Chamber of the Many Worlds, a portal to other realms. It will lead you back to your own world, and you will return to your own body."

"Wonderful! I thank you for your aid, good sir. I am forever in your debt."

"One word of caution, young one," he warned. "50 paces from here, before you reach the moss tunnel, you will pass a section of tunnel which is covered with white dust and sand on the ground. You must be very careful where you step while in that section, or you will awaken the Aztec mummy who was brought here by Manitou to guard this otherworldly realm."

"Then how can I pass unharmed?"

"Follow where the dwarf Fleecy Breast treads," the Old Man said. "Walk in the footprints of the little creature who dwells in this chamber. When you get to the sand and dust trap, look down. You will clearly see where he places his feet when walking through that area. Be sure to step on the same spots. Anything else will summon the deadly mummified guardian."

"I'll remember," she said. "Thank you so much, dear sir. I will never forget your kindness. May Awona'Wilona bless you."

"Good fortune, young one. Farewell."

Kia watched as the Old Man disappeared in a wisp of smoke. *This place is endlessly bizarre!*

Kia exited the chamber, turned right, and counted her steps on the way to the oval tunnel with the moss. She came to the area she had been warned about, where the ground was covered with dust and sand. As she approached, she saw the small tracks of the diminutive Fleecy Breast who had brought her there. *I need to step precisely in his footprints,* she thought to herself, remembering the Old Man's warning.

She walked to the dusty, sandy area and prepared to step in the safety of the footprints, but alas, her unseen tormentor became a problem once again. Still watching the young girl, Ghigau caused a swirl of dirt and dust to arise, making Kia unable to see the ground. She could not see the footprints of Fleecy Breast. *Not again. I hate her!*

With no other choice, Kia did her best to work from memory and tried to step where she thought the footprints were. Unable to see her own feet, she had no way of knowing if she was getting it right. *I hope I do not make a mistake. I wish I could see where I'm stepping.*

Despite her hopes, she made some missteps. Her foot landed outside the safe spots and shifted the magic sand. While she was unaware of this, someone else was not.

In a dark, dank chamber nearby, a stony statue-like figure stood motionless and lifeless in a cubbyhole. When the inanimate being sensed the sand being disturbed, it began to move. Primitive thoughts began to stir in its ancient skull, recalling its purpose—its only purpose. It must protect the caves from intruders, as it had always done. Moving for the first time in centuries, the slow-moving mummified creature lumbered toward the dusty, sandy area, where the intruder would be. The mummy knew that it must destroy any invaders.

The Aztec mummy walked using an ancient sonic vibration technique; the kind used to move the large stones when the Great Pyramid of Giza was built. He emitted an F-sharp below the level of human hearing enhanced by the echoing dimensions of the tunnels. This silent, harmonic power allowed his large, ancient body to move and not break apart from age. The mummy stomped toward his quarry.

Not far away, Kia had finished crossing the sand trap and looked back to see if her footprints matched the dwarf's prints. The cloud of dust cleared as if to tease Kia.

Oh no! I got it wrong! she thought, seeing her footprints near but not near enough to those of Fleecy Breast. *I'd best run quickly! The guardian will be coming, and I don't want to be here when it arrives!*

She was too late for that sentiment. As she turned, she saw the Aztec mummy shambling toward her. Struck with sudden fear by its frightening appearance, she screamed. She wasn't normally a screamer, but she couldn't help it at this moment. The mummy made her give in to a moment of blind panic.

Kia retreated, frantically trying to escape from the fearsome guardian. She hoped Ghigau would not hinder her, but that hope was futile. The silent, harmonic vibrations emitted by the stone man caused Kia's equilibrium to become unstable.

The mummy's slight, unseen vibrations made a connection of an object along an axis between the kinetic motion of Kia's running and itself. This resulted in an electromagnetic field that flipped the magnetic poles of the atoms, so they were attracted together. Kia was then pulled to the ultrasonic vibrations of the stone man.

She tried to flee to the safety of the chamber with the force field, but she could not. She found herself being drawn to the creature. Some force was pulling her inexorably backward, as the mummy simultaneously stalked nearer to her.

Kia panicked. "No! No! Keep away! Please, someone help me! Help!"

Fortunately for Kia, part of the mummy was still a man. Despite its dim, ancient brain having few independent thoughts, it reacted to her. The terror from this small, petite, angelic-looking little girl stirred something inside him that hadn't been stirred in centuries. Mercy! The stone man was moved to pity and chose not to harm her.

The terrified Kia found herself pulled toward the stone guardian until her breasts pressed against his rocky exterior. She couldn't pull herself away. She waited in fear for the beast to strike a killing blow. "Please do not harm me," she begged.

To her surprise, the stone man scooped her up, turned, and carried her away with him. *He didn't harm me. Instead, he's stealing me away. But to where? What does he plan to do with me? What fate am I facing now?* The helpless Kia could only wonder and worry as she was carried off into the darkness.

Pahana lashed out at the bat Camazotz, utilizing the spear Dragonfly for the very first time. He had seen Tawa wield the mystic weapon many times. He had even held the spear as a boy, but he had never had the opportunity to train with it.

It was only hours ago that his father had gifted the spear to him. He wondered if the deathbed of his father was enough to transfer the gift of controlling Dragonfly to him and him alone. As the giant bat attacked, Pahana knew he would have one chance to master this weapon, as he would not live to try a second time.

He saw his mother and Calian watching him. Pinga gasped in dread each time the bat came in for another attack.

I must do this, Pahana thought. *For you, Mother. For my father and for the Itiwana.! I must win!*

CHAPTER TWENTY-EIGHT

Kia was being carried through the tunnels by the mysterious mummy. She feared his intentions. *What does he plan to do with me?*

The Aztec mummy silently carried his young captive into his dim chamber. He put her down on the floor and stood there, looking at her. He seemed curious about her, and somehow protective.

Why is he just standing there? Why is he just staring at me? Why didn't he hurt me like the Old Man said he would? Why did he bring me here? What does he want with me?

She tried to speak to the creature. "Do you understand me? My name is Kia. What do you want with me?"

The Aztec mummy did not understand her. Instead, he backed up and moved into the doorway of the chamber instead of the little cubbyhole he usually stood in. Settling into the doorway, like a sentry on duty, he stared at Kia until he finally slipped back into his former stasis-like state of mindlessness, becoming a living statue again.

Kia tried repeatedly to talk to the creature, but soon realized that it was no longer aware of her. She poked it a few times to be certain. *It seems to be either dead or in some sort of deep trance.*

She inched around the unmoving mummy, stepping back into the hall. She rushed out into the hall and ran for the portal in the chamber of Many Worlds. Although her escape attempt woke the Aztec mummy, she had enough of a head start to allow her to reach the portal and leap into it.

Kia found herself once again back in her physical body in the Sun Temple. Lifting her hand, she was able to easily ignite a flame in the firepit. Kia broke out in relieved laughter, glad to be safe in her village.

She was startled when that small flame flared and grew like a torch. Was she under attack? Worriedly, she saw a face forming in the fire.

"It is I. Your teacher," the flaming face said.

"Shula-Witsa," Kia said, unsure whether she was happy to see the fiery Sky Elder. "Why have you come to me?"

"I've been watching. I have," Shula-Witsa said. "You're in peril. You are. Your father's gone. He's dead. You've been threatened. You have. Protect your tribe. You must."

"I plan to," Kia said. "But the enemy is powerful."

"Indeed, they are. They are," Shula-Witsa said. "You'll need power. Greater power."

"What do you mean?" Kia asked.

"I'll strengthen you. I will," the Elder said. "You'll be stronger. You will. Accept my gift. Accept it. You'll be mighty. Awesomely mighty."

"You can do that for me?" Kia said. "You never said you could increase my powers."

"You couldn't handle it. Not before," Shula-Witsa said. "But you've grown. You have. We'll risk it. We must. Accept it now. Accept it."

Kia could not say no to this offer. Not now. "Very well, I accept. Do whatever you must. Make me stronger. Make me a goddess among mortals!"

Naya-Nazgani, the legendary monster slayer, eagerly walked to the forefront of the defensive line protecting Shipapa-Lina to face an army of monsters. Despite their size, he looked at the bear beasts as nothing more than prey.

Not waiting for the rest of the Itiwana, Naya-Nazgani charged at the stiff-legged big man-eaters, shouting an eager war cry. This seemed to infect the Two Horned Riders, who joined in with his energetic shouts. Naya-Nazgani joined Aholi at the head of the skirmish line and led the attack. Aholi signaled for the rest of the riders to join them.

On their bison mounts, the Two Horned Riders clashed with the bear-like army. The bison seemed a match for the bears, although it took many arrows to slay one of the creatures. Naya-Nazgani, however, had little difficulty. His ax cut a bloody swatch through the enemies, and he laughed with glee as each one fell.

Even Hayoka, who had not been able to slip out of Shipapa-Lina because he was being watched, joined in the fight, although he kept to the rear, keeping Yoki between himself and the beasts, only firing arrows from a distance.

Despite their initial advantage, the numbers were against them. The beasts kept coming and coming in seemingly limitless numbers. For each one Naya-Nazgani killed, two or three more lumbered into the village. The bison were beginning to get tired, and the warriors even more so.

Atira could see that the battle was turning against them and struggled to come up with a plan to save her village, but nothing came to mind. "What can I do, T'Soona?"

"Don't lose heart," he said. "We always survive somehow."

They were interrupted by a sudden bright light. Everyone—the Two Horn Riders, Naya-Nazgani, and the stiff-legged bears—stopped, stunned by the blinding light. It was like a miniature sun floating over the battlefield.

When the light faded, all the Itiwana were amazed to see Kia floating above them, like a petite goddess. She looked down at the bear beasts and shouted, "No more!"

Kia began to emit balls of fire similar to the flaming energy that powered Shula-Witsa. The fireballs engulfed many of the bears, incinerating them. The bear beasts panicked, never having experienced such a thing.

Taking advantage of the bears' confusion, Naya-Nazgani and Aholi rallied the Two Horn Riders to redouble their attack. They courageously took the offense once again, racking up a significant body count. But it was Kia and her flaming attack that really ravaged the bear beasts. Their apparently limitless numbers now seem to diminish. The vast army dwindled to a small group.

The bears sensed that they were outmatched, and despite the mystical urgings of the Breathing Shaman who was mentally motivating them, the stiff-legged man-eaters fled the Land of Everlasting Summer.

The Two Horn Riders cheered as the enemy retreated. Naya-Nazgani dropped to one knee, rubbed his ax, and whispered to it as if it were a loved one. "It is good. Our vengeance against all monsters sustains us. We've won. We always win."

Atira hugged T'Soona. "You were right again, sweet T'Soona. Somehow, we always survive."

"How could you doubt me?" he said mirthfully.

She looked at the battlefield and saw many injuries, but no deaths were apparent. "I think we've been spared casualties."

"But I must go to work now," T'Soona said. "Blood has been slipped and some of our people are hurt. They need me."

"Go," Atira said. "Do what only you can do. Impress me once again with your skill."

"That's why I really do it," he quipped.

The aftermath of battle became one of compassion. Atira looked up at the floating Kia. The girl drifted down, and her feet touched the ground near her grandmother. The girl smiled proudly.

"I told you I had great power," Kia said.

"Yes, you most clearly do," Atira said. And while she was grateful that Kia had the power to protect her people, she was also somewhat frightened. Can a girl her age control such power? And if not, what would happen should she lose control?

Pahana stood over the bloodied remains of the bat, Camazotz. He looked at the bloodied tip of Dragonfly and knew that he was now its master. *I hold the greatest of weapons now. Such a responsibility. Just as I now have the responsibility to lead the Itiwana. I must be worthy!*

"Well done, my brave son," Pinga said. "Your father would be so proud."

Pahana thought about the power of Dragonfly. "This spear represents a bond between myself and the divine powers that have long guided our family. We are the protectors of the Land of

Everlasting Summer. It is part of me. Now, in the name of Tawa and our family, I must restore it."

Pahana tightly held Dragonfly in his two strong hands and lifted it above his head. He abruptly jabbed it deep into the earth. "I command the land. Heal yourself."

All across the land of waking day, a miraculous change occurred. Places that had been barren fields, ravaged and ruined by the plague of the fire locusts, suddenly sprang to life. Roots popped out of the ground. Dead trees were renewed, and leaves began to grow. Flowers sprouted, and grass began to grow. All across the devastated landscape, life began anew.

Pahana, with his divine birth, the sacred power of Dragonfly, and the Land of Everlasting Summer, shared a bond that day, which led to a miracle.

The land healed. Life returned. All became right again.

EPILOGUE

The Breathing Shaman sat dejectedly in the House of Many Hands. She dropped her bone tube, and a salty tear could be seen on her cheek. She had never imagined the power they faced. Between Kia and Dragonfly, the divine energy opposing the shamanic women was overwhelming.

The Keeper entered with a poultice dressing on her arm. She had mostly recovered from the attack. The Keeper was surprised to see her sister looking so defeated.

"We've lost," the Breathing Shaman said. "We cannot defeat them."

The Keeper stroked her sister sympathetically. "I saw. I was watching in the vision pool. We must let this injustice stand. We can't win, and nothing is earned by continuing this useless battle. End this."

"Must we let them go without facing justice?" the Breathing Shaman asked.

"For now," the Keeper said. "Only for now. We will watch. We will wait; we will plan. Eventually, there will be a time when the Itiwana are vulnerable. Perhaps we will find allies of our own. Let them think they've won. We'll be patient. In the end, we'll win. Someday, the Itiwana will fall."

As Pahana rode back to Shipapa-Lina with his companions and his father's body, he received an astral message from Kia. She told him that the battle had been won and Shipapa-Lina was safe. He could now focus on his plans for Shipapa-Lina as their leader.

My father ruled through his intense cleverness and his ability to make his people trust him, Pahana thought. *Everyone had such faith in him. His very being made us rise up to greater heights. Was there anyone among us who did not think him a god among men? But I must rule differently. I cannot inspire the people the way he did. And his death will bring doubts to the masses of the Itiwana. Many will doubt my ability to follow in his great footsteps. I cannot make them believe in me as they did in him. But I can still make plans. I will win their loyalty through my future decisions. I will act alone, if necessary. The Shakowin may doubt me, but once I am officially made the chieftain, they must obey me. It will be their duty. I will plot and scheme alone, and in the end, they will see that I am a worthy leader. They may not love me as they did him, but in the future, they will all accept that I acted for the good of my people and that I was worthy to carry the spear Dragonfly. I will win this war, even though my father could not. I will be the greatest chieftain of all and lead my people to the greatest heights. If I must be an island apart, then I will do so. I will answer to no one. But whatever happens, I will defeat the Enemy Way, by any means necessary.*

Kia was savoring her new powers. She sat in her chamber, conjuring up flaming objects and icy constructs. She even seemed to be able to command the wind. Kia touched the ground, and the Earth shook slightly, and the dirt formed into a mandala. She giggled.

I command earth, air, fire, and ice, she thought. *I am a goddess. No one can defeat me. Those women couldn't despite their experience. I am more powerful than Molowia. I am almighty. Every enemy will fear me. I will be feared!*

Hayoka decided he could now leave Shipapa-Lina. He had won a small bit of respect by fighting in the battle. Many were surprised that he'd joined them, expecting him to flee again. He was ter-rified during the battle, but the aftermath was advantageous.

Perhaps I can convince them that I did not have anything to do with the attack on the Keeper. And if the conflict is over, they will soon forget. At least, I hope they will. And when Pahana returns, I will try to get back into his good graces. I still have not decided whether I will help destroy the Itiwana or not. Their treatment of me certainly moves me toward revenge, especially toward that damnable Calian. Yet must I be a slave to what others want? Agwara, Dagwona, the Coyote, my mother? This is what they want. But what do I really want? Should I do this thing? I do have a fondness for Pahana. Should I betray the Itiwana?

Hayoka noticed that the grass was growing back, and he saw flowers for the first time in many weeks. He found himself unconsciously walking toward the cabin of the Burned-Faced Man although he knew Dagwona was no longer there. He stopped before he reached it, knowing there was nothing left for him within.

"I do miss Dagwona," he said to himself.

"Fantastically flattering," a familiar voice said with a laugh.

Hayoka spun around to see the Witch of the Whirlwind staring at him with a mischievous grin. She gestured for him to come closer, and he did.

"My man's missed," she said. "Much missed. Hayoka's happily here. Dagwona delighted."

"Where have you been?" he asked.

"Watching wistfully," she said. "Always alone. Not now. Hayoka's here. Dagwona desires."

"If you mean..." he began.

"Primal passion," she said. "Immediate intimacy."

Hayoka couldn't restrain a smile. "If you really insist. Who am I to argue with a witch?"

Hayoka lay on the newly regrown grass with the Witch of the Whirlwind. As he enjoyed her affection, he was still unsure of whose side he was on. *This is a benefit that might convince me,* he thought.

Far away, in the bowels of the Shouting Mountains, the ever-present angry wails of Malsumis had abruptly stopped. The powerful, plotting Sky Elder thought about the bargain he had made with Pinga. The Itiwana did not know that two of the omens that would signal his return had occurred. The death of Tawa and the bargain Pinga had made. All he needed now was one more thing and he could escape this long imprisonment.

The echo of boisterous laughter filled the volcanic cave. Triumphant laughter!

END OF BOOK THREE

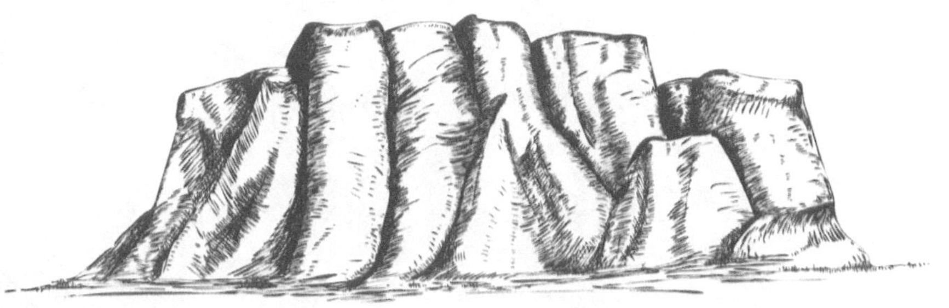

COMING SOON/TEASER

Sky Elders: Book Four: The Desert of Death

It's been 18 years since Tawa died, and Pahana is now an experienced leader. However, he is secretive and calculating, unable to evoke the trust and love his people had for Tawa. He remains secretive and solitary as he makes plans to deal with their growing number of enemies.

His 17-year-old son Gluskap is becoming a respected warrior, determined to live up to his family legacy. Pahana realizes that Gluskap may be the savior the Itiwana are looking for, and so sends his son on a vital but dangerous mission. If he fails, the Itiwana will have no future.

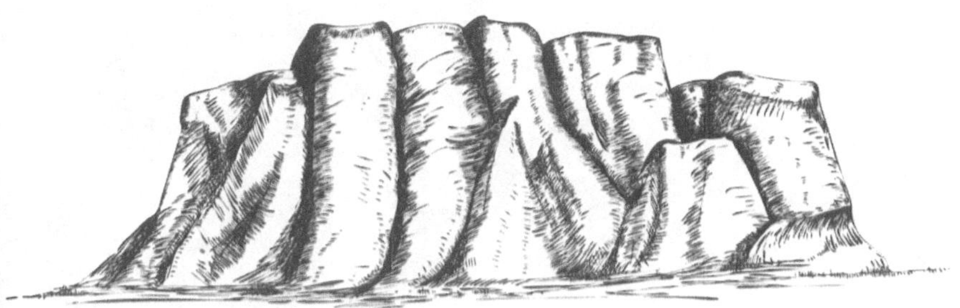

AUTHOR BIO

R.J. Young has been everything from a dog groomer to a custodian to a hospital worker, but his one true love has always been writing. The son of an immigrant, he's had a lifelong fascination with fantasy and sci-fi stories depicting exotic and astonishing locations. The first time he saw *The Wizard of Oz* at seven years old, it was a magical experience. A journalism major in college, he enjoys writing online reviews and articles. R.J. loves discussing fiction with anyone who will listen.

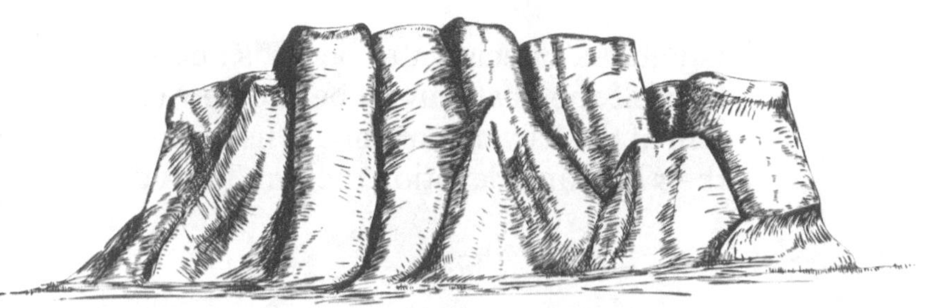

BOOK CLUB QUESTIONS

1. Have the Itiwana been fair in distrusting and ostracizing Hayoka because of what his father did? Is Hayoka justified in considering betraying the Itiwana?

2. Are Molowia and the Breathing Shaman justified in worrying about Kia's power, or should they be more supportive?

3. Given her mental state after the death of her husband, was Pinga's decision to make a deal with Malsumis forgivable? Would you have done the same thing?

4. Should Kia continue to trust Shula-Witsa, considering how much he has helped

increase her power? Does he have an ulterior motive?

5. Is Pahana's decision to be an island unto himself the best way to be the new chieftain of the Itiwana, or should he try to win their love and devotion the way Tawa did?

www.ingramcontent.com/pod-product-compliance
Lightning Source LLC
Chambersburg PA
CBHW021236310726
48971CB00006B/1845